Gridlock

www.transworldbooks.co.uk

Also by Sean Black

LOCKDOWN
DEADLOCK

For more information on Sean Black and his books, see his
website at www.seanblackbooks.com

Gridlock
A Ryan Lock Thriller

SEAN BLACK

BANTAM PRESS

LONDON • TORONTO • SYDNEY • AUCKLAND • JOHANNESBURG

TRANSWORLD PUBLISHERS
61–63 Uxbridge Road, London W5 5SA
A Random House Group Company
www.transworldbooks.co.uk

First published in Great Britain
in 2011 by Bantam Press
an imprint of Transworld Publishers

A CIP catalogue record for this book
is available from the British Library.

ISBNs 9780593063415 (cased)
9780593063422 (tpb)

Addresses for Random House Group Ltd companies outside the UK
can be found at: www.randomhouse.co.uk
The Random House Group Ltd Reg. No. 954009

The Random House Group Ltd supports the Forest Stewardship
Council® (FSC®), the leading international forest-certification organization.
All our titles that are printed on Greenpeace-approved FSC® certified paper
carry the FSC® logo. Our paper procurement policy can be found at
www.randomhouse.co.uk/environment

Typeset in 11.5/16.5pt Times New Roman by
Falcon Oast Graphic Art Ltd.
Printed and bound in Great Britain by
Clays Limited, Bungay, Suffolk

2 4 6 8 10 9 7 5 3 1

For Peter and Jemima

Prologue

Near the end of every month, Bert Ely got up an hour earlier than usual, fumbled into his clothes in the dark so that he didn't wake his wife, clambered into his beat-to-hell Chevy Impala and drove the eighteen miles from his house in Van Nuys into downtown Los Angeles. Getting on to the 101 freeway at six rather than his usual seven o'clock shaved about twenty-five minutes from his commute, although saving time wasn't the real issue. The time he spent in the car on these particular days was something he looked forward to all month.

He loved the ritual of his routine as much as he enjoyed what lay at the end of it. As with any indulgence, half the fun – at least, as far as Bert was concerned – lay in the anticipation.

The 101 took him out of the San Fernando Valley, through Hollywood, the city's degenerate heart, finally depositing him via the Broadway off-ramp into downtown Los Angeles where he worked as a real-estate appraiser for Citicorp. It was a mind-numbing job, based in a soul-crushing grey office building full of good little corporate automatons. Along with the fact that his wife no longer had sex with him, and his kids probably couldn't have cared less whether he lived or died, Bert used the utterly mundane nature of his job to justify his end-of-the-month routine.

This morning, as he turned from North Broadway on to West 1st Street, a Los Angeles Police Department cruiser pulled out behind him. He found his heart rate quickening a little, although he had no real reason to feel guilty – certainly not yet, anyway. He supposed that technically what he would do today was against the law, but that was more to do with the thick streak of Puritanism that still ran through American society than anything else.

The rack of stop lights next to the Japanese American National Museum was at red. The LAPD cruiser pulled up alongside him. Bert glanced at the two cops riding up front. One was half twisted round in his seat, talking to a young Hispanic woman who was perched on the rear bench seat. Judging from her clothes, and her cratered complexion, over which she had smoothed a rough veneer of foundation, she was a street walker.

She saw Bert looking at her and stared back at him, like she knew what his secret was. Bert's heart rate elevated again. The middle finger of her left hand popped up as she flipped him off, then the lights changed and the cop car continued down 1st Street as Bert made the right turn on to South Central Avenue, his heart still pounding.

He shook the image of the Hispanic woman from his head

as he pulled into the parking lot, a sleepy-eyed attendant handing him his ticket as soon as he exited the car with his briefcase.

The sidewalk was still dewy with the water from early-morning street cleaning as he took a left heading down towards Starbucks on the corner of South Central Avenue and 2nd, passing the Cuba Central Café, and Yogurtland. Outside Starbucks a few chairs and tables were already stacked on the patio, ready to be deployed. Bert walked quickly past the three banks of newspaper vending machines next to the kerb, crossed the little patio and pushed the door open. He went straight to the counter and placed his order without glancing up at the board.

'Skinny latte, no foam,' he said, to the barista. 'Oh, and gimme a blueberry muffin.' The muffin was an everyday treat for Bert.

As he waited, he studiously avoided looking outside towards the final bank of newspaper vending machines, their metal posts planted in the sidewalk. A black one, a brown one and two red ones, the last of which held the key to his treat. Inside that machine were copies of this week's *LA Xclusive* newspaper, although the term 'newspaper' was a bit of a misnomer. There was no news inside, only page after page of adverts for escorts, predominantly female but with a scattering of men and transgender prostitutes, all selling limitless variations of the same thing: sex.

It was the endless variation on a theme that captivated Bert. Not just in terms of all the different physical types, ages and races, but in the array of services they offered, some so outlandish that even the thought of them made Bert queasy.

Sometimes the ads had pictures too, although he had learned from a couple of disappointing liaisons that they couldn't always be relied upon to be accurate.

Still, contained within the pages was a wonderland of possibilities, like a huge candy store for grown-ups. Inside those little boxes was an array of women, all of whom would have sex with Bert in return for money. From corn-fed Midwestern runaways, who no doubt told themselves that what they were doing was no different from what they'd done at home in the back seat of a car on a Saturday night, through the twenty-something MAWs (Model/Actress/Whatevers), with their gravity-defying silicone boobs and jaded air of dis-appointment that they weren't even going to make the Z-list, all the way to the hardened professionals, women who had long ago reconciled their hopes and dreams with the reality of making a living by lying on their backs. Over the years, Bert had sampled them all.

Recently, though, he'd begun to find a sameness to the experience, and to feel a dark, lonely emptiness once the encounter was over. Where once he'd felt satiated, now his monthly liaisons left Bert hungry for something other than sex. For intimacy, maybe?

Last month, in the awkward post-coital moments and with ten minutes still officially on the clock, he had lain in bed with a young redhead in a condo in Playa Del Rey. He'd asked her if they could spoon, cuddle in together, his arms around her. She'd looked at him like he was nuts and asked him to leave, reaching into a bedside table and producing a hand gun to emphasize that she wasn't kidding.

Strangely, he had never felt much guilt about paying

women to have sex with him, rationalizing that a real affair, one with emotions and feelings, would be far more upsetting to his wife. That was part of the reason he never visited the same woman twice. Well, that and the fact that he liked the variety. Living in LA you could sample all that the world had to offer in the way of women without leaving the city boundaries. As long as you didn't want a hug at the end.

'Sir? Is this to go?'

The barista's question snapped Bert back to the tiny coffee shop, which was starting to fill with office workers.

'Yeah, thanks,' Bert mumbled, handing over ten dollars and waiting for change. He put the two single dollar bills into the tip jar and kept the coins, which he'd need to pay for his copy of the newspaper. Then he picked up his coffee and the brown paper bag holding his muffin and wandered back outside into the early-morning California sunshine.

He stood for a second, sorting through his change and trying to get back a little of the good feeling he'd left the house with that day; the good feeling that came from his little secret.

At lunchtime he'd sneak to the men's room, peruse the women on offer that week, then make a phone call. With his department offering flexible working hours, he'd reclaim the time he'd banked by getting into the office early, and drive over to the woman's apartment. He was thinking that maybe he'd try someone a little older today, someone who might not find it strange that a man of his age would trade sexual gymnastics for a hug. Or, maybe, he thought, smiling to himself, he'd find a hot little spinner and screw her until her eyes popped out of her head.

It was only then, standing on the sidewalk, lost in his own

thoughts, that he noticed the stack of newspapers sitting at the far end of the vending machines, the pages of the top copy fluttering in the breeze as the beginnings of a hot Santa Ana wind funnelled its way from the natural canyons of the LA basin to the concrete canyons of downtown.

'Huh,' he said to himself, bending down slightly. Someone, a kind of perverted Good Samaritan, must have opened the machine and dumped all the copies out on the ground. With his knees still bent and his head down, Bert grabbed one from the middle of the small pile. Then, as he raised his head, he saw something that sent a jolt of adrenalin surging through him, stealing his breath and leaving a tingle of pins and needles in his fingertips.

Normally, if all the newspapers had been taken, he would have looked through the smeared glass display window to see 'SOLD OUT' printed on a screen at the back of the compartment that held the papers. But that wasn't what he was looking at right now.

Instead he was seeing blood – a lot of blood. And in the middle of the sheet of blood, a pair of eyes were staring back at him.

A head. Someone had taken out the newspapers and replaced them with a human head.

Still gasping for air, Bert straightened up and looked around. A clutch of middle-aged white women dressed in pant suits walked past. One glanced at the paper still clasped in Bert's hand, and gave him a look of disgust. None seemed to look at the vending machine and what was in it.

Maybe it was a prank. Yeah, thought Bert, that had to be it. A mannequin's head and a tube of fake blood. Must be some

goddamn feminists trying to make a point about the exploit-
ation of women or some shit.

He looked back to the head. *Sweet Jesus*. If it was a prank,
they'd made it look really convincing.

The initial shock had passed to the point at which he was
starting to think about what to do next. He should just get the
hell out, he knew that. Then another thought struck him,
keeping him there.

If there were cameras on this intersection and the prank
was found later, the police might think he had something to
do with it and want to speak to him. They might even come
to his home.

However, if he alerted the police right now, he could tell
them he was walking past and just happened to notice it. He'd
be a vigilant citizen rather than someone with something to
hide.

He took a step towards the machine, and had a better look
at the head. Although it was obscured by the blood spattering
the panel he could make out enough of the features – soft, full
lips, blue eyes, a small button nose and dyed blonde hair
running down the cheeks in limp, tangled strands – to see that
it was a woman's.

Get it over with, he said to himself, jamming two quarters
into the vending machine as quickly as he could and yanking
at the handle to open it.

The stench hit him like a truck. Even holding his breath the
sickly sweet cloying odour clawed its way to the back of his
throat, making his stomach spasm and sending the little
that was left of last night's dinner spilling over his shoes
and splashing on to the sidewalk. Behind him a woman

screamed so loudly that he thought his ear drums might burst.

Still gasping, he looked down at the copy of *LA Xclusive* he was holding in his left hand. On the cover there was a young blonde woman, perfectly made up and airbrushed: collagen-full lips, a button nose, deep blue eyes with silky platinum curls. It was the same person.

Slowly, reluctantly, Bert Ely looked again at the front cover of the paper and the headline above the girl's face: 'MEET CINDY CANYON'.

One

Her body slick with baby oil and sweat, Raven Lane whiplashed her neck, sending a thick mane of jet-black hair flying into the air, arched her back and smiled at the three hundred men crowded around the tiny platform, as Mötley Crüe's heavy-metal anthem 'Girls, Girls, Girls' pounded out from two huge speakers mounted at either side of the stage.

Dollar bills cascaded across the metal barrier, which, along with two steroid-pumped bouncers, separated Raven from her public. Ignoring the money, she wrapped herself around the stripper's pole, suggestively pistoning her left hand up and down the cold metal, her mouth open, her head thrown back again, her eyes closed in an expression of erotic abandon.

After years on the road, she had her routine down cold. Every gesture, every pout, every spin around the pole and every hair-flick was choreographed to the second, specifically engineered so that every single man in the club went away feeling that somehow Raven Lane had danced solely for his gratification.

She opened her eyes again, ready to move into the next part of the routine. At the edge of her vision she caught sight of a scrawny weasel of a man with a ratty beard, wearing a John Deere baseball cap, squeezing under the barrier and heading straight for her. Somehow he'd found his way past the two lunkhead bouncers and was now careening towards her at top speed.

Raven tensed as she adjusted her feet, one hand wrapping around the pole for support. Judging the speed of his approach, she took one final twirl and brought up a razor-sharp heel straight into his solar plexus. The man stumbled backwards clutching his chest as the crowd signalled its approval with a primal roar. One of the bouncers jumped on top of him and he was pulled back over the barrier by his hair before being propelled through the crowd by another member of the club's security staff. Despite his obvious physical discomfort, he had an inane grin on his face, as if a kick in the chest from Raven was some kind of come-on.

Raven swept the incident from her mind, working through her routine, her hands running across her bare breasts, her backside thrust out towards the crowd, seemingly lost in a state of rapture. All the while the downpour of dollars cascaded towards her until she almost lost sight of the faces of the men who'd already paid twenty bucks at the door just to see her naked body.

Eight minutes later, and almost as many thousands of dollars richer, she was escorted back to her dressing room, a dingy cupboard at the back of the single-storey roadside saloon. She towelled herself off, reapplied her makeup, put on a short, red silk robe from Frederick's of Hollywood and headed back out to have her picture taken with fans and to sign T-shirts.

The T-shirts cost fifteen dollars; her signature was another ten. Having their picture taken with her cost the men an additional fifteen. Alongside her cut of the door money and the bar, plus all those dollar bills tossed on to the stage, an appearance like this netted her around fifteen thousand dollars. Not bad for a few hours' work by a twenty-eight-year-old who hadn't even graduated from high school, she thought, as another loser stepped forward to have his picture taken with her.

After almost a decade of shedding her clothes on-stage and in movies, Raven still couldn't quite understand why men would turn up to see her. With her long black hair and near flawless body, she knew what the obvious attraction was, but she still didn't quite get it. She always thought it must be like visiting the most amazing restaurant in the world but contenting yourself with standing outside, your nose pressed against the window, as other people ate the food.

Maybe, she guessed, what attracted these men was exactly that: her unattainability. That she was a fantasy made flesh. Someone they could think about when they got home and had to bang the overweight domestic drudges of wives that they themselves had created. Yeah, fantasy was what she sold, she thought, rolling the tension from her shoulders and flicking back her hair; that had to be it.

Two hours later, her right hand aching from several hundred scrawled signatures, her ass numb from perching on so many overexcited laps while they got their picture of her, she was finally back at her dressing room. As she opened the door, she saw a huge bouquet of red roses sitting on the table. How original, thought Raven, plucking the envelope from the centre and tossing it down next to the flowers.

The way it bulged at the corners suggested it contained more than just a note. It was probably a roll of money and a phone number. Guys, usually rich local businessmen, often assumed that a thousand dollars in cash would somehow secure a night of passion for them to regale their buddies with at the local country club when they next played golf.

She dabbed at a bead of sweat running down between her breasts with a towel. These days, her body ached a lot more than it used to when she'd started out. The hair flicks gave you bulging or degenerative discs. Working the pole played hell with your shoulders. You started to damage cartilage from contorting your body into so many unnatural positions, and your sacrum, the large triangular bone at the base of your spine, which most people had never even heard of, started to swell up so bad that you had to sleep on your side. And those were just the physical maladies.

She could have written a book about the psychological damage the job would do if you weren't careful: the suitcase boyfriends who saw you first as a trophy and then as a meal ticket; the constant temptation to drown your feelings in booze or drugs; the hundred and one small indignities you had to suffer on a daily basis, especially from other women.

She reached over and opened the envelope. Inside there was a wad of paper, folded over multiple times. Here we go again, she thought, recognizing the carefully measured printed lettering and the faint whiff of cheap perfume.

She took out the note with a long, manicured fingernail and held it up to the light, scanning the words.

> Please remember, Raven, I did this for you. It's what you wanted. Even if maybe you didn't realize it yet.
>
> You're always in my heart, baby.

Did what? Raven asked herself. Right now all she wanted was for this freak to stop sending her notes.

She dropped the paper on to the table next to the flowers, and looked up, half expecting to see in the mirror someone standing behind her. But the room was still empty.

She was no stranger to freaks, stalkers and weirdos. In this business you tended to collect them like most other women collected shoes. She already had a restraining order out against one ex-boyfriend, and she'd been in contact with the police in Los Angeles about this creep who'd been calling and writing to her for the past few months.

Knowing that the cops would want evidence, Raven took a couple of pictures of the flowers with her cell phone and put the note into her purse. Then she got dressed as quickly as she could.

Once she'd picked up her money from the club owner, she'd asked him about the flowers but he was short on details. They'd arrived at the club while she was out doing her meet-and-greet. The person who'd dropped them off had seemed like a regular deliveryman. No, he hadn't seen the guy before. He gave a description that narrowed down to maybe a quarter of the male population: white, five feet eleven, brown hair, brown eyes. In other words, Mr Average. Yes, he'd take a look at the CCTV they had at the entrance but he doubted it would show anything.

With the best part of fifteen thousand dollars in her bag, and accompanied by two bouncers, she walked to her car, a midnight blue BMW 5-series sedan. The parking lot was emptying as they threaded their way through the pickup trucks and family vehicles (some complete with child seats) towards Raven's.

She dumped her bag in the front passenger seat, got in and clicked the button that locked all the doors. She sat alone in the car, weighed down by the silence, as the two bouncers turned back towards the club. Raven closed her eyes, trying to centre herself. She had a long drive ahead of her and knew better than to start out in an agitated state. She took a couple of long, slow breaths, visualizing her fear and anxiety as a series of small clouds drifting from her mouth with every exhalation.

There was a loud thud.

Her head snapped round and she saw a pair of eyes staring at her through the black slits of a ski-mask. He grabbed at the handle of the driver's door, trying to get it open. That was when she noticed the long sheathed hunting knife dangling casually from his belt buckle. His eyes held hers for a moment, the intensity of his gaze paralysing her. Thick pink lips rimmed by the wool of the mask mouthed something she couldn't hear above the roar of the engine as her foot stabbed at the accelerator.

Then he blinked. The flutter of his eyelids was enough to break the spell. She threw the car into gear, and reversed at speed out of the space, only braking when the beeping of the parking distance control flat-lined to a near-constant tone. She put the BMW into drive and it shot forward, the head-lights framing the man's broad outline.

Yanking down hard on the steering-wheel, she narrowly avoided hitting him with the hood. Keeping her foot on the gas pedal, she pulled out of the club's parking lot and on to the street.

She checked the rear-view mirror: the street behind her was empty. No one was following her. Her hands were still shaking – in fact, her whole body seemed to be vibrating with fear, her heart pounding in her chest. She grabbed for her cell phone, which was next to her on the passenger seat, thought about calling the cops, then decided against it. She wanted to go home, not stand around in a parking lot talking to the police.

She dropped her phone, switched on the radio and turned up the volume, hoping the music would blast away the fear that was settling like a thin film over her skin. She slammed her palms hard against the steering-wheel, rage edging out her anxiety, and pulled over into the driveway of a gas station about a thousand yards from the club's exit, picking a spot near the out-of-service car wash that was pitch black. Then she waited, taking deep breaths, trying to gather herself.

A few seconds later she watched a pickup truck pull out of the parking lot and make the same turn she had. Raven took a deep breath as she caught a glimpse of the driver. It couldn't be him. It just wasn't possible.

The pickup wove across the centre median and, for a moment, she thought she might be about to glimpse some divine justice. But the driver righted the car and continued on his way, like nothing had happened.

She pressed the button to lower her window, lit a fresh cigarette and started the car. Trembling, she pulled out from the darkness of the gas station and back on to the road.

Two

Carved pumpkin jack o' lanterns with jagged teeth and diamond-slit eyes stared blankly at Raven from the front stoops of her neighbours' houses as she turned into the quiet residential street nestled in the foothills south of Ventura Boulevard. Still shaken by what had happened outside the club, she'd used the long drive back to calm herself. Now she was clear about what she had to do.

As she pulled into the driveway, she pressed the garage-door opener, which was clipped to the BMW's sun shield. The door swung up. She took a minute before she drove in, idling on the street, checking to make sure the garage was empty.

Satisfied that it was, she nudged the BMW inside, purposely leaving the door open behind her, then got out and walked to the front of the house. The street was quiet. A couple of cars were parked at the kerb but they belonged to neighbours.

She walked back into the cool of the garage, opened the

passenger door and took out her purse and the holdall that contained her stage outfits. As she closed the door, she glanced back at the BMW, a habit she'd developed when she'd had a bad night and needed to remind herself that her career had its compensations. It had been a gift from a man who had confused what Raven saw as a business relationship with something else. She had waited until he had given her the pink slip that transferred ownership of the car to her before letting him down gently. She couldn't be bought, she'd said to him, with a smile; not in the way he wanted to buy her, anyway. She could only be leased, and even then you never got the full package.

Over the years, she'd learned that you had to keep something back, some small piece of yourself. If you didn't, you got your heart broken, and Raven had experienced enough heartbreak to last a lifetime. She had shut herself off and focused instead on making a life for herself and Kevin, and no one was going to take that away from her now.

Rolling her shoulders to ease the crick in her neck, she walked through the door that led from the garage into the hallway at the rear of the house, then into the kitchen. She put her purse on the counter, took a bottle of water from the refrigerator and drank half of it.

She pulled her work outfits from the holdall and jammed them into the washing-machine, then went back outside to collect the mail, leaving the door open so she could get back in quickly if anything happened. Nothing did, and the mail held no nasty surprises either. There were no handwritten envelopes, no death threats, nothing weird, just the usual junk mail and bills.

She walked back into the house and suddenly remembered something. She'd lost her sunglasses earlier in the week – she'd looked all over the house but hadn't found them. Now she went back into the garage to check the car. Leaving the mail on the hood, she peered into the glove box, then under the seats. Nothing.

She stopped, trying to think where she might have put them down. It came to her. She had been unloading groceries from the trunk the day before and, unable to see in the gloom of the garage, she had taken them off. Maybe she'd forgotten to pick them up again.

She clicked the button to open the trunk, and walked to the rear of the car. The interior trunk light was faulty so she crossed to the light switches on the far side of the garage. The fluorescent tubes flickered into life, throwing fragments of harsh, savage light into the trunk. A horrific still image flashed in front of her. Then the lights steadied and she could see it clearly.

She stared into the maw of the trunk at a semi-clothed body, the stump of the neck covered with clean plastic sheeting, the ends wrapped tightly with string. Then she started to scream.

Three

The minutes dragged as Raven waited in the kitchen for the cops to show up. She smoked a cigarette, then lit a second from the fading embers. She thought about going next door or across the street to one of the neighbours but decided against it. Since moving in she had kept her distance from them, scared that they would work out who she was and what she did for a living. Anyway, no one had come when she had screamed. Not one person. The thought brought her close to tears.

She could have waited outside on the patch of front lawn, she guessed, but she was sure that no one was inside the house. There were no signs of anyone having broken in – no forced locks or smashed windows. Nothing out of the ordinary – apart from the decapitated body in the trunk of her car.

She reached over and turned on the tap, extinguishing the burning red tip of the second cigarette with the jet of water, then rinsing the flecks of wet black ash down the drain, jamming the stub into the waste-disposal unit and turning it on. Then she walked to the front door to wait for the cops.

Another minute passed. A long minute. She rubbed under her eyes, staining her fingers with mascara.

A flashlight swept across the glass pane in the front door, and she started. Then the bell rang. Raven took a couple of deep breaths and opened the door. A lone female patrol officer stood on the threshold. A cruiser was parked at the kerb, its lights dappling the neighbours' lawns and splashing red over the gaudy Hallowe'en decorations that sat in people's front windows.

'Ma'am, you called to report finding a body?' the patrol officer asked, as her partner came into view from the side of the house.

Raven pulled the door wide so they could come in, noticing as she did so that her hands were still shaking. Suddenly everything tunnelled in on her. The red and blue lawn seemed to suck itself up from the ground and race towards her, the silhouetted paper cutouts of spiders, witches and goblins to start dancing at windows. She felt the strength disappear from her legs, and heard, from far away, a woman's voice: 'Ma'am? Are you okay? Ma'am?'

Raven was sitting in the back of an ambulance, an oxygen mask covering her mouth and nose. A paramedic crouched next to her. 'Take it easy. You had a shock,' he said.

Behind him, the street she lived on had magically transformed into a carnival of flashing lights and uniforms. Neighbours stood on the edges of their perfectly manicured front yards in their robes and slippers watching the show. The Hallowe'en decorations were still there but they seemed more festive than frightening. At the centre of the carnival, the main attraction was Raven's house. People in paper suits walked in and out of the front door and yellow crime-scene tape was festooned around it like bunting.

For a second Raven wondered what they were all doing there and then the events of the last few hours came back to her in a series of flashes that made her feel lightheaded all over again. She closed her eyes, and sucked hard at the oxygen.

'She good to talk to us?'

This time when she opened her eyes a man and a woman, both dressed in business attire, were standing next to the ambulance. The guy was African-American, mid-fifties, and had a face that wasn't so much lived in as forcibly occupied: heavy, hooded eyelids gave way to a wide boxer's nose, which was offset either side by sports-trophy ears. The woman was a little younger, late forties maybe, her blonde hair cut in a short bob. She had bright blue eyes.

'This is Detective Brogan,' said the man, 'and I'm Detective Wilkins.'

'We're from Van Nuys Division of the Los Angeles Police Department,' said Brogan, finishing off what seemed like a well-rehearsed introduction.

'Where's Officer Stanner?' Raven asked.

The two detectives looked at each other, puzzled.

'Stanner?' Wilkins asked.

'From the Threat Management Unit? Someone's been stalking me. He's the one I've been talking to.'

Another look passed between Wilkins and Brogan, then Brogan turned away. 'Just going to speak to the watch commander. Be right back,' she said, her hands dipping into her pockets as she walked off.

Wilkins watched his partner's departure, then turned his car-crash face back to Raven. 'You feel ready to take me through what just happened?'

'Where do you want me to start? Finding it in my trunk or before that?'

Wilkins cocked his head very slightly to one side. 'Something happened before you found the body?'

'Kind of, although I don't know if it's connected,' she said.

She took him back through events at the club. When she said she was stripping, he didn't react at all. Normally guys, regardless of their profession or in what capacity they were talking to her, showed something. Apparent disgust. Discomfort. A barely concealed excitement. But all Wilkins had said was 'Uh-huh', like she'd told him she was a waitress in a diner, then moved her on to the next part of the story. She'd liked him for his lack of reaction, even though the whole time she was speaking he seemed to be studying her, like she was a specimen under a microscope.

When she'd told him about the man who'd banged on her window in the parking lot he'd asked a lot of questions. How tall was the guy? What weight? Any tattoos? Once he was satisfied that she'd given him everything she could remember he'd moved her back on, skipping the trip home and getting to the moment when she'd popped the trunk.

By then the female detective, Brogan, was back and they went into a huddle before pulling in a couple of uniformed cops. Then they wandered over to the house where they stood outside talking.

Raven took a deep breath. She reached up and massaged her temples with the tips of her index fingers. At least Kevin hadn't had to witness any of this. For that one small mercy she was grateful.

Brogan and Wilkins traded a look. They'd been partners for five years, long enough to develop a shorthand that didn't require words. They called themselves Minority Report after the science-fiction film. It was a running joke because, between their race, gender and, in Brogan's case, sexual preference, they'd figured they ticked just about every diversity box the LAPD had.

Finally Brogan spoke, pushing a loose strand of hair behind her right ear. 'You buying any of this?' she asked Wilkins.

He looked skywards for a second. 'Nope, but I don't see why she would make the call herself if she'd killed the vic. Why not just dump the body somewhere? Drive down to Baja and stick it in a culvert.'

Brogan thought about it for a second. 'How many of the assholes that we deal with do stuff that actually makes sense?'

Wilkins smiled. 'Expressed as a percentage?'

Brogan nodded.

'Between zero and none.'

'Probably too early to be jumping to conclusions anyway. At least, before we speak to this guy from TMU,' Brogan said.

'Gotta work out who the vic is too,' Wilkins added. 'And what happened to her head.'

Brogan glanced across to the garage as a camera flash went off from one of the forensics photographers. 'Think I can answer that one. Buddy of mine from Central told me they had a caper yesterday morning where they found a woman's head stuffed into a newspaper vending machine down near the Federal building. They thought it was maybe some Islamist shit but it turns out the vic was a porn star. I'll give him a call, let him know we found the rest of her.'

Wilkins gave his partner a grim smile. 'This buddy down in Central tell you the vic's hair colour?'

'No. Why?'

'Well, if the carpets match the drapes then we know for sure it's the same broad.'

Brogan grimaced. 'I doubt her carpet would help us much. Those gals are usually clean as a whistle down there.' She paused for a second. 'Were you on the force for the "Four On the Floor" case?' she asked.

'That was the caper with the porn-star guy, right?'

'Yeah, John Holmes was the dude's name. He was working as a porn actor, doing well, but got into some heavy drugs. Ended up with him and three of his buddies dead in an apartment. Then there was that whole machete-attack deal a year or two back. Those were porn people too.'

'What's that got to do with this?' Wilkins asked.

'Nothing directly, but it's one fucked-up way of making a living. Drugs, disease, a lot of lowlifes. You survive in that world you ain't no innocent,' Brogan said.

Wilkins's eyes narrowed as he glanced back towards Raven. 'Which means that she knows a whole lot more than she's telling us.'

'I wouldn't sweat it either way,' said Brogan.

'Why's that?' Wilkins asked.

Brogan gave another little shrug. 'Body falls in Van Nuys, head falls in Central. That means the whole package is probably going to land on someone's desk down at the Police Administration Building. That means this whole caper is NOP.'

'NOP?'

Brogan smiled at her partner. 'Not our problem.'

Four

Stanner arrived almost a full hour later, his broad shoulders and mass of tightly curled hair visible over the crowd. Raven had met with him twice before, once here at her house and once when she'd taken some of the letters into his office at the Threat Management Unit. She'd liked him. He didn't look at her like she was a piece of meat or like she didn't warrant protection because of what she did for a living.

And as the letters had piled up and the phone calls had started, when no one spoke, he'd done more than she'd expected. He'd organized for a panic alarm to be fitted in her home (although she'd had to pay for it), extra patrols to run by at night, and he'd added the address as a 'special location' to the dispatch system. They'd come up against one problem, though. Unlike the vast majority of these cases, he'd explained, Raven had no idea who the person stalking her was, and neither, even after months of investigation, did Stanner or the LAPD. The letters and silent phone calls had become the criminal equivalent of chronic back pain, something that wore you down and was always in the background. They were also, however, something you learned to live with. Raven had learned to live with a lot of things.

'How you feeling?' Stanner asked.

Raven studied her feet. 'Tired. Shook up. I've had a hell of a night.'

Stanner squeezed a smile. 'Listen, the SID people will be here for a while.'

'SID?' Raven asked him.

'Scientific Investigation Division. Forensics.'

Raven glanced back to her house. Most of the neighbours on either side had retreated into their homes. 'Then what happens?' she asked.

'There'll be a homicide investigation, because we believe the body in the trunk of your car is linked to another discovery in Central Division, which makes it more likely that the case will be passed over to the Homicide Special Section of Robbery Homicide to investigate. There'll be more questions for you.' He sighed, and rubbed his head. 'Sucks, I know, but it's the way it goes.'

'What about me? Do I go into witness protection or something?'

'I'm afraid it doesn't really work like that.'

'But I'm being stalked. I mean, this is more than some creepy letters.'

'It certainly is, but the Threat Management Unit doesn't operate a witness protection programme.'

'So what are you going to do to protect me?'

'You have an alarm. We can up the patrols. Your address is on our dispatch system.'

Raven felt her face flush with anger. Why did no one seem to understand that her life was at risk here? 'You're doing all those things anyway,' she said.

'We can do more patrols.'

'Some woman is dead in the trunk of my car and you're going to do more patrols?'

Stanner sighed again. 'I know it seems inadequate, but we've been through this already. The Threat Management Unit can't offer you close-protection security, or someone to watch over you twenty-four hours a day. We simply don't have the budget for it.'

Raven thought of being on stage, and the predatory way the men she was dancing for stared at her; she thought of the house and how exposed it now felt; and she thought of Kevin and how she'd do anything to protect him.

The garage door was open and she could see her car, the trunk open, men and women huddled around it, one of them taking pictures, the flash from the camera bringing back the full horror of the body and what had been done to it. She looked at Stanner, who shrugged apologetically.

'I don't need more patrols,' Raven said, her voice rising. 'I need protection.'

'I'm sorry. I wish there was more we could do.'

'Well, if you can't help me, then who can?'

'There are lots of private individuals and companies who provide security. The good ones aren't exactly cheap so I'm not sure how much that would help you.'

Raven bit down on her lip. 'I have money. But how do I know which the good ones are?'

Stanner looked around nervously. 'Listen, we're not supposed to hand out recommendations.'

'But you know of someone?'

'He's from back east, but he's been out here working. I don't even know if he's still around, but if I was in your position, he'd be the guy I'd want to talk to.'

Finally Raven felt she was getting somewhere. 'So does this person have a name?'

Five

Ryan Lock lay in bed, listening to the sound of rocks heaving against the giant wooden supports that held the rented beach house suspended in mid-air above the Pacific Ocean. In his first few weeks in the house with his fiancée, Carrie, the fact that the ocean ran directly underneath the house at high tide hadn't bothered him. It was only with the arrival of the Santa Ana winds, and the way that the tides now sucked sand from the beach to expose the jagged black rocks, that he had become unsettled.

There was some small consolation in knowing that he wasn't alone. The dry, hot winds unsettled everything, leaving wild fires in their wake as well as giving rise to the vicious rip tides that clawed away at the sand, dragging it back into the water.

The seasonal winds took their toll on human beings as well. Back in '84 the howl of the Santa Anas had been pierced by the screams of the victims of Richard Ramirez, the serial killer dubbed the Night Stalker, as he carved a bloody trail across the city. This kind of nightmare manifestation made flesh was rare but still every year the winds brought a sharp, sudden spike in violent crime. Perhaps this was why the original settlers had dubbed the Santa Anas 'the devil's winds'.

As the rocks continued to pound against the wood, Lock glanced over to the red digits that burned next to him. It was close to five in the morning. Too early, really, to get up but too late to stay in bed awake.

He got up as quietly as he could, leaving Carrie lying asleep on her side, her hands folded like a pillow under her head, and their yellow Labrador, Angel, sprawled across the bottom of the bed, her jowls twitching as she chased imaginary sea monsters.

Measuring every step with care, he walked downstairs. In the kitchen, he filled a glass with water from the faucet and took a sip.

He opened the dishwasher, and a rush of warm, wet air filtered out. He pulled out the top rack a few inches, jamming the door open. Then he walked to the large sliding door that fronted one half of the house, pulled it open and stepped out on to the smaller of the beach house's two decks.

Looking over the guard rail he could see the white foam of the surf. The air out here was cold. Off to his right Big Rock, a cluster of huge rock formations, lay about thirty feet from the edge of the houses that crowded the coastline. Might as well enjoy all this while it lasts, he thought.

He had come out to Los Angeles a few weeks ago to provide close protection security to an overly paranoid movie actress, who was having problems with an ex-boyfriend who wouldn't accept that their relationship was over. Unusually for one of his protection gigs, Carrie had tagged along for the ride. The work had paid ridiculously well. The beach house, a second home that the star in question rarely used, had been thrown in as part of Lock's remuneration, saving them the cost of a hotel or small apartment.

The troublesome former boyfriend had turned out to be an Australian actor. He played tough-guy action heroes and took the method approach a little too seriously. In the end Lock had got him alone in a parking structure in Westwood and explained the difference between fiction and reality, illustrating his point by dangling the action hero over the edge of the roof while rush-hour traffic sped past five hundred feet below. The guy had taken the hint, and the movie actress had been so grateful to get him out of her life that she had offered Lock the use of the beach house for as long as he wanted. Lock had thanked her, but regular life called, at least for Carrie, and in two days' time they were due to fly back to New York, Carrie to her job as a news reporter and Lock to whatever corporate security gig came up next.

He went back inside the house, pulling the glass door closed behind him. On the kitchen counter his BlackBerry was vibrating. He crossed to it, picked it up, and studied the glow of the screen.

The number was showing as unknown and, above that, the time as 04:56 hours. Out of habit, Lock answered it.

Before he even had the phone to his ear, he could hear a woman on the other end of the line, her voice ragged and husky, as if she had only recently stopped crying.

Lock listened for a moment as, under his feet, another boulder slammed into one of the timber supports holding up the house.

'Ma'am? Can you hear me?' he said softly. 'Are you in immediate danger?'

There was a short silence. Then the woman spoke again. 'Not right this second but, yes, I'm in a lot of danger. You help people in my situation, right?'

Oh, Jeez, thought Lock, here we go. Between them, he and his business partner, Tyrone Johnson, attracted around a dozen crank calls a week. Tough guys who lived in their parents' basements, reading comic books, and wanted the opportunity to go toe to toe with them; tinfoil-hat-wearing conspiracy theorists who wanted to let Lock in on how the government was attempting to control the population's thoughts. And, a third category, which Ty, much to Lock's annoyance, seemed bent on encouraging: a group of women they referred to as Damsels in Distress, who often invented all kinds of threats (abusive boyfriends, prowlers, deranged stalkers) in order to try to arrange a rendezvous.

He had a feeling this was a category-three phone call. 'Ma'am, if your life is under threat you need to call nine-one-one and speak to the police department in your area. I'm sure they'll be able to help you.'

This time the woman sounded almost irritated. 'Who do you think gave me your number in the first place?'

Lock was taken aback. 'Excuse me?'

'My name is Raven Lane. I'm being stalked. I have the LAPD's Threat Management Unit helping me out but something just happened. I need some additional security. They told me to call you.'

Through his work so far in Los Angeles, Lock knew all about the Los Angeles Police Department's Threat Management Unit, or TMU. It dated back to 1989 when California had passed the first anti-stalker legislation. Being slap-bang in the centre of the entertainment industry, the police officers who worked for it were kept busy. When it came to non-celebrities they were only usually involved when stalking or harassment became aggravated. Lock knew that for the most part the victims were fairly anonymous. Sometimes all it took was a sad individual chancing upon a Facebook page for a whole world of misery to open up for the unsuspecting victim. He also knew that stalking cases were messy and difficult. 'But why, if the TMU are helping you, do you need me?'

'The TMU've been great but a panic alarm and a drive-by from a patrol car twice a night isn't going to cut it any more. I need someone who's going to stop this stalker before he hurts me.'

Lock sighed. In the normal run of things, and with the exception of big-mouthed Aussie thespians, he wasn't in the vigilante business. Sure, push him hard enough and he'd push back harder, but he didn't go hunting down stalkers and dishing out street justice. In the real world, behaviour like that tended to land you in prison and, from recent experience when he had been under cover in one, he knew he didn't like prisons very much.

At the other end of the line, the woman must have read his silence. 'Listen, I'm not asking you to kill the guy. Hell, I'm not even sure who he is.'

Lock still said nothing, counting on her to fill the silence.

'I can pay you, if that's what you're worried about.'

'It's not as simple as that,' Lock said, looking up to see Carrie walking bleary-eyed down the stairs, Angel skittering in a figure-of-eight pattern around her heels.

'Then let me help you out here,' the woman said. 'This morning I found a body in the trunk of my car. I'm pretty sure it was a woman's.'

'You think?' Lock asked, suddenly interested.

'It was difficult to tell,' the woman said. 'She didn't have a head.'

Six

As Lock swung his rented Range Rover from the Pacific Coast Highway through the short stub of the McClure tunnel and out on to the 10 freeway, Carrie glanced up from the browser feature on her BlackBerry. 'She's a porn star,' she announced.

'That so?' he said, noncommittal.

The phrase 'headless corpse' meant that Carrie was riding shotgun. A reporter is never officially off-duty, she'd explained to Lock, as they'd both thrown on their clothes. Angel had also insisted on tagging along and had taken up a position in the back, occasionally poking her head through the space between the two seats, hyped up at the prospect of an unscheduled road trip.

'You want me to read you some of her credits?' Carrie asked him.

'Any of them win any awards?'

Carrie scrolled down. 'No Oscar nominations, but *Yank*

My Doodle, It's A Dandy is kind of a snappy title.' She was silent for a moment. 'Are you really going to look after this woman, Ryan?'

Lock glanced over. 'You don't think I should? Y'know, even porn stars have a right to be safe.' He nodded towards Carrie's BlackBerry. 'What else you got?'

Carrie studied the screen for a moment. 'Wow.'

'What is it?' Lock asked.

'Well, she's not how I'd imagined.'

'How'd you imagine her?'

'Blonde, lots of silicon, huge boobs. Kind of plastic-looking.'

'She's not?'

Carrie's brow wrinkled a little. Lock found it reassuring. After all these weeks in LA, he'd grown used to the complete absence of facial movement. Everyone out here seemingly had the Botox look, which left their faces a flat plane devoid of expression. Their happy face was the same as their sad face, which was almost the same as their angry face. Coupled with the habit of framing every sentence like it was a question, even when it wasn't, it rendered the most mundane of daily interactions a veritable minefield.

'No,' Carrie continued. 'She's beautiful, not fake at all, and she looks . . . I dunno, kind of fragile.'

On the dash, the fuel warning light pinged on. Lock checked the GPS for the nearest gas station and switched lanes, ready to pull off at the next exit.

At the gas station on Fairfax, he slipped his credit card through the window to the cashier and went to fill up. Carrie leaned against the side of the Range Rover and watched him.

'You know how you sometimes say that what people call a sixth sense is them adding up all the data but not being able to articulate the conclusion?'

Lock glanced over at her. 'Yeah.'

'Well, if there's a better than fair chance that something bad is going to happen to her, you have one question left to answer.'

'Is she a good person or not?' he said, smiling at her, liking the way she looked, and feeling lucky all over again that she'd decided to be with him.

'And her job doesn't make her a bad person,' Carrie said.

Lock stifled a yawn. Sharp autumn sunshine reflected back off the windshields of the cars travelling in the other direction. Carrie was right. But then she was always right. So why did he still feel uneasy about taking this job?

Although it was daylight by the time they arrived, Raven Lane's street was still awash with emergency vehicles – a couple of Scientific Investigation Division wagons, a van from the Medical Examiner's Office and the requisite marked and unmarked cop cars. Lock parked up twenty yards shy of an LAPD police cruiser and got out. He flagged down a uniform. 'You still have a watch commander here?' he asked him.

Lock knew from experience that with a crime scene like this there was usually a captain designated to co-ordinate the security of the scene so that everyone else could do their job without risking the contamination of any potential evidence. Ever since the O. J. Simpson trial, where footage was played of detectives wading through the front of the crime scene without the appropriate gear aimed at preventing cross-contamination, the LAPD had been shit-hot about stuff like this. A clear chain of command at a crime scene was key to making sure there were no screw-ups a defence lawyer could pounce on later.

The uniform looked at him. 'And you would be?'

Lock gave his name and why he was there.

The uniform stared at him. 'This is a crime scene, sir. You'll have to wait for this young woman until we're finished talking with her. You understand me?'

Lock was neither surprised nor upset by the officer's re-action. If he'd been doing the same job he would have reacted in the same way. Cops viewed private security contractors as wannabe cops. In Lock's experience many of them were.

He walked back to the car to be greeted by a barking Angel. Carrie was down the street, away from the crime scene, chatting up one of the neighbours.

'Any information?' Lock asked her, as she stepped away from the couple she'd been talking to.

'*Nada*. Raven Lane keeps herself to herself. Most of the neighbours had no idea what she did for a living until tonight. Or, at least, that's what they're saying. I'm not sure any man is going to admit he recognizes a porn star when his wife's standing next to him.'

They waited a couple more hours, then Lock called the cell-phone number Raven had given him. She picked up straight away.

'I'm at the end of the street,' he said.

Maybe now that she'd had a chance to collect her thoughts,

she'd change her mind about needing his help. He was hoping she would.

'Let me see if they'll let me leave,' she said. 'The guy from the Threat Management Unit is here too. Would you like to speak to him?'

'That would be great,' said Lock. He got out of the car and took a look down the street. The uniformed cop he'd spoken to earlier and who was now helping to secure the perimeter glared at him. Lock waved the fingers of his right hand at him. The uniform said something to the officer standing next to him. Whatever it was, it wasn't complimentary.

Lock ignored him, focusing on the house in the street with the greatest concentration of vehicles parked outside. It was about six down on the left-hand side.

The San Fernando Valley, which was where they were now, was cheaper than the prime real estate on the west side of the city. It divided up into nice neighbourhoods, and not-so-nice neighbourhoods. It was also further from the coast and, as the name suggested, its topography made for a hotter climate. In high summer the temperature could reach 120 degrees Fahrenheit for weeks on end. However, even with sweltering conditions and a shitty real-estate market, Lock guessed you wouldn't be left with much change from a million dollars for the house he was looking at.

With its neatly trimmed front lawn dotted with flower-shaped sprinkler heads, its newly painted white exterior and freshly varnished white oak front door, it certainly wasn't the kind of place you'd associate with a stripper. Of course, the open garage door at the front lowered the tone of the whole neighbourhood: it was being swarmed over by a whole host of forensics techs. Inside, he could just about glimpse what he assumed was Raven Lane's car, a dark blue BMW sedan.

Lock had been so busy studying the house and all the activity that he had barely noticed the woman walking through the police line towards him. Her dark hair was pulled back into a ponytail revealing delicate features, and the most striking violet eyes he'd ever seen were set above high cheekbones and a turned-up nose. She walked with a sense of purpose, looking straight ahead, but there was a vulnerability to her as well. All of a sudden the million-dollar house made sense to him.

This was a woman whom men would go to war over. And it looked like one, in his own sick fashion, already had.

Seven

Next to Raven, a hefty guy with a bushy head of tight black curly hair, wearing grey slacks and a white shirt with a shoulder holster, struggled to keep up. Lock guessed that this was one of the officers from the LAPD's Threat Management Unit. He hoped he was good at catching stalkers because, judging by the roll of fat spilling over his belt, he sure as hell wasn't going to be much use stopping one if they came after Raven.

As she got within twenty feet of them, he noticed that Raven was carrying a clutch handbag, which was bulging at the seams. Maybe she was packing. He wouldn't have blamed her.

She slowed as she reached him and put out a hand towards him. 'Mr Lock?'

Lock's hand engulfed hers, but she shook with a firmness of grasp that surprised him. 'I'm sorry we have to meet under these circumstances,' he said. 'How are you holding up?'

Raven shrugged.

He kept his eyes on her face. Not looking at a woman's breasts, or lack thereof, was the quickest way of building rapport with a young, attractive female client.

'You Googled me on the way over, right?' Raven said.

'Why do you say that?' Lock asked her, slightly taken aback at her directness.

'The way you just looked at me. Guys who know who I am usually act weird when they meet me. Either they're super-aggressive if they're with their buddies or they act like it's their first day at grade school and their mama forgot to pick them up at home time. But you, you're different. You're trying to give the impression that I'm like any regular person.'

Lock smiled. 'You're not?'

She shook her head. 'Now you're taken aback that I'm not a bimbo. You know, people think because I use my sexuality to make a living that it's the only thing I have going for me. Am I right, Mr Lock?'

Lock smiled again. 'I wouldn't know.'

She turned to the cop standing behind her. 'This is Lawrence Stanner from the TMU.'

Stanner and Lock shook hands.

'Lawrence can fill you in on what they know about the creep who's stalking me,' Raven said.

Lock registered the use of the detective's first name.

'Actually, I can't,' Stanner interrupted. 'We have an active homicide investigation running here.'

Lock nodded. 'I understand.' He could work on the information-sharing once they'd established what his role would be, if any.

An EMS ambulance nudged past them in no particular rush, its siren silent.

'So, you want me to make sure you come to no harm while the police find this guy?' he asked. He was waiting for Stanner to bristle at the suggestion that the LAPD's role might be usurped, but Stanner didn't react at all, save to run a hand through his Brillo pad mesh of tight black curls.

'Got it in one. Now,' Raven said, opening her clutch purse and pulling out a brick of dollar bills still bound by the white paper bank seal, 'here is your first week's payment.' She hesitated for a moment. 'If that's acceptable?'

Lock did his best not to show any surprise at the block of money. 'You always carry this kind of cash around?' he asked her. There was probably close to ten thousand dollars in the brick.

'Usually I'm holding singles,' Raven said, the corner of her lips threatening a smile. 'I mean, this is enough, right?'

Lock took a few steps back, careful to maintain eye contact with her. 'Look, I can save you most of that money. Go get yourself a first-class plane ticket. Don't tell anyone where you're going. Buy a ticket last minute to New York. Then get on another flight to Europe. Go see the Vatican. Get drunk in Ireland. Eat snails in France. But get out of here until the police have done their job.'

Raven closed her eyes, her face suddenly tired. 'I wish I could do that, believe me. But it's not an option. I have responsibilities here.'

'Ms Lane,' said Lock. 'Your main responsibility is to stay alive. Any other responsibilities you may have can't be dealt with if you're not breathing.'

Raven checked her wrist watch. It was a Cartier. It looked like a real one too, not a Hong Kong knockoff you'd find in LA markets. Lock had priced one at Christmas for Carrie, but even with business booming, the amount had scared him off. She looked at him and Lock found himself drawn by the soft violet tone of her eyes. 'I don't mean to be rude here but I need protection, I was told you're the best person to provide it, and I'm prepared to pay your rates.'

Lock held up his hand to stop her. 'Who told you I'm the best?'

'Lawrence did. He knew you were working out here. Now, are you going to help me? Because if you're not, I need to find someone who will.'

Stanner stepped in and pulled Lock to one side, away from Raven. 'We have to cover city officials, all the schools in the LA district, a lot of Hollywood people, plus all the aggravated stalking cases, and you wouldn't like to guess how many of those we have running currently. Now, we would never ask a citizen to pay for extra help, but with the state's budget problems, and if they have the funds . . .' He trailed off.

Lock glanced back towards the house. One of the techs moved away from the trunk of the car and he caught a glimpse of the torso, the stump of the neck sealed with a sheet of clear plastic. 'You have any idea who the body in the trunk belonged to?' He directed the question at Stanner.

Stanner stared at him.

'Sorry, I forgot,' said Lock.

'Procedure,' Stanner said.

Lock took a moment to think things over. Raven was being stalked: Stanner's presence confirmed that much. The body in the trunk confirmed a real threat to her life – if she hadn't put it there herself, which was always a possibility. Leaving that aside, though, there was definitely a job to be done and Raven had the funds to pay him to do it.

On the other hand, there was something off about the whole thing. Why would a stalker dump a headless corpse in Raven's trunk when, for the same amount of effort, he could have kidnapped Raven herself? It didn't add up.

'So, what do you say, Mr Lock?' Raven asked him.

Before he could answer, a red-haired woman in a bathrobe emerged from the house next door. Shrugging a patrol officer out of the way she made a beeline towards them. Instinctively, Lock stepped in front of her, placing himself between her and Raven as she launched into a tirade.

'We know who you are, you know,' the woman was shouting, 'and what you do for a living. No one wants someone like you next door to them. We have kids.'

Lock caught shock and anguish on Raven's face as it reddened. He stepped towards the woman. 'Get out of here.'

Stanner nodded to a nearby patrol officer. 'Jimmy.'

Still screaming at Raven, the woman was ushered away. Lock turned to Raven, but she was already walking back towards the house, her head bent in defeat. 'Hold on,' he called to her. 'I need to make a phone call first. Run this past my partner.'

Digging his cell phone from the pocket of his jeans, he pulled up Ty Johnson's number on speed dial. They had met while serving in the military, Ty in the Marine Corp and Lock in the British Royal Military Police, but now they both worked in private security, Ty serving as Lock's second-in-command. Ty was not going to be happy about being woken, and even less happy about Lock asking him to cancel the vacation he was about to take.

Ty picked up on the fourth ring. 'I'm visiting family, dude.'

'I need you back in LA right now.'

'I don't know if I can do that, brother. Who's the principal? Listen, if it's one of those Hollywood types you can forget it. They're way too high-maintenance.'

Lock smiled to himself, ready to play his trump card. 'Well, she is an entertainer. And she's definitely going to be high-maintenance.' He sensed he had piqued Ty's curiosity.

'She?'

'That's what I said.'

'What's her name?'

Lock told him. There was a spluttering sound at the other end of the line.

'*The* Raven Lane? You mean – the porn star?'

'Don't worry about it,' Lock said. 'You're visiting family. I shouldn't have bothered you.'

In the background, Lock picked up what sounded like Ty getting out of bed. 'No, it's okay, man. The lady's in trouble. Family can wait.'

Eight

A blood-orange sun hung above pristine red-tiled rooftops as the van from the Medical Examiner's Office withdrew, the headless body riding out of sight in the back. Along the street, daylight had robbed the Hallowe'en lanterns perched on front steps and the paper decorations of ghosts and goblins tacked inside windows of their menace.

Along with the early-morning sunshine, the Santa Ana winds had begun to pick up again, the hot breezes bringing with them a fresh swarm of paparazzi – word had leaked out of the headless body's identity. Latent heat, pushed into the ground by nightfall, seeped from the sidewalks, raising the temperature and fracturing tempers. More patrol cars arrived with uniformed officers to manage the blossoming crowd.

Word was also coming in of a brush fire north of Malibu, the first of the season, and Lock was glad that they'd brought Angel with them rather than leaving her back at the beach house.

At the sawhorse barriers erected at the end of the street, one of Raven's neighbours was trying to negotiate his way through the crush. A more aggressive paparazzo started snapping pictures of him, and the guy got out of his car to remonstrate, letting loose with a torrent of F-bombs. 'What the fuck, man? I mean really, WHAT THE FUCK?' he bellowed. 'I got my kids in the back of the car and you're taking pictures. Fuck you, you fucking lowlife piece of shit.'

The patrol officer whom Lock had spoken to earlier stepped in to quell tempers with a threat to both men to either calm down or do the rest of their talking in jail. It was going to be a long day, thought Lock, who had grabbed five minutes with Carrie.

'I think I have a name for the victim,' Carrie said, lowering her voice. 'Cindy Canyon. Her real name was Melanie Spiteri. She was an adult performer, like Raven.'

'Was she being stalked as well?' Lock asked.

Carrie shrugged. 'All I have is a name so far. You think it might be the same guy?'

'You don't think it's a possibility?'

'I thought stalkers tended to fixate on one person.'

'They also tend to be less of a nuisance than someone prepared to cut someone's head off, then stick the body in the trunk of a car.'

'True,' Carrie said. 'I'm going to head back to Malibu and make sure the house is okay. Should I see about us extending our stay?'

'You want to stay out here?' Lock knew that Carrie had work commitments back in New York.

'I spoke to the network. They're happy for me to be here for a few more days.' She turned, taking in the familiar media circus with a sweep of her eyes.

'I'm going to have to hang out here,' Lock said, apologetic.

'Don't worry. I already ordered a cab. I'll take Angel with me.'

Lock leaned in for a kiss. Carrie's acceptance that when he was on a high-risk job it took precedence was one of the things he loved about her. 'Thanks.' He put an arm around her shoulders. 'Are you really okay with me doing this?'

Carrie reached up to stroke his cheek. 'I trust you. And, like I said, every woman has a right to be safe in her own home.'

He took her hand and gave it a squeeze. 'I love you. You do know that, right?'

Carrie smiled. 'I know. Now go give some bad guy the good news.'

She turned away from him and whistled for Angel, then started towards the cab that was pulling up at the police barrier. He watched her go with a twinge of anxiety, wishing he didn't have a job to do right now. Then he turned back towards the house. There was a lot to do in a very short space of time.

The techs from the LAPD's Scientific Investigation Division were finishing up their initial work as Raven emerged from the house, her face concealed by a hooded top, baseball cap and sunglasses.

'They seem to be done talking to me,' she said to Lock, walking past him. 'I need to pick up my brother. We can use your car, right?'

Lock put out a hand. 'Hold up. Your brother?'

Raven stopped and turned. 'He was staying at a friend's last night. I need to go pick him up.'

'How old is he?'

'Seventeen.'

'He doesn't drive?'

'You'll understand when you meet him,' Raven said softly, smiling at Lock.

'Is there anyone else, or is it just you and your brother who live here? It's important that I know.'

'It's just us.'

'No boyfriends?'

Raven peered over her sunglasses at him. 'I'm kind of burned-out on men.'

'Okay then.' Lock squared his shoulders, bracing himself to face the squall of media attention. 'Wait here. I'll bring the car over.'

The drive gave Lock an opportunity to talk to Raven about the stalker, and to begin making some basic arrangements. Guarding her twenty-four-seven, even for a short period, was going to be a challenge.

If he'd been a cop, he would have tried to brow-beat her into going into hiding, not that it would have done much good, judging by her attitude to it so far. But he wasn't a cop, he was a close-protection operative, and the reason people hired CPOs was to keep them safe while they went about their daily business.

To their left they could glimpse the large white buildings of the Getty Center up on the hill. Even though she lived less than seven minutes' drive from the place, Raven was staring at it like she was noticing it for the first time. Lock took the relative calm inside the car as his cue.

'So,' he began, 'tell me how this all got started.'

She exhaled, and ran a hand through her jet-black hair while the sun caught the deep violet of her eyes. 'In my business, you can attract weirdos. I mean, dancers and porn stars are like freak magnets, right?'

'I know you've been through this all before with the cops, but the more I know the better I can protect you.'

Raven ran her hands down her face and settled herself. 'Okay, so I get a lot of letters, you know?'

'To your home?'

She shook her head. 'No. And I never talk to anyone about where I live. I don't have guys back there either. Not with Kevin.'

'That's your brother?'

'That's right. So anyway' – she was quick to shift subjects, Lock noticed – 'I have a company. RLC. The Raven Lane Company. That's where I run my fan club from. Most of my mail goes to a mailbox I've set up.'

It was all very corporate. The more she talked, the more Lock was getting a picture of someone who was very much in control. He'd always assumed that people in Raven's line of work were flaky, but she seemed to approach the entire thing primarily as a money-making enterprise. 'You said most of your mail. Where does the rest go?'

Raven dug into her clutch purse, pulled out a pack of gum, and offered a stick to Lock. He declined. 'If I'm dancing at a club, people send me stuff there. Like the note.'

'Was there anything else with the note that led you to

believe it was the same person who'd killed Cindy Canyon?'

Raven sank down an inch in the passenger seat. 'That was her name? The girl in my trunk?'

'Her stage name, yeah. Did you know her?'

'I'd heard of her.'

'Ever met her?' Lock pressed.

She rolled her eyes. 'No. Jesus, what's with all these questions? Are you a bodyguard or a cop?'

Lock sure as hell wasn't a cop and disliked the term 'bodyguard' so he shrugged off the question. 'The more I know about this situation, the more effective I can be in keeping you safe. Before the body turned up in your car—' He stiffened. For the past few minutes a Blue Honda Accord had been behind them on the freeway. He had accelerated and switched lanes and it had followed suit. Now, as he slowed and indicated that he was leaving at the next exit, its blinker had come on.

'What's the problem?' Raven asked.

'Blue Honda about three cars back. It's been tailing us since we left your house.'

Nine

Raven turned in her seat to take a look but Lock caught her arm. 'Best if they don't know that we've spotted them,' he said, switching lanes suddenly, and pulling in behind a black Volkswagen Bug. He checked the mirror again. He had a visual on the driver of the Accord. White or light-skinned Hispanic. Early twenties. Kind of scruffy. Keeping a real sharp eye on them but trying not to be too obvious, and doing a bad job of it.

From what Lock guessed the LAPD's profile of the stalker was, he imagined that several boxes had just been checked. There were other possibilities as well but in these situations it was always safer to assume the worst and work back from that point.

He sank back in the driver's seat, watching the traffic behind them in the side mirror as the Honda moved up on the outside. The driver had his eyes on them, no doubt about it.

In an ideal world, he would have had time to get a full

briefing from the LAPD so that he could run a full risk assessment. He would have been able to go over Raven's daily routine, bolster the security at her house, make sure they had the appropriate men and equipment, including up-armoured vehicles if they were required. He could have studied her plans for the week and recced every venue ahead of time so that there would be no surprises. But the world wasn't ideal. If it had been, the job he did wouldn't exist.

Normally Lock would have been reaching down to rack the slide on his Sig Sauer 226, but this was Los Angeles and a concealed-carry permit for someone not resident in the state of California was almost impossible to come by. You could carry illegally, but if you were stopped and caught without a permit you were probably looking at jail time. So, given the risks involved in the job he had flown out to do, he had chosen to forgo his usual weapon. And right now, legal or illegal, he was starting to regret it. Los Angeles was the city of the car gun and the bad guys tended not to worry about administrative details such as concealed-carry permits.

He looked over at Raven. Her face was pinched and anxious. 'Do you have a number for Stanner or any of his people in the TMU?'

'Why?'

'Like an emergency number?'

She snapped open her bag and pulled out a pack of cigarettes. 'I thought that's why you were here. In case there was an emergency.'

'Do you have one or not?'

'If I felt scared and I wasn't near the panic alarm, they told me to call nine-one-one.'

Of course they did, he thought, taking out his cell and putting in the call himself. He gave the dispatcher their position on the freeway, which was about two miles from the Sepulveda exit, and jammed the phone back into his pocket. As he did so, he caught a glimpse of the Accord in the rear-view as the driver waved at him to pull over.

'What's he doing now?' Raven protested.

The Honda was a single car behind them and, from the brake lights of the other cars around him, making moves to get closer. Lock tensed. There was still no sign of the Highway Patrol or any other members of law enforcement, and if their pursuer was going to do something to harm Raven, he was her only defence.

As the Honda moved up on them, he got a better look at the driver. Long, greasy hair, a hipster patch of facial hair below his bottom lip, and a pair of chunky earrings.

Up ahead the traffic was beginning to concertina to a halt, hardly an unusual occurrence in a city where the freeway system regularly ran at over ninety per cent of full capacity. The next exit where, presumably, the Highway Patrol would be waiting for them was still a half-mile away.

Lock nudged ahead of a soccer mom who was driving her Saturn with her elbows while applying lipstick with one hand and talking on her cell phone with the other. He edged into the inside lane.

The driver of the blue Honda was still muscling his way through the columns of slowing vehicles towards them. Lock watched him as he took one hand off the wheel and started to rummage around on the front passenger seat.

Eyeing the breakdown lane next to them, Lock suddenly

spun the wheel, and accelerated at the same time. The driver of the Honda followed suit, careening down the empty lane, as people stared at them through their car windows.

'Get down,' Lock shouted to Raven, pushing her seat back, so she could squeeze into the footwell in front. 'Damn it!' Ahead of them in the breakdown lane a hulking recreational vehicle loomed up through the windshield. Lock jammed the brakes on, scoping out the possibilities for evasive action.

To the right of the RV the cement wall next to the emergency lane was too steep for them to go round. On their left was a solid wall of traffic.

Looking behind them again, Lock could see the driver of the Honda closing in tight on them. He was scowling, angry, his shoulders hunched as he crouched over the wheel; a raging bull, everything about his body language signalling aggression.

'Okay, we're going to stop in a moment and when we do you're going to stay as far down in the footwell as possible. You got me?'

Raven nodded, her face pale with fear.

Lock's Range Rover was still moving as he reached down and yanked on the parking brake, throwing off his seatbelt at the same time. The vehicle shuddered to a sudden halt and he clambered out. Staying low, he ran to the corner of the car, then popped his head up to take a peek.

The Honda had stopped too, and the driver was starting to get out, only his left arm and hand visible.

Lock stayed low. Then the driver spotted him and they stared at each other for a long moment. Lock noted the driver's right hand was still moving inside the Honda.

The movement made up Lock's mind for him. Pushing off on his back foot, he sprinted towards him. As his vision tunnelled he saw a black shape in the driver's hand.

Lock jumped, tackling the driver high around the top of his chest, the kind of tackle that in most contact sports would have earned you some pretty serious time on the bench or even a lifetime ban.

The driver gave a shout of pain, his shoulder slamming against the edge of the open car door, then Lock was on top of him, searching for the object in the driver's right hand and coming up with a black digital single-lens reflex camera with a telephoto lens, the strap wrapped around his wrist.

'What the fuck, man?' the driver protested, as Lock got to his feet. 'Are you out of your mind?'

In the distance, Lock could hear the sirens. All around them people seemed to be on their cell phones. He guessed that they weren't calling home to check on what was for dinner. He knelt down next to the driver. 'Where does it hurt?' he asked, feigning sympathy.

'Here,' the driver said, rubbing at his shoulder.

'There?' Lock asked, slamming a fist into the wounded area. The driver howled. No words. Just a guttural noise of torture.

Across the concrete barrier, a patrol car was steaming towards them down the car-pool lane on the opposite side of the freeway, against oncoming traffic, lights and siren blazing.

Lock stepped in close behind the driver. 'What's your name?'

The driver started to glance round but Lock nudged a knuckle into the base of his spine hard enough to get his attention. 'Name.'

'Raul Dominguez.'

The patrol car was pulling up close by, so Lock chose his words with deliberation. 'Okay, Raul, listen to me carefully. Until this psycho is captured, I will assume that anyone pursuing or stalking Raven Lane is a threat to her life and I will respond with the level of force appropriate, including deadly force, to ensure her safety.' He paused for effect, his tone low and even. 'So, I want you to pass that message on to anyone else who thinks they can make a quick buck taking her picture. The glint from a camera lens and the light that bounces off a rifle scope aren't all that different. And that's what I'll be telling the judge. Do you hear me?'

Raul stared straight ahead. 'Assault me for doing my job, that's some bullshit right there. Man's got to make a living.'

Lock looked back at Raven, who had stumbled from the Range Rover, her face pale and drawn after this latest ordeal. 'It's going to be even harder making a living if I break both your legs.'

Ten

The almond-shaped eyes were the giveaway, the skin folded over so that it almost entirely obscured the inner corners. Set in an overly rounded face, above a slightly protruding tongue, the eyes told the story of Raven's unwillingness to leave the country, and therefore her need for the services of someone like Lock. Her brother, Kevin, had Down's syndrome.

Kevin and Raven hugged, the warmth of their relationship evident for all to see.

'Did you and Wendy have fun?' Raven asked her brother. Lock noticed a slight tremor in her voice. The strain of recent events was catching up with her.

'Yeah. We watched a movie,' Kevin said.

As he broke away from his sister, Kevin stared at Lock for a long second, almost as if he were waiting for the flicker of pity in his eyes. Lock wondered what it was like going through life where the first reaction people had to you was pity or shock or, in some cases, discomfort. In that single split second before they drew the curtain of politeness over their initial reaction there must have been a thousand tiny wounds.

Brought up to treat everyone the same, he smiled and put out his hand. 'Kevin, I'm Ryan Lock. I'm a friend of your sister.'

A single crease etched across Kevin's palm confirmed, if any were needed, his condition. It also confirmed Lock's feeling that he'd been correct in accepting this assignment. Protecting the vulnerable was what he did best. And, however you cut it, and whatever politically correct platitudes society offered, Kevin was more vulnerable than most seventeen-year-old boys.

Behind Kevin stood a girl around the same age, with the same physical characteristics. 'I'm Kevin.' He thumbed over his shoulder at the girl. 'This is Wendy. We're getting married when she's eighteen.'

Behind Lock, Raven and Wendy's mother raised their eyebrows simultaneously. Clearly, thought Lock, this was not news.

'Kev, can you get your stuff together?' Raven prompted.

Wendy's mother, a woman in her early fifties with short-cropped blonde hair, smiled at them both. 'They have separate rooms when Kev sleeps over.'

'Mom!' Wendy protested, her face turning red: Miss Teen Drama 2011.

'Thanks for taking him,' Raven said.

'It's not a problem. But I do kind of need to talk to you in private,' Wendy's mother said.

Raven turned to her brother. 'Kev, what did I ask you to do?'

Kevin grabbed Wendy's hand and pulled her out of the room and up the stairs. She giggled at this show of possessiveness as Raven rolled her eyes, more mother herself than older sister.

Lock sensed that this was a conversation the two women would want to have to themselves. 'I'll go make sure he behaves himself.'

'Thanks,' Raven said, with an awkward smile. Lock trooped up the stairs following the sounds of Kevin's bravado all the way into a small spare bedroom where he was busy jamming his clothes into a rucksack.

Downstairs, he could hear snatches of conversation. Wendy's mother seemed to be doing most of the talking.

'I think it might be best.'

'At least until all this blows over.'

'You know how fond we are of Kevin.'

'It's nothing personal.'

It had started already. The gradual isolation of Raven and her brother. No matter how nice someone was, how kind, how understanding or empathetic, no one wanted themselves or their child drawn into even the furthest orbit of the psychopath who had dumped Cindy Canyon's body in the back of Raven's car. Raven's stalker – assuming they were one and the same as Cindy's killer – had chalked up another victory.

Lock had seen it before with stalking cases: the slow and steady isolation of the victim. Human predators knew as well as their counterparts in the animal kingdom that half the battle was isolating their prey from the herd. Even if it wasn't conscious, Raven's stalker must have known that his gory display would have that effect. He stepped into the spare bedroom. 'You want me to help you with that?' he asked, nodding to the Superman backpack on the floor next to his feet.

Kevin and Wendy looked up at him but didn't say anything. He wondered if they'd also caught some of the conversation from downstairs. After a few moments, Kevin shrugged his assent.

'Superman, huh?' Lock said, picking up the backpack. 'You know, I reckon I could kick Superman's ass if I put my mind to it.'

Kevin got up. 'No way. Superman could kick your ass.'

Wendy giggled, and covered her mouth with her hand. Lock liked her. In fact, they made a cute couple. There was more genuine warmth and affection between the two of them than there was in ninety per cent of the adult relationships he saw.

'I'm telling you, man,' he said, walking towards the door. 'There's no way Superman would survive if we went one on one.'

'Are you a cop?' Kevin asked.

'Something like that.'

'So how come you don't have a gun?'

'Because I don't need one.' Lock crossed his fingers behind his back, hoping this was true. 'I'm like a cop who protects people.'

'What do you mean?' Wendy asked.

'I guess it means that I make sure bad things don't happen to good people.'

Raven shouted up the stairs, her voice sounding strained, 'Kev, we gotta go.'

Kevin started down the stairs with Wendy, Lock to the rear, Kevin's backpack slung over his shoulder. He caught a whisper of 'Superman would so kick his ass,' from Kevin to Wendy, and smiled.

Raven was waiting for them by the front door. She put an arm around her brother. 'Come on, let's go home.' Then she looked to Lock. 'Can you maybe call and see if that's gonna be okay?'

'Why wouldn't it be okay?' Kevin asked.

'We had a little accident back at the house. Some water got into the garage. That's all.'

Lock stepped out of the house and stood on the front porch. Not even midday, and the heat was building. It was like breathing soup. He called the Van Nuys Division headquarters. 'Am I clear to bring them back to the house?'

'Yeah, the techs are just finishing up. We had to take her car in as well.'

'Understood,' Lock said, hanging up.

He stepped back inside. 'I just spoke to the plumber,' he said to Raven. 'You're good to go.'

While Raven hustled Kevin out of the door, he took a quick check of the street and hung back for a moment.

'Can I speak to you for a moment?' he said to Wendy's mother, handing his car keys to Raven. 'I'll be real quick.'

He watched Raven and Kevin walk slowly towards the Range Rover, then turned back to the woman. 'I understand your concern with everything that's going on. And I just want you to know that if you send your daughter over to see Kevin I guarantee you she'll be safe.'

Wendy's mother nodded, but avoided eye contact. 'I appreciate that. However, I'm not sure that's a chance I want to take. When you have a child like our daughter, they mean more to you than a regular kid, not less.'

'You know what Raven does for a living, right?' Lock asked.

Another nod and floor stare. 'This is the Valley, Mr Lock. You'd have to be pretty naïve not to know what goes on with some people around here. But she's a good sister to Kevin. Most people would have put him in a home, walked away and not looked back, got on with their life. She has to get credit for that.'

'And he's a good kid. They both are. But this isn't about what's happened in the last twenty-four hours, is it?' Lock asked her, already knowing the true answer. He'd seen the subtle shift in her expression when Kevin and her daughter had talked about marriage.

She finally made eye contact with him. 'This talk about them getting married. We laughed it off at first. But they're serious.'

'Then if that's the reason you don't like them seeing each other at least be honest about it. Right now it's looking like it's some kind of judgement on Raven's lifestyle. You know she didn't invite this crazy into her life.'

Wendy's mother's face hardened. 'Are you absolutely sure about that?'

Eleven

When they arrived at Raven's house, Ty's purple 1966 Lincoln Continental was parked at the edge of the police cordon. Ty was slouched against one of the car's huge, tapering rear fins, his eyes obscured by mirrored Aviator sunglasses. The lettering on his T-shirt read: 'You Look Like I Need A Drink.' Even with the sunglasses, Lock could tell that he was checking out Raven from head to toe. As Raven helped Kevin unload his overnight bag from the car, Lock went to talk to his partner.

'Brought the Pimpmobile, huh?' Lock said. Ty's car was a source of constant irritation, undermining his belief that the first duty of a close-protection operative was to blend into the background.

'Speaking of which,' Ty started, 'where's that piece of shit you drive?'

Lock nodded towards the black Range Rover parked across the street.

'No way,' Ty spluttered. 'What happened to blending in?'

'This is LA,' Lock explained. 'Here, this blends.'

'Man, you're full of surprises. Kind of young for a mid-life crisis too. Porn stars. Sweet rides.'

Lock shifted uncomfortably. 'Ty, can we keep the porn-star talk on the down-low for now? She's a client. That means we have to treat her with a certain degree of respect.'

'I'm all about the respect, Ryan, you know that, brother.'

Behind the cordon, the last of the forensic techs were putting away their gear. The garage door was open and Lock could see that Raven's BMW was already gone.

'So? Wanna give me a sit rep?' Ty was looking at Lock over the top of his shades.

'Twenty-eight-year-old white female being stalked by a person or persons unknown. The cops think that whoever is obsessed with Raven is the same person who killed Cindy Canyon, and that this stalker has it in his head that he's already in a relationship with Raven. That's version one.'

'And version two?'

'That she did it,' Lock said.

Ty tipped his sunglasses up on to his forehead. 'Man, that's kind of hot. You think it's true?'

'If I did, I wouldn't have taken the gig.'

Ty looked around at the suburban street. 'You know, brother, there are two kinds of crazy in this nation of ours.'

Lock smiled. 'Go on, Brother Johnson, preach it.'

'Well,' Ty said, 'there's regular crazy, and then there's LA crazy. And LA crazy beats regular every time.'

Ty wasn't wrong, thought Lock, glancing up as two television helicopters buzzed overhead. A couple of the neighbours were gathered on their lawns, watching the show. A few more peeked through blinds from inside their homes. Lock watched a soccer mom snatch away a younger child from the front window of a ranch-style house that was opposite and a few doors down from Raven's place.

He wiped a hand across his face, the sweat beading on his brow dampening the back. What he really needed was a nap but he wasn't about to get one. There was too much work to be done. 'We have someone who's very determined and capable of taking human life. We need to be on the top of our game here, Ty.'

'So why don't we get her the hell out of here?'

'She won't do it.' Lock looked back towards his car where Kevin was still standing with Raven. 'Her brother has Down's syndrome. She doesn't want his routine disrupted.'

Ty filled his cheeks with air, then exhaled loudly. 'Our boy comes through the window at two in the morning with a hunting knife, that's going to disrupt everyone's routine, not to mention create a whole bunch of other medical problems.'

'Then we'd better do our job properly. I want to recce the house. You go introduce yourself.'

Ty straightened up. 'Be my pleasure.'

Lock called him back. 'Ty?'

'Yeah?'

'Don't go making things more complicated than they already are.'

Ty gave Lock his would-I-do-that? smile and wandered off.

Lock turned back towards the house. The SID team were finishing up, loading their gear into a panel truck. Contrary to the TV shows, most of their equipment, certainly at this stage of an investigation, was decidedly low-tech: swabs, plastic bags and digital cameras. The high-tech stuff was saved for the lab.

He wanted to walk through the house while it was completely empty. Although nightfall was around nine hours away, it was very unlikely that Raven and Kevin would be taking their advice and spending the evening somewhere else, so he needed to make sure the place was locked up tight before the sun fell over the Valley.

He walked around the property from the outside, approaching it as an intruder would. The front door was properly secured with a mortise-lock and separate chain. They could use a camera out here. He added it as the second item on his list, the first being a couple of motion sensors for the lawn area at the front. If anyone stepped on to the property, he would want to know about it. With the foothills of the San Gabriel Mountains close by, they would have to adjust the sensitivity and height of the sensors for the coyotes that no doubt roamed the neighbourhood after dark.

Next he walked to the windows at the left of the property – the living room windows. They had locks on them and sensors that would trigger the alarm if anyone tried to jemmy them open. There was some sagebrush off to one side. It wasn't planted close enough together to offer any great degree of cover so he determined that it could stay where it was.

He took off down the side of the house, noting the position of every drain, every window. Any inanimate object made it on to his plan of the house. The large plastic wheel-mounted garbage cans would have to be secured and any paperwork shredded. Not only would they inevitably be trawled by the media but they were a potential treasure trove to a stalker. A misplaced credit-card or bank statement could tell someone where you shopped, the gym you worked out at and the stores where you bought your clothes and groceries. A carelessly discarded phone bill offered up your family and friends, as well as business acquaintances, who you spoke to, how frequently and what times you called them. Armed with these two items you could build a fairly comprehensive picture of someone's life relatively rapidly.

This reminded him of something else. He jotted down a separate note to ask Raven about any social networking accounts she might have. If she had a fan page on Facebook, which anyone could join, the stalker might be there already. By definition stalkers were obsessive by nature so it should be possible to run a search to see who was monitoring the fan page most frequently. He guessed that Stanner and the other officers at the Threat Management Unit would already have done this, especially given the events of the past few days, but there was no harm in double checking.

There was a door at the rear of the house that led out on to a deck, which offered up an impressive view of the Los Angeles basin. Jumping off it, he used his Maglite, one of the big heavy torches used by cops, to check the crawl space underneath. It was clear but he would get a contractor in to seal it off.

Beyond the deck a steep slope led down to the property on the street below. The front of the deck hung out over this space, and the property line was demarcated by a chain-link fence. It was climbable but it would take some effort.

Lock started down the slope, walking sideways on the edge

of his heels. Halfway down, he started as a dog appeared on the other side of the fence and barked, its teeth bared. It was smaller than a German Shepherd but had the same profile and markings. It was probably a Belgian Shepherd – not the ideal dog to have for security. In truth, small, yappy dogs were a bigger pain in the ass to intruders as they were more easily threatened, and tended to make more noise, thus warning the householder.

Lock continued down the slope. When he got within ten feet of the fence the Belgian Shepherd, which had been backing up, suddenly lunged towards the fence, putting its paws up against the chain-link, throwing its head back and alternating a throaty growl with an I-mean-business bark. A woman in her early sixties, wearing slacks and a University of Southern California Trojans T-shirt appeared at the side of the house. She had gardening gloves on.

Lock put his hands up by way of apology. 'Sorry to disturb you, ma'am.'

She called the dog back to her side. 'I wish you people would just finish up what you're doing.'

Of course. She'd assumed he was with the LAPD. Presumably they had already been down here to take a look, keen to give the appearance of thoroughness.

'Just one question,' he said. 'Then I'll get out of your hair.'

'I already told you I didn't see anything.'

'Does the dog stay out in the yard all the time?'

The woman looked to the skies like it was the dumbest thing she'd ever heard. 'No point having a guard dog if you don't let him guard.'

'Doesn't the barking bother the neighbours?'

The question earned Lock another withering look. 'He's trained not to bark at every little thing. He only goes off if there's someone where they ought not to be. Like you right now.'

He made his apologies and retreated. Like every other single security measure, guard dogs could be subverted, but the dog's presence on that side of the house would make their job a little more straightforward.

He reached the top of the slope, finished his external inspection, then walked into the house. There was one major detail he still had to plan for. Assuming the worst-case scenario of a homicidal stalker inside the house, they would need a plan B, and plan B came in the shape of a panic room.

He moved through Raven's home searching out the most appropriate room. Ideally, he would have had something specially designed and installed but there wasn't time for that. He would have to pick a space and work around what he had.

He climbed the dark oak staircase, noting the absence of pictures on the walls. That fitted with the rest of the place. Everything was neat to the point of sterility. The faint whiff of bleach hung in every room.

On the upstairs level there was a master bathroom and three large bedrooms off a long rectangular hallway. One bedroom was set up as a home office-cum-junk room. It was on the left-hand side of the house adjacent to the master bathroom. He ruled it out. One of the most important attributes of a panic room in a small domestic setting was how quickly you could gather everyone and get to it. If an intruder was halfway up the stairs before you knew they were inside the house, the last thing you wanted to have to do was make a mad dash across a hallway.

He checked the room and the bathroom, then walked into one of the other bedrooms. This, he guessed, was Kevin's, although the décor was more appropriate to a child than a teenager. Superman dominated the walls, from an elaborate mural emblazoned by the bed to the posters tacked up everywhere else. Even the bed sheets and pillow cases had a Superman theme. There was one window, which overlooked the rear yard. One window was good. Just off to the left there was a small en-suite bathroom. No evidence of Superman here, although on opening the bathroom cabinet Lock was confronted with an array of prescription medicines. Clearly Kevin had some fairly heavy-duty secondary health issues. He could understand why Raven was insisting on staying put.

Standing in the middle of Kevin's room, he wished she had just told him about her brother from the get-go. He guessed, however, that to live the life she did, Raven had built defence upon defence around herself, and didn't see the need to explain or justify her decisions. The stalker's intrusion must have made things doubly difficult.

Lock closed the door softly on Superman, and walked into Raven's bedroom. Here, the style was decidedly feminine. The bed was a California King with crisp white Egyptian sheets. In fact, pretty much everything in the room was white, including the walk-in wardrobe next to the en-suite. With a change to the wardrobe's door, it would make an ideal panic room, even though there was barely space for Raven, Kevin and whichever bodyguard was on duty at the time. But it would only have to hold them safely for an hour at most.

Even if the stalker was in the house, an hour was more than enough time for the LAPD SWAT team to move in and take him out.

Pulling out his cell phone, Lock made a call, arranging for someone to come round and replace the door.

He took another look around the closet. All of her clothes were arranged neatly on hangers or in drawers, and many items still had the plastic dry-cleaner wrappings covering them. Replacing the door would be a messy business. Some of this stuff would have to be moved into another room.

Lock heard footsteps behind him and looked over his shoulder to see Raven come into the bedroom.

'Kevin seems to be hitting it off with your partner,' she said.

Lock smiled. Everyone got on with Ty. 'I'm afraid we're going to need to clear this closet out so we can make it into a panic room.'

Raven looked nervous. 'I thought I was paying you guys so it wouldn't come to that.'

'We already know that your stalker is violent and determined. We need to plan for every eventuality.'

Raven hesitated, then nodded reluctantly.

'You want to help me clear it? Maybe move it into a spare room?' he asked her.

'Sure.'

Stepping past him into the closet, she scooped up a half-dozen outfits from the rail and dumped them on her bed. 'I kind of need to go through this stuff anyway. Get rid of some of it.'

She stepped back into the closet, then looked away from the rail, where she'd just removed a bunch of clothes, to Lock. 'Is this someone's idea of a joke?' she asked, her violet eyes cloudy, her face taut with fear.

'What are you talking about?'

'I'm talking about this,' she said.

Lock noticed that her voice was shaking, as she passed him a short black designer dress. A note was pinned to the front. Neatly etched in printed letters was a short message.

I thought you'd look nice in this.

Twelve

The cops were back. Not in the same numbers that they'd been when Raven had discovered Cindy Canyon's body in the trunk of her car – a dress with a handwritten note didn't have quite the same pulling power as a headless corpse – but they were back just the same. A forensic tech removed the dress and note for further examination while a couple of detectives spoke to Raven in her bedroom. Lock let them get on with it.

Feeling uneasy, he went downstairs to check on Ty and Kevin. The discovery of the dress took things to a whole new level. For starters it meant that someone had been inside the house. Worse, there was no sign of a previous break-in, and no evidence of their presence, apart from the dress and the note. The police had already checked the doors for signs of someone picking the lock, but there were none of the telltale scratch marks left by an amateur. If that method had been used it had been used by someone who knew what they were doing.

Ty glanced at Lock from the couch.

'How's everything upstairs?'

'All good,' Lock said, aware of Kevin's presence.

Ty clapped a hand on Kevin's shoulder. 'See? I told you, K-Lo, nothing to worry about.'

Kevin retreated into his TV show. It was impossible to know how much of this he was taking in but Lock guessed it was more than he was letting on.

Lock hadn't been around someone with Down's syndrome for any length of time before. In some instances they might have the mental age of someone much younger. At seventeen, Kevin came off like a nine-year-old, but anyone who knew anything about nine-year-olds was aware that they were far from dumb, and they picked up on stuff. In many ways they could be far more perceptive than adults or, at the very least, more willing to share their perceptions.

The front-door bell rang and Lock went to answer it, leaving Ty with Kevin. He was hoping it was the locksmith. The dress and the attendant note meant that changing the locks and improvising a safe room were priorities if they were to stay where they were.

Outside, Stanner, from the LAPD's Threat Management Unit, stood sweating, his curly hair glistening in the afternoon sun. Lock opened the door.

'Sure as hell doesn't feel like late fall,' Stanner said.

Lock stepped outside, waving towards the inside of the house. 'We're trying to keep as much of this from the kid as possible.'

'I got you,' Stanner said.

At that moment a van bearing the logo Valley Locksmiths

drove up, and Lock gestured for the guy to pull into the drive before turning his attention back to Stanner.

Stanner combed his hair with his fingers. It sprang right back into place. 'So, it looks like someone's been inside the house,' he said.

It was revealing that Stanner framed it as a statement rather than a question. 'Sure does,' said Lock, noncommittal. 'But the question is, when are they coming back?'

'You think they will?' Stanner asked.

Lock didn't buy Stanner's doubt. He was doing what smart cops did sometimes, playing dumb.

'He's fixated,' Lock said. 'And determined. And he's upping the stakes.'

Stanner made another futile pass at his hair. 'We do have one lead.'

'What happened to procedure?'

'There's some things I might not be able to share, but this is something I think you should know,' said Stanner. 'Her last appearance at the club out in Arizona. The guy who tried to get to her when she was on stage. She told you about that, right?'

'You pick him up?'

'Not yet. But we will. We have a name. I can't give it to you right now.'

'There's only one thing that bothers me about it being him,' Lock ventured.

'And what's that?'

'There was also a guy in the parking lot who threatened her, but she told me he looked taller.'

Stanner shrugged. 'It was dark. She was scared.'

'So you think they might be the same guy?'

'It's all we have right now.'

Lock had to concede that it made some sort of sense. The guy in the parking lot could have transitioned from his fantasy to making contact with her, and he'd certainly been around to plant Cindy's body in Raven's car. And he supposed that the dress could have been put in Raven's closet at any time in the past week without her necessarily noticing it, though how the culprit had managed to get into her house without leaving any other trace was anyone's guess.

So that was the case for the prosecution. But the case for the defence was even more compelling. Lock was no profiler, but if you started from the point of view that criminal profiling, like close-protection work, boiled down to the rigorous application of common sense, then the guy was a million miles away from the person behind all this.

For a start, the person who had killed Cindy Canyon, then planted her head in a newspaper vending machine and her body in the trunk of Raven's car, was extremely accomplished at what he was doing. He was methodical, a planner. Bat-shit crazy but bright. Trying to assault Raven in a packed strip joint was none of those things. And if he'd been in the parking lot, why hadn't he hidden inside the car and abducted her there and then?

No, the real perpetrator was getting off on the terror and uncertainty that he was leaving in his wake. The torso and the dress were clear demonstrations that he could and would do what he wanted, when he wanted. More than anything, he was focused on demonstrating that he was in control, that all anyone else could do was react.

A pencil-thin middle-aged man had got out of the lock-smith's van and was opening the rear of the vehicle. He took out a tool box, then walked over to where they were standing. 'So, what do you want changed out?' he asked.

Lock glanced back towards the house. 'Everything.'

Thirteen

It took three of them to move the panic-room door up the stairs and into Raven's bedroom. Composed of a solid core with internal steel framing and non-removable hinge pins, it must have weighed close to two hundred pounds. By the time Lock, Ty and the locksmith had wrestled it to the landing they were soaked with sweat.

Lock walked back downstairs. Kevin was on the couch watching cartoons. Raven was on her cell phone, pacing the length of the house.

'What do you mean your insurance won't cover me? . . . Then let me speak to Jimmy . . . Okay, well, tell him to call me back.'

She terminated the call with a jab of her thumb. 'Assholes.'

Lock waited for her to finish her tantrum. He didn't ask what the call was about. If she wanted to share, he figured, she would. 'I guess this isn't a good time to give you this,' he said, handing her the invoice for the newly delivered panic-room door.

She took the piece of paper and scanned it. 'Three thousand bucks? For a door?'

'That's actually pretty cheap. I negotiated a fairly hefty discount. These things can go for as much as twenty grand. Short notice like this, I was kind of amazed that the guy negotiated at all. We got lucky.'

Raven went back into the living room and slumped into a chair, the invoice still in her hand. She rubbed at her temples with her thumbs. 'The phone call. It was the club I was supposed to dance at later this week, pulling the plug.' She had lowered her voice. Between the hammering from upstairs and the blaring television, Lock doubted that Kevin could hear what they were saying, but Raven wasn't taking any chances.

She leaned forward in the chair, visibly stressed. 'Will they take a credit card?'

Lock perched next to her. 'Listen, I'll get it out of my ten. You can pay me when this guy's caught and you start working again.'

Raven turned her head towards him, her violet eyes hard and dark. 'I can pay my own way,' she said, getting up and stalking out of the room.

Lock sighed. He'd broken one of his own rules by assuming too much familiarity. That was a bad idea with any client. It was an extra-bad idea with someone like Raven, who fought so hard to retain control and keep people at a distance.

In less than a minute she was back. 'I'll cover the invoice. It's not a problem. I don't need your charity.'

'It wasn't charity. Someone who charges the kind of money I do doesn't have much interest in charity.'

'Me either,' she said, her voice softer and more placatory. 'Now, seeing as I'm paying you so much, can you give me a ride to pick up mail? Plus I need to get some groceries. All I managed to eat earlier was some cereal and I'm starving.'

Lock smiled. It seemed she had forgiven him. 'Give me a second. I need to check on the locksmith and the guys fitting the panic-room door before we leave.'

'Sure,' Raven said. 'I have to get changed anyway. I won't be long.'

He walked into the living room where Ty was now watching Kevin, who in turn was watching TV. 'Can you keep an eye on things while I'm gone? I have to run a few errands.'

Ty barely looked up. 'Okay, brother. We'll hold the fort here. Won't we, Kev?'

Kevin glanced round. 'Yeah,' he said, and went back to his show.

'Kev's been telling me about this little hottie he's been seeing.'

Kevin's face broke into a wide grin. 'She's my bitch. Isn't she, Ty?'

Lock shot Ty a look.

'Dude, you might not want your sister or Wendy to hear you using that word,' Ty said.

Kevin looked puzzled. 'You used it.'

'Yeah, Ty, you use it all the time,' Lock said, laughing.

'I know. But I shouldn't. It's disrespectful.'

Kevin's head cocked to one side as he thought this over.

'Okay. So I won't say it again.' Once more he went back to his show.

If Kevin was troubled by all these changes, he didn't seem to be showing it. Lock wondered if Raven had overplayed the effect that relocating temporarily would have on him.

The sound of footsteps on the stairs made him turn around. She was wearing boot-cut jeans, a plain black T-shirt and a pair of sneakers. She had removed any last vestiges of makeup and her hair was pulled back into a ponytail, which emphasized her natural beauty. He caught Ty staring at her, slack-jawed.

She smiled hesitantly at Lock. 'I heard you talking to Ty earlier about blending into the background. It's not exactly what I'm used to doing but I thought now might be a good time to give it a try.'

The way she looked, Lock wasn't sure she was capable of disappearing into the background. 'Ready?' he said, after a moment.

She nodded, and turned to Kevin. 'Best behaviour, okay?'

'Sure,' Kevin grumbled.

She walked over and gave him a hug, then followed Lock, who was standing by the front door. 'Now I'm ready.'

Fourteen

The remaining photographers camped outside the house kept a respectful distance as Lock emerged into the bright sunshine with Raven. News of his confrontation with Raul, the paparazzo who'd pursued them on the freeway, had spread. They got off a few shots but left it at that, and Lock used the Range Rover's powerful engine to quickly lose the one photographer who made a half-hearted attempt at following them.

The place where Raven directed her business mail was a small drop-in store in a nearby strip mall. The drive took less than ten minutes and passed in silence, which didn't surprise him. She had probably experienced more white-hot fear over the past forty-eight hours than many people did in a lifetime. A narrowly avoided assault or rape in a parking lot and a body in the trunk of the car were bad enough – single events that might well lead to a rippling anxiety capable of over-whelming a human being's ability to function. But, Lock guessed, what was really spooking Raven now was the knowledge that someone had been inside her home. Burglary was seen by the law as a crime against property. In reality, it was far more than that. The intruder had gifted the dress but stolen any shred of her belief in her home as a sanctuary. It would take a long time for that to return, if it ever did.

He glanced at her. The side of her face was pressed against the cool of the window and her eyes were closed. He thought about asking her how she was but stopped himself. Right now the best thing he could do was his job. Anyone who was being threatened needed, above all else, to see the person charged with their security alert and focused.

Inside the mailbox store, he watched as Raven took out the key from her purse, with a slight tremor in her hand. Then she stepped back. Cindy's head had been found jammed into a vending machine and the last time Raven had opened the trunk of her car she had found the matching torso. The mailbox wasn't big enough to hold a head, but he sensed that she still felt nervous.

'You want me to open it?' he asked her.

Behind them the tiny lobby of the Mailboxes R Us store was empty.

'Sure,' she said, handing him the key.

Inside there were maybe a dozen letters. He held them up. 'Shall I check them?'

She stared at the floor. 'No, it's fine.'

He handed them over and watched as she rifled through them. 'Anything interesting?'

Her eyes creased with concentration as she kept flicking. 'Doesn't look like it.'

'You have any regular correspondents?'

'A couple.'

'Anyone who's threatened to harm you or others?'

'Apart from the stalker?' she asked.

'Yeah.'

She shook her head, then seemed to study him for a moment. 'You were a cop originally, right?' she asked him.

'Military one.'

'I thought MPs and the investigators were two different things.'

'They are here. But I served overseas.'

He gave the street a quick scan, then turned back to her. He had to keep his vigilance up, especially in places she was known to frequent. 'I served in the Close Protection Unit of the Royal Military Police.'

'They're good?' she asked.

'The best.' Something caught in his throat and he coughed. 'There's something I've been meaning to ask you.'

'What's that?'

'Have you given the TMU people access to your email and any social networking sites you use?'

'Yeah,' Raven said. 'I gave Stanner all the passwords but I don't think the stalker's been in touch that way.'

'Good. Then are we done here?' he asked.

Raven tapped the edge of the final envelope against the palm of her hand. 'I guess so.'

'So where next?' he asked.

'Food!'

'It's better if we don't order takeout. The fewer people we have coming to the front door the better. But it's your call.'

She frowned. 'That makes sense. Grocery store it is, then.'

*

Five minutes later Lock pulled the Range Rover into the parking lot of the Vons supermarket on Laurel Canyon Boulevard. He stopped near the front and got out first. The early-October heat was brutal. The Santa Anas must have picked up again. He walked round to open Raven's door.

Stepping out, she left the mail she'd collected on the passenger seat. 'So what do you and Ty like to eat?'

Lock put his hand just behind her back, escorting her into the cool of the store. 'You spend time in the military, you learn to eat what you're given.'

'So, tofu,' she said, then added, with a nervous smile, 'I'm kidding. Let's get some steaks.'

'Sounds good,' Lock said, his eyes flitting over everyone who rolled a cart past them. The customers were predominantly white with a scattering of Hispanics and very few African-Americans. The distinct racial profile of Los Angeles' sprawling neighbourhoods was one of the things that had most struck him about the city. It contrasted sharply with New York, where every race, creed and colour were stacked, almost literally, on top of each other. Here the boundaries of social class and race were sharply differentiated.

As they turned the corner at the end of the aisle, Lock noticed a middle-aged man wearing business casual attire of slacks and a white shirt with no tie, staring at them. His hair was matted from the heat and he had a nice little paunch going. Lock met his gaze – but he didn't look away, as most men usually did when Lock made eye contact in a way that suggested he, and anyone he was with, wanted to be left alone.

Raven must have noticed the man too because she gave a little shudder.

'Ignore him,' he reassured her. 'He's probably starstruck. If he's something else, I'll deal with it. Relax. Do what you were doing.'

They were next to freezer cabinets full of ice cream. 'Could you grab me some Rocky Road?' she asked him.

'Sure.' He reached in, pulled out a tub and placed it in the cart for her. The guy was still staring. They moved on down the aisle and he followed, trying to make it seem coincidental.

Next to him, Lock heard Raven mutter, 'This is bullshit.' Then she started towards the man. 'Can I help you?'

He was clearly surprised to be confronted. He stepped back, then looked around as if searching for a hidden camera. 'Excuse me?'

'You were staring at me,' Raven said.

The guy recovered his composure. 'Maybe I thought I recognized you.'

'And do you?' she asked him.

The guy smiled. 'Actually, I live across the street from you. Hal Bradley. You might have seen my kids coming to visit on the weekends.'

Next to him, Raven relaxed a notch, but Lock kept his guard up.

Hal said, 'Sorry, is this your boyfriend or something?'

'No,' Raven told him. 'Just a friend.'

Hal's face hardened. 'Great. Well, perhaps we could get together some time. Have dinner, maybe.'

Raven cleared her throat. 'I have a lot going on right now.'

Hal made a face. 'So, I'm not good enough for you, is that it? I didn't think women like you were that selective. I could make it worth your while financially.'

Lock took Raven's elbow as she started to protest. 'Go get those steaks.'

She shook him off. 'I can fight my own battles.'

'I don't doubt it,' Lock said softly. 'But I'm on the clock, which means I deal with this.'

Raven shot Hal an angry look but walked away, leaving the two men together. Hal seemed oblivious to the fact that Lock was glaring at him. There were times for Lock when dealing with a situation was purely professional. There were others when it became personal. This was one of the others.

If you wanted to make judgements about other people based on what they did for a living that was fine. This was America. People were entitled to their opinions. But when you shared those judgements, you had better be prepared for the person you're talking to, in this case Lock, to reply.

'She's just a hooker, right?' Hal protested, as Lock's right hand moved slowly from his side and formed into a fist.

Raven was paying for the groceries at the checkout when Lock caught up with her. Behind him, a couple of store employees were gazing at him with open mouths, having just witnessed the one-sided altercation he'd had with Hal. He'd been careful to make sure that the other guy threw the first punch but it was all one-way traffic after that.

'You okay?' he asked Raven.

She nodded as the packer loaded the final bag into their cart.

'You have a clean-up in aisle three,' he said to the cashier, as she handed Raven her receipt. Then he took the trolley and escorted Raven out of the store.

Fifteen

The glow from a neon store sign traced across Raven's face as they pulled out of the parking lot. She turned away from Lock and he knew she had started to cry. He drove in silence for a while, keeping an eye on the traffic. If she wanted to talk, she would. It wasn't his job to force the issue.

After a few moments she grabbed her purse and fished out a packet of tissues, dabbed at her eyes, then blew her nose. 'I'm sorry,' she said finally.

Lock's eyes flicked between the rear-view and the road ahead. 'You're allowed to be upset.'

'It's just a lot to deal with sometimes. If I had only myself to worry about I could probably get by, but with Kevin as well . . . There's a lot of pressure.'

'A lot of people would have left him when he was younger,' he said.

She cleared her throat and her eyes darkened. 'They already had. That's why I couldn't.'

He reached down and grabbed a bottle of water from a cup holder and handed it to her.

'Thanks.' She took a sip. 'I don't often tell people about what happened. But if you want to hear it?'

Now Lock felt she needed to talk. He gestured to the wall of red brake-lights ahead. 'It's not like we don't have time.'

'We grew up in northern California, right up past San Francisco. Dad split right after Kevin was born when he found out he was different. Just walked out on us without an explanation and never got back in touch. So that was one person who bailed on Kevin. Our mom did her best but she got involved with one deadbeat after another and most of them didn't want kids around, never mind one with Kevin's problem. So I guess all we had was each other and I ended up taking care of him a lot.' She stopped. 'Are you sure you want to hear this?'

He nodded.

'Mom started getting more and more into drugs. Coke at first, then crank – y'know, methamphetamine – sleeping pills, pretty much anything she could get her hands on. Stuff started going missing from the house. She'd take it and sell it so she could buy drugs. I used to cover for her because I didn't want us to be taken into care. By the time I was seventeen I'd dropped out of high school so I could bring in some money waiting tables. I started entering local beauty pageants too and making some spare cash that way. But it still wasn't enough.'

'That was how you ended up in your present line of work?' he asked her.

She sighed. 'Do you mind if I smoke?'

'Go ahead.'

She dug into her handbag again, came up with a pack of cigarettes and lit up. After the first puff she closed her eyes. 'It's not like any little girl grows up thinking they want to do this for a living. You kind of fall into it. One day I was waiting tables when these three bikers came in. One of them was, like, mid-twenties, real handsome, and we ended up dating. Mom was too far gone to care and I was young and dumb and head over heels in love.'

'He got you into stripping?'

Raven laughed. 'He dumped me for a stripper, so I went and got a job where she worked to get back at him. Like I said, I was stupid. Anyway, turned out that an eighteen-year-old beauty queen can make a lot of money in one of those places – as long as you realize that the less you give the customers, the more cash they'll throw at you.'

She took another puff on her cigarette and lowered the window to blow the smoke out. 'All of a sudden I was making more money than I knew what to do with. I could get a place for Kevin, pay for someone responsible to look after him while I was working, and cover all his medical bills. And all I had to do was take off my clothes and pretend like I was interested in what some horny businessman was talking to me about.'

'So why not just stay doing that?' he asked her. 'Why get into movies?'

Raven smiled again, but this time there was a tinge of sadness in her eyes. 'That's a really good question. I started out doing photo shoots, and the more of those I did, the better the clubs I got invited to dance at and the more money

I could make. It all made sense at the time. It's little bitty steps, Ryan. You strip, then you get offered a centrefold and you think, Well, I'm already naked in front of guys anyway. Then someone comes along and asks if you want to be in movies. So you do that. Then someone says, "If you do a little bit more next time they'll pay you more." So you do that little bit more. And it's not like it feels weird because you're surrounded by people who it's totally normal for. That's their life. They have sex on camera, they get paid, then they go home. It's a job. That's what people don't understand about the business. There's nothing erotic about it. We don't sell sex, we sell the idea of sex.'

She turned to face him, holding his attention with a steady gaze. 'Does that make any kind of sense?'

'It does. I've worked for people I shouldn't have, taken on jobs I'd have been better off avoiding.'

Her smile was back. 'And it's not like I plan on doing this for ever. I have the house almost paid off. Two, three years, and I'm good. I'll have enough money to look after me and Kevin, and go back to college. It's what keeps me going. Making sure that we'll have a secure and worthwhile life.' She stopped. 'If I live that long, right?'

'That's one thing you don't have to worry about. Not while me and Ty are around anyway.'

Sixteen

Inside Raven's home, a faint smell of wood shavings hung in the air: the airborne residue of the newly changed locks, which glittered next to the handles of every door. Eight new cameras with infrared lamps beside them sat high on each wall of the house, feeding back a flickering loop of green-tinged images to two monitors, which sat inside the newly functioning panic room.

Kneeling on the wrong side of the closed door, Ty tapped against it with his knuckles. 'Kevin? Can you hear me?'

There was a muffled response, which Ty could just about make out as 'Go away.'

'Brother, you need to come out of there before Ryan and your sister get home.'

Kevin didn't respond.

'Come out and we can talk.'

Ty sank down, his back to the door. Lock was going to have

a shit fit when he got back. 'Okay,' he said. 'I'm just going to wait here until you want to talk to me.'

Then he got up and paced to the window. The glass threw his reflection back at him. He killed the lights and stared down to the deck below. At the bottom of the slope, on the other side of the fence, a dog prowled – a guard dog of some kind. A Shepherd. Ty sighed and rolled his shoulders. Kevin had been in a funk ever since he'd called his girlfriend, Wendy. It had been a short exchange.

Ty had overheard some of it. It had sounded like Kevin had been talking to someone, maybe the mom, who wouldn't put Wendy on the phone. Kevin had started out polite. Then he'd pleaded a little. And then, when he'd grasped that the person he was speaking to wasn't about to change their mind, he'd become petulant.

Finally, he had put the phone down and disappeared upstairs. Ty had assumed he'd headed to his room. He must have done at first because Ty saw him a few seconds later on the landing, clutching a backpack with Superman on the front. Ty was expecting him to come down the stairs and maybe head for the front door, but instead he'd disappeared into Raven's room. A few seconds later, Ty had heard the heavy door of the panic room slam shut. By the time he'd got there, Kevin had locked himself inside and was refusing to talk.

Ty walked back to the door, running a finger down the edges. As hiding places went, it was damn near perfect. Ty tried the handle but the door was shut tight. The only way to get in was probably through the roof or by taking down some walls with a sledgehammer. Given all the recent disruption in the house, Ty doubted that Raven would appreciate this. They would have to sit it out.

The only drawback to this plan was that it left the feeds from the security cameras inside the panic room un-monitored. The plan had been to move Raven into the spare bedroom at the end of the hall overnight. That way, Lock and Ty could take shifts watching the screens. It also kept them close to their principal. Raven hadn't been wild about the idea at first but Lock had won her round.

There was one thing left for it. Ty dug out his cell and called Lock.

'Everything okay?' his partner asked.

Ty glanced back towards the two hundred pounds of reinforced-steel-framed door. Right now it looked about as impenetrable as the kid on the other side of it.

'Kevin got a little upset. He's shut himself inside the panic room.'

Lock went quiet. Ty knew that this meant he was really pissed off. When he was irritated he might curse. When he was really upset he went quiet and folded in on himself. The mood lasted as long as it took him to work out a solution. Then he was back to normal and carried on like nothing had happened. But that period when he was in quiet mode, he wasn't any fun to be around. There was always something murderous that lay under the surface with Lock. As long as Ty had known him that had been his way.

'Why did he get upset?' Lock asked.

Ty moved further away from the door and lowered his voice so that Kevin wouldn't catch what he was saying. 'He called his girlfriend but her mom wouldn't let her talk to him.'

Lock sighed. Ty heard him relay the information to Raven. Then she came on the line. 'Ty?' she said.

'I'm here.'

'He gets like this sometimes. Just leave him. We'll be home soon. He's okay, right?'

Ty hollered over to the door. 'Hey, K-Lo, your sister wants to know that you're okay.'

There was a grunt, which Ty took as a yes.

Ty got back on his cell. 'He's chillin' in there with Superman.'

'We'll be with you as soon as we can.'

In the background Ty heard the Range Rover accelerate. He ended the call, then strolled back to the panic-room door.

He and Kevin had been getting on so well too. At first Ty had been unnerved by Raven's brother having Down's syndrome. It had made him uncomfortable. Like a lot of kids growing up, Ty had thrown around words like 'retard' without considering their full weight. Kevin must have sensed as much because he'd seemed to make an extra effort with Ty – at least, he had at first. It was like he had tried to make sure that Ty was comfortable rather than the other way round.

He was a funny kid. He seemed to be missing the filter that adults had and which was usually well in place by the time someone hit their late teens. While they were watching cartoons, he had turned to Ty and said, apropos of nothing, 'Is it weird being black?'

Ty had had to fight back a laugh. He wasn't sure whether he should be offended or not.

'How'd you mean?' he said, parrying the question.

'Well, people treat me differently, you know, because of

how I look and things. I was just wondering if it was the same if you're black.'

This time Ty did smile. 'You're pretty deep, man.'

'That's not an answer,' Kevin said.

'Well, I look at it like this. If someone wants to treat me differently because of the colour of my skin, then they got a problem, not me.'

Kevin seemed to reflect on Ty's answer. 'You get that off of Oprah?' he asked.

Ty burst out laughing. 'Man, you're a trip.'

'I know,' said Kevin, with a self-deprecating little shrug.

Of course, then had come the phone call and the storming upstairs. Now he was shouting through the door. Ty wondered if he'd decided to come out but couldn't figure out how to open it.

'Kevin? You okay in there? What you say?' he yelled.

'There's someone creeping around outside.'

Seventeen

Inside the panic room, Kevin watched, transfixed, as the shadowy figure exited frame left on the first monitor. A second later they entered frame right on the second screen. They were making their way from the front to the rear of the house where a set of french windows opened directly into the living room.

His arms wrapped around his knees, he rocked back and forth a little. On the other side of the door Ty was shouting at him, making Kevin's heart pound even more than the person outside was doing.

He opened his backpack and pulled out his wrist bands, which he wore when he got stressed. They had Superman on them and the letters WWSD, which stood for 'What Would Superman Do?' Raven used them to help him decide what was appropriate or inappropriate behaviour. That meant something you could do or something that would make people mad and get you in trouble. He hated it when people were mad.

There was a loud thump on the door. Kevin reached down

and twisted the wrist band, watching the WWSD spin round. He wished Wendy was here with him. She always made things better. But her mom was mad at him and he didn't know why. He didn't know what he'd done.

On the screen the man was approaching the doors.

'Where is he now?' Ty was shouting.

But Kevin was getting confused. He wished Ty would stop shouting at him. It wasn't his fault that someone was creeping around outside. If only Superman was really here. Or his sister. They'd know what to do. Because, right now, Kevin was too scared to do anything.

With no response from Kevin, Ty made for the bedroom door. There was a panic button in the hallway. He slammed his palm down on it, then called Lock again.

'We got a prowler outside.'

'Where?'

'I don't know. Kevin's still locked in the panic room so I can't see the screens. I'm gonna go take a peek now.'

'Okay, keep me posted.'

'Roger that. Lock?'

'I'm here.'

'If I get the drop on him and I think this is our guy?'

'Do what you have to do. We have precedent with this one.'

Ty knew exactly the precedent Lock was talking about. Back in 1995, a private-security contractor working for Madonna had shot and wounded an intruder at her compound in Malibu. No charges had been filed by the district attorney. The intruder posed a threat. He was on private property. The bodyguard had done what he was paid to do. There had been a few civil-rights lawyers who'd made some noise in the *LA Times*. But there was no debate to be had.

Lock had made a point of not carrying a gun while they were in LA. Still technically a resident in California, even though he worked out of state a lot of the time, Ty didn't have that problem. He had the permit courtesy of a local sheriff in a county near where he'd grown up in Long Beach. He and the sheriff had served together in the Marine Corps.

Ty drew his weapon, turned to his immediate left, hit the light switch, plunging the hallway into a gloom that matched the deepening twilight outside, and started down the stairs.

Lock spun the wheel, one-eightying the car, taking them north again and away from the house. Raven's head snapped round. 'What the hell are you doing?'

'If the person who's stalking you is at the house, I don't plan on delivering you to him.'

'But my brother's there.'

'He's locked in the panic room, Ty's there and the LAPD are on their way. Me slinging you into the mix, what do you think that's likely to do? Make things better for your brother or worse?'

Raven's eyes flashed with anger. 'I don't care! I want you to turn this car around.'

'Too bad,' said Lock, his hands tightening on the wheel.

Ty skirted around the side of the house, his gun held low. At the corner, he stopped and listened. Down the slope at the back the neighbour's guard dog was barking, a constant stream of canine invective. But it might have been spooked by his movements.

He rounded the corner. He couldn't see anyone. The deck and the area around it were empty. He hunkered down and crept slowly forward. In his left hand he had a Maglite, but he kept it off. A light gave away your position: a bad idea when the enemy was unseen.

A noise.

Someone or something was moving about. A coyote come down from the hills to scavenge? The sound was coming from near by.

He stared towards the vortex of the crawlspace, which lay under the deck. It was too dark for Ty to see anything.

Then he heard another noise.

There was definitely something down there.

He angled the Maglite so it was facing towards him, then pressed it into his body and switched it on. A vague circle of light leaked on to the centre of his chest.

As quickly as he could, he laid the torch on the ground with the beam punching out towards the area under the deck. Then he moved fast in the opposite direction. Falling into a low crouch, left leg forward, right knee bent, he aimed towards the crawl space lit by the Maglite.

The figure was curled almost into a ball, chin tucked on to the chest, the black hood of a sweatshirt covering the face, hands dug into pockets.

'Armed security!' Ty bellowed. 'Put your hands where I can see them.'

No hands moved but a head was raised. Burrowed into the

cowl of the hood, a pair of almond-shaped eyes stared back at Ty, the pupils wide with fear.

Ty's stomach turned over as he realized how close he'd come to shooting Kevin's girlfriend, Wendy.

He hunkered down, his hands shaking.

'Come on out of there,' he said, beckoning her towards him.

She didn't move. If anything, she seemed more afraid now than when he'd had the gun pointed at her.

It took Ty a second to register that she was looking behind him. Grabbing for his gun, he spun round in time to see a man's darkened outline running past and down the side of the house.

'Wait there,' he said, leaping to his feet and taking off after the fleeing figure.

He took the corner wide at the side of the house, the gun punched out ahead of him. All he caught was the man's heels as he fled towards the driveway.

He heard the clatter of metal on stone, then a muffled curse, more footsteps and the sound of a car door slamming. An engine fired and tyres squealed as the vehicle took off at speed.

Ty stood in the driveway, breathing hard. There was a solitary flash of brake lights at the end of the street and then the car was gone.

He walked back to Wendy. She was rooted to where he had left her. He ran the beam of the torch across the area where the intruder had been. On the fifth or sixth pass, he caught a glint of metal on the deck near the rear doors.

He walked over and bent down to retrieve a brass house key. He turned it over in his hand, then tried it in the new lock. It didn't fit. But he'd bet any money in the world that it fitted the old one.

Eighteen

Kevin and Wendy sat sheepishly on the couch. He had put one arm around her protectively, but removed it as soon as he saw Raven heading towards them. Lock hung back as she threw her arms around her brother, almost squeezing the life out of him. Then she hugged Wendy. 'You know you're both going to be grounded for this, right?'

Both Kevin and Wendy nodded, their eyes wide and troubled.

An LAPD patrol officer motioned Lock and Ty towards him. He was a Hispanic guy in his mid-forties with an easy smile that was more social worker than cop. 'She can't stay here. You realize that, right?' he said.

'I know,' Ty said, 'but let's just give 'em a minute or two. I'll make sure they behave themselves.'

The cop shrugged and went to talk to his partner.

Lock pulled Ty towards the window. 'You get a look at the guy outside?' he asked.

Ty shook his head. 'White, I think, but could have been light-skinned Hispanic. Big. Like over six feet. Beyond that I got nothing, really. I'm just happy no one's hurt.' He scratched his chin. 'She was hiding under the deck. I almost lit her up.'

'Cops take the key that was dropped?'

'First thing they did was bag it.'

'Maybe they'll get something from it.'

'I hope so, brother,' Ty sighed, 'because this shit feels real messed up to me.'

'Everyone's safe. You did your job. That's all that matters.' Lock clamped a hand on his partner's shoulder. 'I'm going to go take a look outside.'

Out front a red sedan pulled up and Stanner got out, his frizzy mop of hair making him instantly recognizable. He waved and headed towards Lock. His shoulders were slumped and Lock had a feeling that he wasn't there to tell them they had Cindy Canyon's killer in custody.

'How's the brother's girlfriend?' Stanner said, glancing behind Lock to the house.

'Shook up but fine.'

Stanner chewed his bottom lip. 'Young love. Think I just about remember what that feels like. Been married twenty-plus years.'

'You got any news?' Lock prompted.

Stanner studied his shoes. 'Nothing on the prowler but we think we're getting closer to the guy in Arizona – the one who threatened Raven in the parking lot last night.'

'Assuming he's still in Arizona.'

'Even if he's gone, he might have left enough behind to give us something more to work on. We have someone from the FBI on board out there to check it out and feed back any extra intel.'

'How come?' Lock asked. He wasn't an expert in the finer points of law-enforcement procedure and who took the lead, but with only one body and a case of ongoing aggravated stalking on the table it seemed a little early for the Feebs to be beating the bushes on behalf of the LAPD or the cops in Arizona. If it was, say, a serial killer they were looking for, the body count usually had to hit four before a federal investigation was triggered.

'There's an unsolved case going back a few years that we think might be linked to this.'

Lock exhaled. 'I know you get in some major shit if you say too much, but the more I know, the better I can do my job. And if the FBI are getting involved there's no way in hell they're going to tell me anything.'

Stanner motioned for him to move a little further away from the house and on to the sidewalk. 'About four years ago an adult-film director by the name of Gary Fairfax was found dead at his apartment in Van Nuys. He was pretty rough with the female talent. Liked to knock them about sometimes.'

'And this ties in with Cindy Canyon how?'

'It doesn't.' Stanner hesitated. 'Not exactly anyway. But it might tie in with Raven.'

'She knew the guy?'

'She knew him. She worked for him. She threatened to kill him.'

'Was she interviewed at the time?'

'She had an alibi. A good one. Watertight, in fact. It all checked out. Plus people who make threats tend not to be the ones who back them up with action.'

'So we're back to square one.'

'Not quite,' Stanner said. 'I got a call yesterday from someone else in the porn business, another director who worked with Raven, an even bigger scumbag than the guy who got snuffed – if such a thing is imaginable. He said he'd been getting some fairly heavy-duty threats. Notes showing up in his mailbox.'

'So what? He's a porn director. Wouldn't he be used to threats?'

'Maybe so, but the handwriting was a direct match for the note that was left with the dress.'

Nineteen

Lock stood in the darkened living room, listening to the house creak and groan as, outside, the wind whipped up a storm of late autumn leaves. The first time he took residential guard duty at night he always tried to tune himself into the location. Every house or office building had its own little quirks: a squeaky floorboard or an air vent that whistled in the wind. The better you knew them, the easier it was to click when something was out of place. The same went for people.

Upstairs, Raven, Kevin and Ty were asleep, sheer exhaustion trumping fear in the case of the first two. Being scared or on the edge for any length of time drained the body of energy. It was why men in his job quickly learned to take control of anxiety and fear. He visualized his response level in colours. Green was normal, amber corresponded to no immediate threat but a heightened level of awareness, and red was game on. If you stayed on red for too long, eventually you'd crash and burn.

After dinner, he had agreed with Ty that he would take a first shift of residential security lasting four hours. Then Ty, who hadn't had the early start Lock had had, would pick up a final five-hour stint. Four or five solid hours of sleep were plenty. Lock had gone days at a time on far, far less.

Taking the first shift would give him the opportunity to think over the day's events and settle them in his mind. As long as the intruder didn't choose to come crashing through a window with something deadlier than an old house key. His recent appearance had ratcheted up the threat level. It wasn't a question now of if he would be back but when. And, to make matters worse, he now knew that he would be facing opposition so he'd come prepared.

Lock walked to the french windows at the rear of the house. Beyond the deck was the sweeping panorama of city lights and he wondered if the stalker was down there some-where, planning his next move, or whether the spectre of something more sinister, which Stanner had raised, had substance. Could Raven be implicated in all of this?

The fleeing figure Ty had chased said she wasn't. Her threatening a movie director who had then turned up dead suggested she might be. The note with the dress could have been planted by anyone. And now another director was being threatened. The cops would be looking into it – but with how much manpower? Perhaps this was Lock's opportunity to get off the back foot at last and start to make some progress of his own. He'd need help, and he had just the woman on standby.

Walking back into the living room, he pulled out his cell phone and called Carrie.

She sounded slightly groggy and he worried for a moment that he'd woken her.

'Hey,' she said. 'Everything okay?'

'All shut down nice and tight for the evening. Listen, I know it's late, but Stanner came by and he mentioned the name of someone I could use some more information on. He's a guy who's worked with Raven in the past.'

'Sure.'

He gave Carrie the name, then told her what Stanner had said and what had gone down at the house.

'I'll get right on to it,' Carrie said.

At the other end of the line he could hear waves breaking against the shore and closed his eyes, wishing he was there with her. 'It can wait until morning,' he said softly.

Carrie sighed. 'It's fine. I can't sleep anyway.'

'If you're worried about me, don't be. It would take a lot more than one crazy to take me down.'

'I know,' Carrie said, clearly unconvinced.

'Is something else worrying you?'

He heard her sigh again. 'It's nothing. Forget it.'

'Carrie? I'm not here alone with her, if that's what you're worried about. Ty's upstairs.'

'You really think I'm that insecure, Ryan?'

'No. I was only saying that—'

'Well, don't. You want me to look into this director? Because if you do, I should get going.'

He reached up his left hand and worried at the scar on the back of his head, a souvenir from a door that had been rigged to a shotgun. 'I don't want to say goodnight like this.'

A moment of silence passed between them. Upstairs, he

could hear someone snoring loudly enough to compete with the Santa Ana winds. It sounded like Kevin but it might well have been Ty. In any case, he should probably go up and take a look, maybe close a bedroom door if one was open.

'Neither do I,' Carrie said at last.

'So, we're good?' His heart rate speeded up as he waited for her to answer. No job was worth putting their relationship on the line for.

'We're always good, Ryan.'

'I love you. You know that, right?' he said softly.

'I love you too, cowboy.'

Twenty

After the phone call, Carrie stepped out on to the deck, Angel padding after her. She hoped the fresh air might clear her head. Until now, with Ryan Lock, she had felt she was with a man truly as his equal. It wasn't something they'd ever discussed; that was just the way it had happened. And now she was feeling like some kid who was worried her boyfriend was after the school slut behind her back.

She hated herself for feeling jealous. She hated herself for acting insecure. But most of all she hated the way that, as soon as someone threatened her relationship with Ryan, especially a woman like Raven, all her feminist convictions, all her confidence, had flown straight out of the window.

When Carrie thought about Raven she didn't think about how women in the porn industry were treated like pieces of meat. Neither did she consider how amazing it was that Raven had not only survived that but made a life for herself and her brother. No. She had only one thought about the woman he was protecting: What a skank.

Carrie walked back inside and crossed to the dining table, which faced one of the large floor-to-ceiling windows that looked out over the blue-black Pacific stretching to infinity. She flipped open her MacBook Air and sat down. Angel settled with a snuffle at her feet.

She opened the browser, which defaulted to Google, plugged the name Ryan had just given her into the search engine and pressed enter. The search returned over a million results. She clicked on the Wikipedia entry first. Wikipedia might not always be completely accurate but it would give her a general overview. Both she and Lock were delving into a world that neither of them knew and, as a journalist, she wanted to be objective. As she read the entry, though, objectivity dissolved into a thick stew of revulsion.

It began:

Vince Vice (born Paul Aronofsky on 6 August 1956 in Salt Lake City, Utah) is an adult film performer, producer and director who gained notoriety with his gonzo-style movies which usually feature female adult film actors who are new to the industry. While all the performers in his movies are over the age of eighteen, the scenarios usually depicted in the films revolve around underage girls. Female performers in his movies frequently appear dressed as schoolgirls and Girl Scouts and he has said that he deliberately casts actresses who 'look like they're underage, like they're your babysitter, because guys get off on that stuff even if they won't admit it'.

Vice has been criticized, even by people within the adult

industry, for the simulated violence in his movies, which frequently feature actresses being forced to perform sexual acts apparently against their will. Choking, vomiting and simulated rape are frequent features of his movies. Some actresses have alleged that Vice has sexually assaulted them during filming but no charges have ever been brought.

Vice's production company, along with his freelance work, have made him a multi-millionaire.

There was more but Carrie stopped reading. She got up and slid back the glass door to let some air in, then walked back to the computer, scanning as quickly as she could through the rest of the entry. It didn't get any better. Even with the sanitized descriptions of a Wikipedia entry she felt ill. Then she realized that this man's name (if the term 'man' could be applied to someone like this) had generated more than a million results and that he'd grown rich producing movies that deliberately set out to degrade and debase women.

There was a long list of some of the performers he'd worked with, women with improbable names, like Candy and Kitten. Raven Lane's was near the bottom. She clicked on Raven's name, which defaulted to her Wikipedia entry so she pulled the Google home page up again and did an image search, hoping for a picture of this guy.

There were lots on the first page.

The first took Carrie to a head shot of Vince Vice. He had a gaunt face, as if his skin was stretched way too tight over his skull, short-cropped peroxide-blond hair, and cold blue eyes. His lips were parted over his teeth in a theatrical snarl.

Not all the pictures were of Vice: some were of his co-stars, if that wasn't too grandiose a term. One in particular caught Carrie's eye. The actress had her hair in pigtails, and makeup had been plastered on to her face as if she was trying lipstick and mascara for the first time. It was smeared by the tears that had left thick black streaks running down her cheeks. Her eyes were dead.

Over the woman's shoulder, and slightly out of focus, stood Vince Vice, with the same snarling expression. This time you could see more of him: he had a powerful, sinewy physique, a broad chest and bulging biceps. He looked exactly as he was: a man who clearly delighted in inflicting humiliation on women.

Carrie felt simultaneously sick and angry. If someone had threatened to kill him, she thought, good for them.

Twenty-one

FBI profiler Levon Hill hunkered down in the back of the Arizona State Police radio car and watched as an angry red tinge blossomed on the edge of the eastern horizon. Sunrise was minutes away and the SWAT team was already creeping into place, ready to storm the house and braced for a fight. Reports from Los Angeles suggested the target was already gone, but at this stage nothing could be taken for granted. They had a suspect. They had an address. It was worth checking it out, and making assumptions with someone like this was always dangerous.

His right hand shielding his eyes from the rising sun, Hill studied the target location. If the man inside was responsible for the murder of Cindy Canyon they had to be prepared for the worst, although in Hill's experience serial killers were often surprisingly meek when they knew the game was up. Oftentimes, they played a part in their own capture, their ego driving them to be discovered so that they could then share more fully in the glory of what they'd done. At least, those were the theories.

Ten years into his work with the Bureau, Hill had been present at the arrest of a serial killer only once before. That case had ended in a shack near an abandoned cattle ranch in Montana and the uncovering of a gory collection of trophies. Years later, Hill still had nightmares from the images of that morning. He was hoping that this time they were wrong, that the man they believed was threatening Raven Lane was just a regular asshole. He could deal with regular assholes.

Hauling himself up, Hill stared down the street at the target location: 1425 Rattlesnake Trail was so far on the wrong side of the tracks in Tempe, Arizona, that even if the trains had still been running you wouldn't have been able to hear them. Clapperboard houses spoke of hasty construction and decades of neglect. Weeds filled every yard, snaking over rusting engine blocks and decrepit children's climbing frames.

No one was about. No one was walking drowsily to their car, or to catch a bus and head off to work. This was a community on the wrong end of the American Dream, a place devoid of ambition beyond the last toke of marijuana, or slug of malt liquor, a place where the small hopes people harboured of a stable family life, or of a child attending college, or of a house where both parents raised their kids with love and respect, had come to die. This block was small-town ghetto to its core.

A black-gloved hand tapped the windscreen. The SWAT team was getting ready to make its dynamic entry. Four men stood by the front door, two of them hefting a battering ram. Other SWAT officers were fanned out around the house, squatting low beneath windowsills and folded in tight against exterior walls, body armour making their movement seem strained and lumbering.

Hill opened his door and got out. Once they were inside, and the suspect was in custody, he would be able to take a look around. He raised first one foot off the ground, then the other, slipping on blue plastic shoe covers. Nervous, he ran a hand through his hair. He waited, a man given to going about his work in a quiet and methodical manner without making too many waves. His nature reflected itself in sombre brown eyes and a loping gait, which seemed designed to minimize his six-foot-four-inch frame. A full beard provided him with further camouflage. Levon Hill was about as far as from the clean-cut preppy types the FBI usually attracted as it was possible to get.

At the front door of the house, a member of the SWAT team counted down from five with his hand. At one his thumb folded down, forming a fist, and he stepped back, out of the way of the battering ram. The door flew open on first impact. The SWAT team poured inside, guns drawn, an officer hoisting a pump-action shotgun leading the charge.

Behind them, Hill listened intently but all he could hear were the barks of the SWAT team calling to no one in particular.

Shit.

He's gone.

We're too late.

He started walking towards the house. The shouts went on. Then he half caught someone scream, 'In here!' and quickened his pace, hope rising with every step, only to fall away as he reached the entry and stepped into the dark stump of a hallway. Helmets off, guns reholstered and shoulders slumped, a couple of the SWAT team stood in what passed for the living room. A TV in one corner crackled with static.

The metallic smell of blood filled the air. At the opposite end of the room, their target, Larry Johns, slumped in an armchair. His trousers and underwear were missing. Hill could see them lying in a heap behind the chair. It didn't take a genius to work out that Larry hadn't been watching *Good Morning America.*

His head was still attached to his body but, from the blood patterns on his body, the chair and the floor, he was far from intact. Both testicles and his penis had been hacked off, leaving a gaping wound in his groin. The missing items were nowhere to be seen.

Outside, beyond the front yard, more law-enforcement vehicles were starting to arrive as word seeped out that the main suspect was dead – a victim, one could presume, of the real killer.

Hill glanced back to Larry Johns's body. The head was attached but the killer had made a pretty unambiguous statement, if in a less graphic way than he had with Cindy Canyon.

A blindfold masked the eyes.

Hill didn't dare touch it but, skirting the wads of congealed blood on the floor, he moved closer, then leaned down so that his face was level with Johns's. The gap between the blindfold and the eye socket confirmed his hunch. The killer had gouged the man's eyes from their sockets before blindfolding him.

The contradiction made no sense. Why remove someone's

eyes and then go to all the trouble of placing a blindfold over the empty sockets?

He pulled his BlackBerry from his pocket and made a note of it, then snapped a few quick pictures of the scene. One thing was clear: the killer wasn't simply interested in killing Larry Johns. They were sending a message. A screwed-up, garbled, crazy message, but a message all the same.

He walked out of the house and stood on the sidewalk, his gold-on-blue FBI windcheater ensuring he was left alone. People were slowly emerging from their houses, bleary-eyed, in ragged bathrobes or shorts and T-shirts. Local cops were fanning out to secure the area around the house. A couple were beginning to canvass the neighbours. Doors were being closed now. In places like this the cops were viewed with distrust and suspicion, and no one wanted to be seen speaking to one.

There was, he thought, an obvious explanation for what had happened to the man inside the house. The motive was one of the most powerful: revenge. Larry Johns had threatened and humiliated Raven Lane at the club. Then he was found dead. And not just dead but mutilated. The cutting off of his genitals emasculated him, rendered him impotent.

That still left the eyes, though. Where did gouging them out fit in? Was it something about the very act of looking? Feminist theory talked about objectifying women, about the male gaze and how it reduced women to objects of desire rather than human beings. Could that be something to do with it?

Removing the man's genitals and eyes suggested one thing

quite strongly to Hill. That the person who had done this was a woman.

But how did Cindy Canyon fit in with it? Was there a link between her and Larry Johns after all? Their bodies had been altered after death, which was significant. But the ways in which they had been altered were very different.

Assuming, for the sake of argument, that the cases were linked, there was one thing that Levon Hill was quite clear about. This was a person with a lot of rage. It was probably well concealed, hidden deep within them, but it was there, it was potent and it was overwhelming. The killer was operating in a frenzy. They might have killed before. They might not. But one thing was a hundred per cent guaranteed.

If this individual wasn't caught, there would be more bodies.

Twenty-two

When Lock walked into the kitchen, Kevin was slumped over a bowl of cereal, still upset over the fallout from Wendy's unscheduled appearance. Wendy's mother had not appreciated her daughter sneaking out to see him – especially not when she had turned up to a house surrounded by cops. Lock had brokered a deal that meant Raven and Wendy's mother agreed that Kevin and Wendy should take a break from each other for a few weeks. Neither Wendy nor Kevin had seemed thrilled at the prospect and Wendy had had to be practically dragged into her mother's car. It had taken both Lock and Ty to restrain Kevin, who had eventually retreated to bed in a sulk. This was one situation that even Superman didn't have an answer for.

Lock grabbed some water from the fridge dispenser. Raven, dressed in sweats and with her hair pinned up, was wiping down the counters.

'Do you have a moment?' he asked her.

'Sure.' Raven followed him out of the kitchen and out of Kevin's earshot.

'I had a call earlier about the guy in Arizona, the one who hassled you inside the club.'

'They caught him?'

The early-morning sunlight was streaming in through the french windows at the rear of the house. The temperature had dropped by a couple of degrees – the Santa Anas had died down, at least for now. It was the kind of mid-seventies-perfect day that drew the huddled masses west to California.

Lock took a deep breath. Delivering bad news was like ripping off a plaster: best done swiftly. 'They found him dead this morning at a house in Tempe.'

Raven's shoulders slumped. 'But the guy who was here last night?'

'They think the person they found in Tempe had been dead for a while, possibly since the night he approached you in the club. The guy last night might have been the one from the parking lot. You said they looked different, right?'

'I think so . . . The guy in the lot looked a lot taller. But it wasn't well lit out there and it happened so fast.' She sighed. 'So we're back at square one?'

Lock took a moment to think her question over. 'It ups the stakes for all of us, which means more manpower and more attention from the cops, so that's positive. But we still have to keep our guard up. The more your stalker thinks that people are after him, the more dangerous he'll be.'

Raven checked her Cartier watch. 'And what will that mean?'

'If it brings him out into the open, we'll be waiting for him.

Until then you try and go about your business as best you can.'

Raven shot him a tight smile. 'I did have a meeting scheduled for later this morning with the old production company I used to work for. And something out of town this evening. But I'm not sure it's a good idea with all this attention.'

Lock waited.

'Can we go outside?' she asked.

'Sure.'

She stopped at the edge of the deck, resting her elbows on the edge and staring out over the cityscape. 'When I told you I wasn't seeing anyone, I wasn't being entirely truthful.'

She turned to face him, then went back to staring at the view. 'There is someone I see from time to time, but it's more of a business arrangement – if you know what I mean.'

Lock squared his shoulders. Anyone who followed the news knew that women in Raven's line of work often supplemented their income by partying with high rollers, whether they were Hollywood A-listers or sports stars or just guys with more money than sense. 'You don't have to draw me a picture.'

'He called me this morning,' Raven said. 'He wants to see me in Vegas tonight. He said he was worried about me.'

'You want to go to Vegas tonight?' he asked her, momentarily taken aback.

'It's a lot of money.'

Lock nodded reluctantly. 'Whatever you want to do. Ty can keep an eye on Kevin here and I can come with you. You shouldn't travel alone.'

Raven turned to him with a sad smile. 'I'll have to clear it with my client first. He has his own security. He said there would be a private jet waiting for me at Van Nuys at four o'clock.'

But an obvious question was troubling Lock. 'You know, if this guy has his own security, and a private jet on standby, does it not occur to you that he might have something to do with' – he gestured to the house and garage – 'all this?'

Raven shook her head. 'Believe me, if he wanted me dead, I wouldn't be here talking to you.'

'So why isn't his security here now?'

'He pays me well for my time, and I make sure he gets value for money, but that's as far as it goes. He's not someone I want to be indebted to.'

'Well,' Lock said, raising his hands, 'it's up to you. If you want me on that plane, I'll be there.'

'Thanks,' Raven said. 'I'd better go get changed for my midday meeting.'

He watched her leave. Through the glass he could see Ty mussing Kevin's hair. With every new revelation about Raven's tangled life, the gnawing sense of unease grew. But it was too late now to pack up and walk away. For better or worse, he was in for the ride all the way to the finish.

Twenty-three

But before any private flight to Vegas there was the matter of Raven's first business meeting. Lock wasn't sure what to expect from the head office of the world's richest porn production company (dozens of toga-clad supermodels? scenes of debauchery to equal the last days of Rome?) but this sure wasn't it.

The company's headquarters was a two-storey windowless concrete bunker two blocks east of Van Nuys Boulevard. It was flanked on one side by an industrial unit housing an aircraft-parts maintenance company and on the other by a low-rent Mexican restaurant. Like good bodyguards, wealthy adult-movie producers clearly recognized the wisdom of blending into the background.

Lock parked the Range Rover in back, and took a quick scan of the nearby cars before walking round and opening Raven's door. She stepped out into the blazing heat, black hair frizzing at the ends with the humidity. They walked to a door at the back of the building, and Raven hit a buzzer. A camera whirred round towards them. A second later there was a click.

Lock pushed the door open and ushered Raven inside. They found themselves facing a reception area. An obese middle-aged woman, who looked as if walking upstairs would make her sweat gravy, came out from behind the reception desk and enveloped Raven in a hug.

On the way over, Raven had explained to Lock that, after she had started out in the business, she had been one of the first 'contract girls' for Vixen Entertainment, meaning she had made movies exclusively for them. They operated at the higher end of the industry with a revenue stream from distributing their movies via the Internet, cell phones and hotel chains that would have pleased the head of any major Hollywood studio. One thing was for sure, though: they hadn't spent their money on their head office. Looking around at the faded linoleum and bare walls, Lock wondered what the low-end places were like.

'Oh, honey,' the receptionist was saying to Raven, 'we're all so glad you're okay. After what happened to you yesterday, we were so worried.'

'Thanks.'

The receptionist seemed to notice Lock for the first time. 'New boyfriend?' she asked Raven.

'Security,' Lock said, then put out his hand. 'Ryan Lock.'

'Cherry Brandowski,' the receptionist said, scanning him from top to toe. 'You ever done any acting, Ryan?'

Lock smiled. 'The people in these things act?' he asked her, waving at the movie posters that lined the walls. They looked like real movie posters, except they all featured naked women and the titles ranged from the comedic, *Sheepless in Seattle*, to the more straightforwardly graphic, *I Own Your Ass VI*. Clearly *I Own Your Ass I* through *V* had been sufficiently successful to merit a further sequel.

Raven frowned. 'Believe me, it's the women who have to do the acting most of the time.'

'Just like real life,' Lock observed, drawing a snort of a laugh from Cherry.

'Is Dimitri around?' Judging by Raven's body language, and the way she was lifting up and down on her heels, she seemed eager to cut the conversation short. 'He did say it was important.'

'Yeah,' Cherry said. 'He's in his office.'

Raven led the way down a long corridor off which there was an array of doors. Some were open and a variety of people sat behind desks, working on computers or on the phone, or filling in paperwork. If you took away the women on the posters, it appeared like any other business. The employees looked like those in any Hollywood production company: young, tired from the long hours, a little more casually dressed than in other parts of the corporate world, with more than the usual share of tattoos and piercings. Other than that they could have been making movies with Keanu Reeves.

The final door was unmarked. In fact, Lock had noted a complete absence of signage on any of the offices as he'd walked by. Raven knocked and, without waiting for an answer, went straight in.

From the name and the job title, Lock had been expecting

a burly Greek-American with lots of chest hair and a gold medallion, puffing on a cigar. But Dimitri appeared to be in his mid-thirties, an LA fashion victim dressed in an understated combo of designer jeans and a white shirt. There were no medallions, or any other jewellery, in sight.

Raven made the introductions. Dimitri was the CEO of the company.

'You want me to wait outside?' Lock asked.

'No, we're good,' Raven said, aiming a smile at Dimitri, who shrugged that he didn't mind either way.

Of course he had to be with Raven right now. She couldn't have gone to the meeting unescorted. He also sensed that not only did she and Dimitri have a history but that he was being used. As he saw it, Raven had hired help, and not the kind of dumb meathead who usually turned up as boyfriend or manager. She had brought the real deal: a man who had killed.

After air-kissing Raven and nodding curtly to Lock, Dimitri motioned for them both to take a seat across from him. Beside his computer he had one of those executive stress-relief contraptions with balls that clacked back and forth. Lock wondered if it was some kind of post-modern attempt at humour but didn't ask.

'I'll cut to the chase, Raven,' Dimitri said. 'I want you to come back and work for us.'

Raven's answer was swift but delivered with a smile. 'For ten thousand bucks a month? Forget it. There are more pleasurable ways of getting screwed.'

Dimitri opened a desk drawer and Lock tensed.

'Relax. I'm pulling out a deal memorandum,' Dimitri said, looking up at him.

He conjured a single piece of paper from the drawer and slid it towards Raven. 'Think about it. With this kind of money you can forget the club appearances and all the other bullshit. We handle everything for you. All you have to do is one movie a month, some promotional work, and stay in shape. Beyond that, your life's your own. You'd be back in the fold. And we wouldn't let anything bad happen to you. I guarantee it.'

Lock's focus shifted to Raven. He studied her face, looking to see if it would betray a reaction. The fact that it didn't confirmed, in his mind, that she was having thoughts similar to his own. That maybe there was no serial stalker beating a bloody path to her door. Maybe it was a classic piece of extortion.

While Carrie had been looking into Mr Vice, she'd found something else she had passed on to Lock earlier that morning. Something that had taken on a new meaning in the past few seconds. The last company Cindy Canyon had worked for was Vixen Entertainment. They'd been building her as the successor to Raven Lane.

As sure as night followed day, Dimitri was a front man, the acceptable face for much of the money that was coming into his industry. And the money behind porn was usually linked to crime. The distributors might be upstanding hotel chains and blue-chip tech companies, but the money behind the product would be something else. There was no way that organized crime wouldn't be involved with a morally dubious business that generated more money than Hollywood at a fraction of the cost and therefore with a much higher profit margin. You didn't need to be a forensic accountant to work out that much.

If Vixen Entertainment and its backers wanted their cash cow to return to the fold, scaring her would be one way of doing it, although even Lock's natural paranoia didn't allow him to believe that they would start killing people to achieve that goal. More likely they were using a situation that was already in play as leverage. Cindy was going to be their new star until she'd been murdered. So Vixen needed to go back to its old star, using the protection it could offer as the carrot.

Raven studied the piece of paper. Lock was hoping she'd say she would think about it, and they could leave. But Raven was not a woman to take the path of least resistance.

'Never go back. Wasn't that what you told me when you terminated my contract, Dimitri?' she asked now, her violet eyes blazing with fury.

Dimitri placed his hands palm down on the table. 'Circumstances change. You have a lot of heat around you, with everything that's going on. Why not cash in?' He took a breath, then lowered his voice. 'Raven, you've got maybe five years left. This stalker situation is a once-in-a-lifetime opportunity. We can all make out if we play this right.'

Raven stood up abruptly. 'That's what this whole deal is to you? A marketing opportunity? Or are you thinking of how much you'll get for my movies if this guy kills me?'

As she spoke, Lock kept his eyes on Dimitri. He was affecting a look of detached amusement. He stayed sitting but raised his hands, palms out. 'Okay, okay, I was asked to put the offer to you. You don't have to go postal on me. It's a good deal, Raven. A great deal, in fact. But it won't be on the table for ever. You and I both know that.'

Lock got up, ready to end the exchange. 'It was nice meeting you.' He nodded towards the door. 'You have to be somewhere,' he reminded Raven.

Lock fell into step behind her as she stalked out of the room and down the corridor. In the reception area, Raven gave Cherry a goodbye hug, which was when he noticed the poster behind her desk, separate from the ones lining the walls of the corridor. It showed Raven Lane. Next to her was Cindy Canyon. They had their arms wrapped around each other, and they were staring into each other's eyes, lips not quite touching.

Lock kept walking. This was the Cindy Canyon whose head had ended up in a newspaper vending machine and whose body had been pulled from the trunk of Raven's BMW; the Cindy Canyon whom Raven didn't know. For two people who didn't know each other, they looked pretty close.

Lock had a decision to make. Either he could ask Raven why she had lied or he could keep his mouth shut. In the parking lot, Raven's cell phone beeped. She took it from her bag and read the text. 'They confirmed. The plane will be ready for us at Van Nuys at four o'clock.' She looked at him. 'Are you okay? You seem kind of quiet.'

'Just thinking about something.'

'Want to share?'

'Not right now,' he said, holding open the door of the Range Rover. They had a long day together. There would be plenty of time to try to work out which parts of Raven's story held up – and which didn't.

Twenty-four

'Cool car,' Kevin said, rocking back and forth in the passenger seat of Ty's purple 1966 Lincoln Continental, his sulk about Wendy seemingly forgotten.

'Thanks, brother. Now, you got everything you need?'

'I think so.'

'Lunch?'

'In my backpack.'

'Okay, then, we're good to go, I guess. You ready?'

'Ready.'

Ty flattened the accelerator and they took off with a roar, leaving behind a belch of exhaust fumes sufficient to give Al Gore an aneurysm. Halfway up the street, a soccer mom had to jostle her MPV almost on to the sidewalk as Ty laid waste to any sense of careful driving in a semi-suburban neighbourhood.

'You drive faster than my sister,' Kevin observed, a grin plastered over his face as Ty continued to carve a swathe through the traffic.

'She drive fast?'

'Oh, yeah. Not as fast as this, though.'

Kevin stared out of the passenger window, eyes focused in the middle distance, his tongue pushing out from his mouth a little. 'Raven's not her real name. She made it up.'

Ty moved back down the gears as they came to the stop light on Wilshire Boulevard, the engine reduced to a low series of grumbles. 'You mind that?'

'No, it's kinda cool.'

The stop light shifted to green and Ty took off again, tumbling down a hill towards the freeway on-ramp. 'So what was her real name? If you don't mind me asking.'

'Well,' Kevin said, straightening up in his seat. 'Our name is Lane, but my sister's real name is Sarah.'

Ty mulled it over. It kind of made him wonder about the real deal of how Kevin and Raven were brought up. Crazy families usually went in for crazy names, and 'Sarah' was about as strait-laced as they came. 'Sarah's cute. Hey, you know Superman's girlfriend was Lois Lane. Is that why you like him so much?'

'No,' Kevin said, resting his head against the cool of the glass. 'I like Superman because he kicks ass.'

Ten minutes later, Ty stopped the Continental up outside the day centre. It was a Spanish bungalow-style white concrete building with red tiles, neatly trimmed grass out front, everything spick and span. A yellow school bus pulled up outside, disgorging its cargo of young adults.

Ty thought back to high school, when he and his buddies might have been standing on the sidewalk, making jokes about the Short Bus or the Goof Troop. But here and now, with Kevin next to him, those jokes didn't seem so much funny as pathetic. Maybe, he thought, kids used that kind of humour about people like Kevin to distance themselves because the reality was too uncomfortable. Or maybe he and his buddies had just been assholes when they'd cracked those jokes.

After a couple of beers, Lock had once told Ty about his approach to such stuff and it had stayed with him: 'If you'd feel like a complete asshole saying something to someone's face, then don't say it behind their back.' Lock the philosopher, thought Ty, smiling.

The bus pulled away and a number of the teenagers were pointing at Ty's car. Most, but not all, had Down's syndrome. Kevin waved at them, enjoying the attention. Then Ty noticed his brow furrow and he looked away.

Wendy's mother was escorting her daughter into the building. Ty rested a huge hand on Kevin's shoulder. 'You okay, brother?'

Kevin gave a weak nod.

'Listen, remember what I told you. It'll work out. There's no guy a girl likes better than the one her parents don't want her seeing. Take it from me.'

Ty started to escort Kevin across the road, but their path was blocked by a convoy of three more school buses, this time carrying what seemed to be high-school kids. It was only then that Ty noticed the building less than a half-block away from the adult learning centre where he was dropping Kevin. His car was drawing attention from the high-school students too, but a couple of skater kids sporting shaggy hair on the last bus were more focused on Kevin's friends on the other side of the road. One of the skaters jutted his jaw out, letting his face go slack, aping the expression of someone with Down's. His buddy cracked up. The group waiting to go into the learning centre looked away.

Ty made a mental note of the two skater kids, then walked Kevin across the street and inside the building. When he came back out, some of the high-school kids were still milling about, grabbing the last few minutes before they had to be inside.

Ty walked down the road towards the high school. The two skater kids he'd made a note of earlier were still outside, passing around a joint. The slightly taller one waved the joint in Ty's direction as he closed in on them. 'It's okay, man, we're good.'

Black guy outside a high school has to be a drug-dealer in their world, thought Ty. He let his jacket, which he'd weighted with coins earlier so that it wouldn't ride up and reveal his gun, slip to one side.

The kid's expression shifted in less time than it took Ty to pluck the joint from his hand and crush it under his boot. He stared at them.

'It's only a little weed, man,' the smaller one offered.

Ty kept staring, enjoying their discomfort. He nodded down the street. 'You think the people over there don't have enough bullshit to deal with without assholes like you making fun of them?'

Their teenage bravado evaporated.

'Answer me,' Ty said.

'No,' said the taller of the two.

'What about you?' Ty said, addressing the shorter one, who seemed busy willing the ground to open up and swallow him.

'They probably didn't even see us.'

Ty took a step forward. 'Say what, motherfucker?'

The kid remained silent, his face flushing.

'And look at me when I'm talking to you, bitch,' Ty continued.

The other kids had melted away.

'No.' The kid's voice was starting to fracture as he fought off tears. 'I'm sorry. We won't do it again.'

'Damn straight,' said Ty, and walked back towards the Continental.

Twenty-five

Dodging the airport's main terminal building, Lock drove the black Range Rover towards a gatehouse-controlled side entrance where a guard checked his and Raven's ID before directing them to a nearby aircraft hangar.

A dozen jets were parked on the apron, mostly Gulfstreams and Cessnas. The cheapest one probably cost more than five million dollars, Lock guessed. If the world economy was in difficulty, clearly no one had told the people who owned or rented them.

Lock knew from prior experience that security at private airports was generally more relaxed than at the ones that serviced the general public. Most people would never have cause to come near a facility like this. Raven's stalker wasn't most people, though, so he kept a close eye on everything around them as they got out of the vehicle.

The jet to take them to Vegas, a Gulfstream G250, was waiting for them, stairs down, fuelled, crewed and good to go.

Raven led the way, clearly familiar with the drill. Two female cabin crew greeted them at the top of the stairs. Their overnight bags were spirited away to a front storage area as they walked into the main cabin. Plush cream carpet swallowed them ankle deep as they made their way past a sparkling stainless-steel forward galley and a black-marble-topped bar towards the creamy-soft leather seats. At the back, Lock could see a bathroom, complete with shower, the size of ten cramped conventional aircraft restrooms, the interior walls covered with soft leather.

The luxurious surroundings lent a soporific quality to the atmosphere, as if you were stepping out of the conscious world and into a dreamscape where nothing bad could possibly happen.

Lock took a seat facing the front while Raven sat opposite him. One of the smartly dressed female cabin attendants asked if they wanted anything. Lock asked for water.

'Vodka tonic. Ice, no lemon,' Raven said, stretching out her long, jeans-clad legs.

The flight attendant disappeared into the galley with her colleague as Lock took another look around. 'Guess this beats Economy,' he said. He dug into his pocket for his cell phone and started to pass it over. 'Thought you might want to call your brother before we take off.'

Raven smiled and opened a console next to her. She pulled out a telephone handset. 'I was going to wait until we were up.'

It was the first smile he'd seen from her in a while. Her full lips parted to reveal perfect white teeth and her eyes sparkled with life.

'Not your first time on one of these,' he said.

'Like I explained, it's an ongoing relationship. Although,' she said, looking round, 'this plane is a new one.'

The flight attendant returned with their drinks, both of which were served in crystal glasses. Raven took a sip of vodka and closed her eyes. 'I'm amazed Kevin still wants to stay in the house after the other night.'

'Kids are resilient,' was all Lock could offer. He was amazed that Raven had left him. After all her protestations about not wanting to leave town, here she was on a private jet headed for Vegas. It just didn't synch.

The jet was moving now, taxiing out towards the main runway, a soft winter sunset lying like crystal against the horizon. Lock put on his seatbelt and Raven followed suit.

'Can I ask you something?' she said.

He shrugged. 'Sure.'

'Ty has a gun, right?'

'You know he does.'

'So if the stalker comes back to the house, and Ty has the chance, will he kill him?'

'If Ty considers that his or Kevin's life is threatened, then yes, absolutely.'

'And what about you, Ryan?' she said, fixing him with those deep pools of violet.

'Would I kill someone who posed a serious threat to the life of the person I'm protecting or to me? If I had to, yes.'

She took another sip of her drink, as if she were bolstering her courage to ask the next question.

'The man you killed in that stairwell in San Francisco.'

Lock shifted uncomfortably in his seat. He wondered how

she'd found out about that. Maybe Stanner had mentioned something. Or she could have worked it out from an Internet search. It was hardly a secret even if he was the only one who knew the real story.

They were moving down the runway now, the landscape of patchy grass and chain-link fence whipping past at a furious pace.

'What about him?' he asked her.

Another sip of vodka. 'Do you think about him?'

Lock shook his head. 'I took a decision. I stand by it. So, no, I don't think about him, and before you ask, I don't regret it either.'

Raven nodded, seemingly satisfied. 'That makes me feel a lot safer.'

Twenty-six

Carrie got out of her car and stretched the kinks out of her back. She hesitated for a moment, car keys dangling in her hand. Directly ahead of her, perched at the end of the steeply sloped cul-de-sac in the Hollywood Hills, lay her final destination, a sterile, post-modern monstrosity of concrete and glass: the home of adult-movie director Vince Vice.

Her background checking into Vice had yielded his address easily enough but there was no phone number to go with it so she had decided on impulse to drive over from Malibu. She had a feeling that Vice lay at the dark heart of a world that might provide the clue as to who was terrorizing Raven. But Carrie recognized that there was more to her desire to confront Vice: she wanted to observe the monster up close. She'd started out with a belief that she would find a pathetic creature, that the reality of Vice would be at odds with his sadistic image. Now she was here she was less sure, and regretting that she had told no one, Lock included, about her plans to visit.

But something in her wouldn't allow her to turn back now. Vice might have scared a bunch of insecure runaways but he wouldn't scare Carrie.

At the bottom of the steep driveway there was a pair of heavy black iron gates. They were open. She could have driven through them and parked directly outside but she chose to leave the car where it was and hike up the slope. *Always secure your escape route.* It was one of the many things that Lock had drilled into her.

Through the glass walls she couldn't see anyone moving about inside. At the front door, which was positioned to the side of the house, two phallic-looking cacti stood in planters. A sticker in one of the windows advertised that the house was protected by an armed security company. So far so LA.

She rang the bell and waited. A full minute passed. She was about to wander around to the front of the house to take a closer look when the front door was flung open. A man she recognized as Vince Vice stood in front of her, legs splayed, arms folded. He was wearing skintight Speedo swimming trunks and a cowboy hat. A Native American-style feather necklace hung from his neck.

He looked her up and down, lingering on her breasts. He still hadn't opened his mouth and she was already creeped out.

'Mr Vice, I'm Carrie—'

He cut her off with a wave of his hand. 'You're late. Come in.'

Telling herself that she'd dealt with bigger scumbags than

this guy, Carrie stepped into the foyer. White tiles stretched through the house, adding to the overall coldness and sterility that seemed to seep from the walls.

'Mr Vice?' she shouted, as he walked away from her, then around a corner.

She heard his voice somewhere in the distance. 'How come you actresses are always late?'

She took a deep breath, cursing herself again for failing to let anyone know that she was coming here – but it was too late for that now. And to turn back would leave her feeling foolish. She pressed on.

As she rounded the corner, the corridor opened out into a vast open-plan living area. There was a black leather couch, a glass coffee-table with a tiny mound of white powder and a razor blade, a fifty-inch plasma-screen television, tuned to what Carrie guessed was one of Vice's movies, and a video camera mounted on a tripod.

Vice was behind the camera. 'Take your clothes off,' he said. He sniffed and rubbed at his nose. Carrie noticed that his movements were jittery and agitated, his eyes hollow from lack of sleep.

She straightened. 'Your real name's Paul Aronofsky. Correct?'

Something in Vice's expression shifted. He checked his watch. 'Ronnie didn't send you over, did he?'

'I've no idea who Ronnie is, or who you think I am. And I don't appreciate you barking at me like I'm a piece of meat.'

Vice's face darkened and he moved out from behind the camera. 'So who are you?'

'I'm a reporter. I wanted to ask you some questions.'

'What kind of questions?'

'When was the last time you saw Cindy Canyon?'

Vice's right hand started to slide down the back of the couch. 'I don't know anyone by that name.'

'Yes, you do. You made a movie with her.'

'Do you know how many actresses I've worked with? Hundreds. Thousands over my career.'

'I'm sure you have,' Carrie said, watching his right hand as it came back up with a handgun. A big one. A Magnum .44.

'Everyone out here wants to be in movies,' Vice said. 'What about you?'

'I'll pass,' she said, trying to inject a note of confidence into her voice.

'You sure about that?' he asked, pulling back the hammer and casually raising the gun so it was pointed at her.

Carrie took a step backwards, almost stumbling over the corner of a rug she hadn't noticed on the way in. She had expected him to be hostile – his bio had told her that. She hadn't expected a reaction so extreme, though.

'Tell you what,' he said, his voice soft and reasonable. 'I'll put the gun down and you can ask me all the questions you like.'

'Okay,' said Carrie, her heart pounding as she waited for the catch.

'But when you're done, I get to ask you some questions. We have a deal?'

'I'll have to take notes. And you have to put down the gun. I can't concentrate with it pointed at me.'

'Sure,' he said, with a smirk, the gun dropping to his side.

Carrie thought back over the ground she'd covered when

she'd walked into the house. She had to take maybe four steps until she was round the corner and back in the hallway. He might be able to raise the gun and get off a shot in that time . even in his coked-up state but she'd probably make it. The problem was the long stretch of corridor to the front door. He would be ten or twelve paces behind. She could gain a couple more steps if she got the jump on him. But how long was the corridor? Twenty steps? Thirty?

Then there was the question of the door. She had followed him inside so he couldn't have secured a chain. But it was closed, and she had no idea how long it would take her to get it open. Ryan would have known. But he probably wouldn't have followed the guy inside without an exit strategy. How she wished he was with her now.

'Why don't you sit down, make yourself comfortable?' Vice said, patting the sofa.

'I'm fine right here.'

Vice shrugged. The paranoia that had flared in his eyes a moment ago seemed to be receding. His movements were still jerky and staccato but Carrie felt herself relax a notch.

'You wanted to know about Cindy Canyon,' he prompted. 'But there's just one thing before I tell you.'

'And what's that, Paul? You don't mind me calling you by your first name, do you?'

'I'd prefer if you called me Vince. Paul's dead.'

'What happened to him?'

'You mind if I . . . ?' He nodded to the cocaine on the table. 'It's your house.'

Vice made a big show of chopping out two lines with the razor and hoovering one up into each nostril. His nose flared

red and his eyes watered and it took him a moment to settle. 'What happened to Paul?' he said, repeating the question. 'You might as well ask what happened to whoever Cindy Canyon was before she became Cindy Canyon.'

Carrie cleared her throat. 'Her original name was Melanie Spiteri.'

He laughed. 'You see . . .' He paused.

'Carrie Delaney. I only have one name.'

'You see, Carrie,' Vice said, slumping back into the couch, 'the adult industry is a place where people come to reinvent themselves, to escape from who they were, to become someone or something else. That's the first thing you have to understand. It's not about sex. Not really.'

'So what is it about?'

'I just told you. It's about freedom. The freedom to be who you truly are, not who your parents or your teachers or the Church want you to be.'

Even with the gun, Carrie wasn't about to let this pseudo-philosophical bullshit fly. 'So, getting some teenager fresh off the bus to dress up as a schoolgirl, then forcing her to have oral sex until she throws up is about freedom?'

Vice held up his non-gun hand, palm open. 'Do you want to learn or do you want to preach?'

'You know what happened to Melanie Spiteri?'

He nodded towards the huge TV. 'Caught it on the news,' he said matter-of-factly. 'Shit happens in this business.' He stroked the .44 Magnum, which was next to him on the couch. 'That's why you can't be too careful.'

'Had you heard about anyone threatening her? A stalker, maybe?'

Vice smirked. 'How the hell would I know? I worked with her once.'

'And you don't get much repeat business?'

'Once is usually enough. Most of them can't take the pace of a Vince Vice flick.'

Carrie sighed. 'I bet. What about Raven Lane?'

Vice ran his fingers through his short cropped hair. 'What about her?'

'You worked with her at the start of her career too.'

'Yeah, me and Raven go way back, but I haven't seen her in years. Not since she threatened to kill me anyway.'

Carrie felt relief that he had brought up Raven's threat without being prompted. 'You weren't worried by her threatening you like that?'

'Not enough to want to harm her. I've already gone over all of this with the cops. Listen, you might not like what I do or how I make my living, but I'm the one whose life is being threatened.'

'What do you mean? Raven made that threat years ago.'

Vice lifted the gun again, holding it in two hands. 'I've had phone calls in the past few weeks. Why do you think I have this?'

'You tell the cops about these calls?'

'Sure. They sent out some fat, frizzy-haired retard to talk to me.'

'You think the phone calls were from Raven?'

'Not directly.'

'What does that mean?'

Vice stood up. Carrie kept still, although her heart was pounding again.

'It means that Raven is good at playing the victim, drawing people into her little world, but she's no angel, believe me. Now, I've answered all your questions, so what do you say? Should you and me get to know each other a little better?' He leered at her, his tongue flicking over his lips.

Carrie tensed as she watched his hands. She was waiting for him to raise the gun. Trying to judge the best moment to make a break for it.

She took a deep breath. 'You know, I don't think I'm suitably attired for one of your productions.'

'The outfits are upstairs. Why don't you go pick one out?'

The stairs had been facing the front door. Without waiting, she started to walk out of the room, towards them. She could hear him getting up to follow her. But as soon as she was around the corner, she took to her heels, her shoes slapping hard against the tiles. At the door she allowed herself a split second to look back.

Vice was at the far end of the corridor. The gun was nowhere to be seen. He saw the panic in her face and laughed. 'Say hello to Raven for me, would you?'

Carrie wrenched the front door open and then she was gone, half running, half stumbling down the drive. But as she neared the gates, she saw them starting to move.

Most electronic gates had a sensor to stop them closing on vehicles or people. Once they were shut, though, that was it. All she had to do was get there before they sealed entirely.

Not looking back any more, she focused entirely on the last few feet, making it just in time. As she squeezed through, the gates stopped.

Shaking, she clicked open the car and clambered in,

activating the central locking as soon as she was inside. Then she sat, her head in her hands, feeling sick with fear and disgust.

She'd promised herself that a lowlife like Vice wouldn't get to her, but he had. She looked to her right, back up towards the house. But the front door was closed and he was out of sight.

Even looking at the house made her shudder. Something about the place had chilled her. She thought of the dozens of young women, no more than children really, who must have stepped inside that front door, and left as very different people.

She took one last look, thinking for a moment that she had glimpsed Vice standing at one of the upstairs windows. But as the sun glinted against the glass, he was gone again, back into his nightmare world where women existed only to satisfy the darker, depraved urges of men who would run a hundred miles from a real relationship.

Twenty-seven

The Gulfstream taxied off the runway and came to a stop. The engines were shut down and the steps lowered. Next to the aircraft, a shiny black limousine waited for them, its engine idling with a low rumble. A driver and a single bodyguard sat inside.

As Lock escorted Raven down the stairs, the bodyguard had emerged to open the door. He was a huge guy, not tall but wide, with a thick neck and a Lego-block head. He was wearing a tight-fitting suit, which Lock presumed was meant to emphasize his muscles but would only cripple his ability to move if anything happened. A Fu Manchu goatee and pair of wraparound shades completed his look. While everything about him screamed 'bodyguard', Lock knew that if anything did go down, this guy would be about as much use as a cat-flap on a submarine.

As the bodyguard opened the door of the limo for them, his suit jacket rode up to reveal his firearm, a Glock 9mm.

Professional operators usually weighted their suit pockets so they didn't put their weapon on show when they moved. This guy'd made it clear that he was armed – and equally clear that the jacket restricted movement, so that by the time he was ready to fire his gun, an attacker could have put him down.

Close-protection work was about reaction time, and reaction time wasn't helped by bulk. Ty was a powerfully put-together individual but he was also athletic. This man, Lock thought, was like a goddamn hippo. Yeah, if he got close enough he'd do some damage, but he'd never get near someone who knew what they were doing. He was like a cartoon version of what a tough guy should look like, and his presence instantly made Lock nervous.

The rear passenger door of the limo closed with a bass *thunk* heavy enough to let Lock know that the vehicle was up-armoured. Another bad sign: up-armoured vehicles tended to be used by high-net-worth individuals who carried a high risk. If you were all about bling and had no enemies, you'd save the cash and go for a soft-skinned regular limousine.

Raven sat opposite him, pulled some makeup and a compact mirror from her bag and went to work. It was time to ask her the question he'd been avoiding.

'So, are you going to tell me who this guy is before we get to the hotel?'

Raven smiled. 'He'd prefer I didn't.'

Lock sighed. 'It goes no further. Scout's honour.'

Raven pursed her lips and blotted some lipstick on to a tissue, then checked herself in the mirror. 'He's a businessman.'

'American?'

She glanced at him over the top of the compact. 'Why the sudden interest?'

'Would you mind answering the question?'

'He's Russian, if you must know. Or Ukrainian, I'm not quite sure.'

Lock's heart sank a little. From his experience with Eastern European businessmen, the phrase was interchangeable with Mafia. Even if they ran a clean operation here, the risk of an overlap with elements of organized crime from back home was inevitable.

Raven must have read his unease. 'Look, he's a perfect gentleman. And, like I already said, if he wanted to harm me, he'd have done it already.'

'And what about people close to you? Does he have any reason to harm them?'

'People close to me?'

Lock took a deep breath, knowing that his question might finish his involvement with her. He'd brooded over whether to ask it since the visit to the production company. 'Like Cindy. You denied knowing her but you were in a movie together, weren't you?'

Raven's only reaction was to straighten in her seat and cross her legs. 'Where's all this coming from?'

'At the production company I saw a poster with the two of you on the wall.'

She smiled. 'That's it? That's your evidence that I've been lying to you? I hope you're a better bodyguard than an investigator.'

He stared straight at her. 'So how do you explain the poster?'

'You don't watch a lot of these movies, do you, Ryan?'

'I never considered that a bad thing,' he said, reading her body language, which stayed perfectly relaxed and free of any tics that suggested she was nervous.

'It's true that Cindy and I were in the same movie, but we never shared a scene. They were shot on different days. That poster was a composite put together after the shoot.'

'But I assumed—'

Raven flicked her jet-black hair. 'People always assume things about me. Usually they assume the worst.' She stared down at her hands. 'I thought you might be different.'

Lock's jaw tightened. 'I'm sorry, but a couple of things didn't add up. The poster was only one of them.'

She sighed. 'Then you might as well ask me about the others.'

He glanced out at the shoals of overweight Midwesterners in slacks and T-shirts filtering in and out of the casinos in the broiling late-afternoon heat. 'You were adamant that you wouldn't leave your brother alone. That he was the reason you couldn't get out of town. Yet here we are.'

She pulled her cigarettes from her bag and lit one. Lock reached over to press the button to lower the window but when he pushed it nothing happened. He tapped on the glass divider that separated the rear of the limo from the driver's area where the bodyguard was sitting.

A second later it slid down and the man's face filled the gap.

'I'd like to open the window a little,' Lock said to him.

There was a grunt, then the face was gone and the glass slid back into place. A second later the window nearest Raven came down a few inches.

'It's one night,' she said finally. 'And he's with Ty. If we moved now it would freak him out even more than he is already. If I have to move I will, but right now he needs the familiarity of home. Plus, with the kind of money I'm spending on security, I couldn't afford to pass this up. Happy now?'

Lock met her eyes, still unsure. 'Yeah, I am,' he lied.

Twenty-eight

Five minutes later they pulled up at the Bellagio, the billion-dollar hotel and casino that was the playground for the really high rollers. The bodyguard left Lock to carry the two small bags and led them through the lobby. The overly plush décor was offset by a huge multi-coloured chandelier, which made the place look, Lock thought, like a bad acid trip to seventeenth-century Venice.

They followed the bodyguard towards the elevator that would take them up to the bedrooms.

'He's in the Chairman's Suite,' the bodyguard said. He produced a key from his jacket pocket and used it to call the elevator – standard procedure for the private suites where it often opened straight into the accommodation. Lock made sure to keep a close eye on where he put the key, although usually getting down was a simple matter of pushing a button.

The bodyguard ushered them inside and they started their

ascent to the top of the hotel. As the doors opened, Raven's features shifted into a thousand-watt smile – like an actress walking on stage, Lock thought.

They stepped out into a marbled foyer. The bodyguard gestured towards a set of double doors, but as Lock moved towards it, a beefy arm shot out in front of him blocking his passage.

'The lady goes inside. We're over there in one of the entourage suites,' the bodyguard growled, with a nod to a door across the corridor.

Lock stared at the guy's arm. 'Put that down before I break it off.'

The bodyguard cleared his throat. 'I don't think my boss was looking for a threesome, which means you have to wait outside.'

Lock turned to Raven. 'It's your call.'

Raven smiled. 'Relax. If I need you, I'll holler.'

'You're sure?'

She nodded, opened the doors and was gone.

The bodyguard patted his shoulder with a hand the size of a fire shovel. 'You've done your job. Got her here in one piece. Come on inside and chill out. She's going to be a few hours.' He smirked. 'The boss has a lot of energy for a guy his age.'

The entourage suite, as the bodyguard had called it, was four times the size of any regular hotel suite. Another marbled foyer opened into a huge living area, which was dominated by a vast television tuned to a pro football game. To either side of the living area there were two bedrooms, complete with separate his and hers bathrooms.

Lock had already noticed that the bodyguard seemed to get

off on the wealth of his employer, and the power that he clearly thought it bestowed. The guy was naïve. Money could buy muscle. Protection was a different matter. People who were interested in staying safe didn't go in for lavish demonstrations of their buying power.

He made a show of taking in the suite and let out a low whistle. 'The bill for all this must run pretty high.'

The bodyguard fiddled with the touchscreen remote for the television. 'Yeah, guess you wouldn't see much change from fifteen or twenty grand for the night. Chump change for this guy.'

'How long you been working for him?'

The fiddling stopped and the bodyguard's head rotated slowly towards him. 'Why you wanna know?'

Lock held up open palms. 'Don't worry, I'm quite happy with the gig I got. I'm not looking to get in on your action here.'

The bodyguard's lips peeled back to reveal a gummy smile and a couple of gold caps. 'I bet you are. You sleep with her yet?'

'No, man.'

'You sure? I could see the way she looked at you.'

'And how was that?'

'Like you was a pork chop. So, you ain't hit it?'

Lock laughed and shook his head.

'You gay or something? Not that there's anything wrong with that as a lifestyle choice, know what I'm saying?'

Lock was going to mention Carrie, then realized he had an opportunity to put the guy a little off balance. 'Yeah. I am. I'm gay. How'd you guess?'

The bodyguard's eyes widened and the smile evaporated. 'For real?'

'That's one of the reasons she hired me, brother. Didn't want someone hitting on her.'

'I'll be damned. I ain't never heard of a gay bodyguard before,' he said, checking his watch and pushing up the volume on the TV.

There was something about the gesture that put Lock on guard. The two actions seemed premeditated. Who looks at their watch before they decide to turn up the volume on the TV? he asked himself. There was only one answer. Someone who knew that there was about to be some kind of loud noise they didn't want the other person in the room to hear.

He hoped he was wrong – and he needed a way to check his suspicions without antagonizing the guy.

'The Redskins' game on?' he asked.

The bodyguard shrugged. 'Thought they were playing later.'

'Here, I know the channel number,' Lock said, plucking the remote from the edge of the couch before the other had a chance to object.

He quickly hit the mute button. The blaring crowd noise and chatter of the commentators gave way to a woman's piercing scream. Then everything in the room went on to fast forward.

As the bodyguard grabbed for the remote, Lock spun round, put his hands on the man's shoulders, pulled his head and torso down and brought up a knee as hard as he could into his groin.

The bodyguard let out something between a yell and a

grunt. Lock kept the man's downward momentum going, grabbed the back of his neck and pulled his head down to the level of his waist. Then he kneed him as hard as he could in the face. Once. Twice. The third time there was the splinter of teeth.

Lock let him go and he fell to the floor. Moving quickly out of his reach, Lock bent down to retrieve his gun, which he jammed into the folds of fat at the back of the guy's neck. 'Get up.'

Shakily, the bodyguard rose to his feet. Lock pushed him towards the door of the suite.

In the corridor, Raven's screams were louder.

Lock shoved him towards the door of the Chairman's Suite. 'Open it,' he said.

One hand massaging a broken nose, the bodyguard used the other to slide an electronic key card into a slot. The door opened and Lock pushed him through it.

Inside, the screaming went on. Lock looked round for other security personnel but the suite seemed to be empty, apart from the man who had Raven pinned down on a vast super-king-sized bed in a room fifty feet to their left. He was bare-chested, middle-aged, but with a squat, powerful physique. He straddled Raven who was clawing at his chest with her long nails as he raised his open palm to slap her.

'Tell me,' he shouted. 'Tell me who's doing this.'

Raven struggled, shifting her face as best she could to avoid the blow. It caught her hard on the side of her head.

Lock thrust the bodyguard out of the way – he fell over a coffee-table and landed on the marble floor. Then he raised the gun and pointed it at the back of the Russian's head. 'Hit her again and I'll blow what few brains you possess all over this nice room,' he said.

The Russian looked up at the mirror that hung over the bed. He must have caught Lock's reflection straight away because he relaxed enough for Raven to struggle out from under him. As she fell to the floor, she grabbed one of her shoes and whacked the Russian with the heel. 'You asshole.'

'Get dressed,' Lock said to her, pointing to the clothes strewn on the floor.

He turned his attention to the Russian, who stared at him, terror stamped on his features. 'Please,' he said. 'How much? I'll give you as much as you want. Just don't kill me. She's yours. I know. I'm sorry.'

Lock ignored him. Clearly he had Lock mixed up with someone else. 'She's coming with me. And I want you to know that, even if you kill me, I have a friend who will make it his life's work to ensure that very bad things happen to you very slowly before you die.'

'Please. I know all this. Just leave. Take her.'

At the edge of his vision, Lock could see the bodyguard crawling on to a plush couch, next to which was an end table with a phone on it.

Lock aimed the gun at him. 'Same goes for you. You're an accessory to felony, assault and rape. You make that phone call, I might be going to prison but you're coming with me and the sentence will be a lot less for me.'

The bodyguard slumped down on to his knees.

'Go into the bathroom and wipe some of the blood off,' Lock said to Raven. 'Quick as you can. Don't worry about makeup.' He turned to the bodyguard. 'Check the closets.

Find me a sweatshirt or something with a hood. And remember what I said.'

The bodyguard lumbered off and returned a minute later with a hooded top. Raven came out of the bathroom and Lock threw it to her. He could see she was still shaking, a reaction to the adrenalin pumping through her system from the shock of being attacked. 'You have sunglasses?'

'Yes,' she choked out.

'Then throw those on as well after you put the hood up.'

He waited as she grabbed her things and got herself together as best she could. The Russian and his bodyguard stayed where they were.

'I'm ready,' she said finally.

Lock kept hold of the Glock until they were out of the suite, then dropped it into Raven's bag. They took the elevator down and moved swiftly through the lobby, which seemed even more surreal this time. There was no sign of hotel security or anyone else who mattered. The Russian was clearly too smart or too scared to pursue them – for now, anyway.

Outside, the Bellagio's trademark fountains surged hundreds of feet into the night sky. A crowd stood transfixed, watching the show.

Lock moved Raven through the crush and hailed a cab. They took off towards the airport and the first flight back to LA. The neon lights shimmered ever more brightly as night took a hold. He would have to wipe down the gun and stash it before they went through Security.

He looked across at Raven, who was snuggled against the door, her face almost entirely obscured by the hood and sunglasses. She seemed small and vulnerable.

What happens in Vegas stays in Vegas. That had been the marketing slogan a few years back. Lock had a feeling that this time it was wishful thinking.

Twenty-nine

It was one in the morning and Vince Vice had been awake for forty-eight hours when the doorbell rang. These days, his sense of time was about as reliable as one of Salvador Dalí's melting clocks. He thought for a second that it might be the blonde reporter, back to take him up on his offer of a starring role. Then he remembered that she had left seven or more hours ago.

The coke was mostly gone and he had been upstairs, rifling the medicine cabinet in his bathroom for something to bring him down. Bottles and pills lay scattered over the black marble counter top of the vanity unit. He caught a sliver of his own face in the mirror and recoiled at the sight. Then he went to search for his gun. He wasn't opening the door at this hour without it. Not with that crazy bitch or one of her buddies out there.

The gun. Where was the gun? Where had he left it?

He walked back into his bedroom where he'd been

reviewing some of his old work on the plasma screen he had mounted over the bed. He'd heard on the grapevine that one of the girls he'd worked with had killed herself a few weeks back, strung out, no doubt, in some trailer back in Idaho. The idea had excited him.

Pulling the pillows from the bed, he flung them across the room as the doorbell rang again. The sheets, so encrusted they crinkled like low-grade cardboard, joined them. Then he remembered: the gun was downstairs where he had left it.

He grabbed a robe and put it on over his trunks and marled grey T-shirt. In the upstairs hallway he killed the lights. He didn't want whoever was outside seeing him as he came down the stairs.

Taking the steps two at a time, he almost slipped, grabbing the handrail at the last second. Walking fast into the living room, he saw the gun lying on the glass coffee-table. He picked it up and went to the front door.

He peered out the glass panel at the side of the door, catching only his own reflection for a second. Squinting, he got a view of outside, the white steps leading up to the door.

No one there.

Looking further down the driveway he could see that the gates were open. They must have sprung back when the reporter had left and he'd forgotten to hit the button again, which would have sealed them.

There was no car to be seen either in the drive or at the bottom, in the street. No car and no one. Yet the doorbell had rung.

Whoever it was must have gotten bored and left.

Vince turned and started back up the stairs. Four steps

from the door the doorbell clanged again. 'Motherfucker.'

Now he was pissed. Someone was screwing around. Well, he'd show them. Open the door and shoot them right in the fucking face.

He sprinted down the stairs, reached forward to open the front door and flung it open.

No one there.

What the fuck?

He took a step forward, the gun in his hand level with his waist, his finger on the trigger, his nerves not wholly sub-sumed by rage.

Still no one. He angled his head left, looking at the door-bell. Maybe it had short-circuited or something. But the tiny black box seemed fine.

He took another step outside. Then another. Only then did he hear the front door begin to close on him. He turned round, getting his hand to it only in time to feel it click into place against the frame.

'Shit.'

He sighed. Just freaking great. Now he was locked out. He tried the handle. It turned but the door didn't open. His cell phone was inside. So were his keys. All he had was what he was wearing and the gun.

This gave him an idea. He stepped back and looked at the lock. Maybe he could shoot it out. Then he thought about what might happen if the round rebounded towards him.

No, if he was going to shoot anything, it had better be a window. Then he could smash the rest of the glass and climb back in.

He started round the side of the house, searching for a

suitable candidate. Most of the windows were full-size sheets of reinforced glass, expensive to replace, probably three or four thousand dollars a throw. Vince knew he would struggle to explain the circumstances to his insurance company – 'Well, you see, I was coked off my face, and then the doorbell rang, but there was no one there. Paranoid? Me?' He laughed at the thought of how that conversation might go.

A concrete lip ran around the footprint of the house. It was narrow. Maybe only three feet wide. Wide enough to walk as long as you were careful.

At the back of the house the concrete lip fell away almost immediately to a steep slope and beyond that were the lights of Hollywood. Vince took a little time out to study the view. He could trace Sunset Boulevard, Hollywood's main artery, which snaked through what everyone imagined was where the magic happened but which was in fact a low-rent neighbourhood of sleaze and grifters. Most of the girls Vince worked with he found below in Hollywood – young and dumb was how he liked them.

Damn, this was a great city.

Along the narrow lip there was a panel of two thinner rectangular windows, which fronted the kitchen. These were ideal. He might find himself with his ass in a sink of dirty dishes when he climbed in but that would be the worst of it.

The problem he had now was finding an angle. The Magnum was a cannon by handgun standards and he was worried that if the angle was too acute the bullet might blow through the window and the external wall on the other side of the house and end up in his neighbour's home, which would harm more than his insurance premium.

Holding the gun in his left hand, he could just about make it work. All he needed now was a little more distance.

He took a single step, the gun feeling awkward in his left hand. Then one more, as the heel of his supporting leg slid out from under him, over the edge of the lip and he lost his balance.

Vince's heart pounded and his arms flailed like those of a tightrope walker playing for the crowds below. Then, just before he slipped over the edge and down the slope, he felt a hand fold around his right biceps and steady him. Vince weighed close to one eighty pounds but the arm held him there then hauled him, with no great effort, back over the edge. It was like a junkyard crane picking up a Pinto and depositing it in the car crusher.

Oh, thank God. He closed his eyes, a cool tide of relief sweeping over him.

He barely felt the gun being taken from his shaking left hand. He opened his eyes, twisting his head round, ready to thank the stranger who had appeared from thin air to save him – and a whole new terror engulfed him.

Thirty

The flight from Las Vegas to Los Angeles passed without incident. Raven had caught some anxious looks going through Security, but this was Vegas. People left every day of the year looking far worse. Lock had checked her over in the cab. She had some facial bruising and she was shaken, but miraculously nothing was broken.

On the flight, she had told him that once the door had closed, her client had offered her a drink and asked her why her 'friend' was threatening to kill him if he ever saw her again. She assumed he meant the stalker and tried to explain the situation, but he had flown into a rage and kept demanding a name as he beat her. She screamed as loud and as long as she could until Lock had broken in and taken control.

At LAX they had jumped another cab to Van Nuys to pick up the Range Rover. Then, both starved, they had stopped at an all-night diner for something to eat. Raven paid the bill and they headed back to the house.

As they got closer, Lock felt the muscles in his neck and back tighten. Something was off. He could feel it.

He didn't believe in a sixth sense, or extra-sensory perception, or any of that mumbo-jumbo. But he did believe that, after years in the job, your senses sometimes constructed a feeling that your brain couldn't articulate into a single thought. You just knew you were walking into trouble. This was one of those times.

Turning into Raven's street, he took his foot off the gas pedal, the car slowly coasting past her neighbours' houses. There was no one outside, although that was hardly unusual in a quiet residential neighbourhood.

About three houses back from Raven's, and on the opposite side of the street, a grey sedan was parked at the kerb, with two men in the front. White. Middle-aged. Wearing suits. They didn't look like serial killers but their presence at this hour, just sitting there, was off.

Lock tapped his foot on the gas pedal and accelerated past them, watching in his rear-view mirror. Nightfall made picking out their faces next to impossible, but as he drove past Raven's home, he noticed them both moving in their seats. Their heads rose so they could get a better look at the back of his car, then turned very slightly towards each other.

That was enough for Lock to keep driving.

'Hey, you missed the house,' Raven protested, waving towards where they should have stopped.

'I know.'

'What the hell's going on?'

'Call the house for me. Let me speak to Ty.'

She was starting to panic. 'What? If Kevin's in there, we should make sure he's okay.'

Ahead of them the road dead-ended. If they wanted out, Lock would have to drive back past the two men. Judging from their reaction the first time, he wasn't sure they would let him.

'Ty's with your brother. He'll be fine. Now call him.'

Raven retrieved her cell phone and made the call. 'Kevin, you okay? . . . Well, put Ty on, would you?' She handed it to Lock.

'I have a car with two guys parked across the street. Not directly. A few houses down.'

At the other end of the line, Ty sounded tense. 'They just rolled up. I was about to call you.'

Lock felt the muscles in his shoulders tighten yet another notch. 'Look like cops.'

'I already spoke to Stanner. He doesn't know anything about it. He said the only police we should be seeing are the uniforms coming by every few hours to take a peek and make sure everything's cool.'

'Okay, sit tight.'

Lock went to hand the phone back to Raven but changed his mind. He hit the contacts list.

'Hey – what are you doing?'

'You've got Stanner's number on here, right?'

'I don't want you going through my address book.'

Lock was taken back by the defensiveness of her tone. 'Fine,' he said, tossing her the phone and digging out his own. 'Give me the number.'

He jabbed in the digits as she called them out.

Stanner answered on the third ring.

'It's Lock. Do you have anyone out at Raven's place?'

'No. Why?'

'What about the Sheriff's Department? Or anyone else?'

Stanner responded with a torrent of questions of his own: 'What's this about?', 'What's going on?', 'Is Raven with you?', 'Are you at the house now?', barely giving Lock the chance to answer before he rapidly shifted to the next. Lock took it as a sign that Stanner was panicked.

The cul-de-sac ended with a loop of pavement. Lock spun the car back round with one hand while he held his phone with the other. 'Slow down, would you, Stanner? I just drove past the house. Can you get someone out here to take a look for me?'

'We'll be there in under five. But give me your precise location. Okay?'

'I'm at the westerly end of Pine Lane. You'll see the car. Raven's with me.'

'Okay. Sit tight.'

Lock kept the engine running, though there was no sign of the grey sedan coming down the street towards them. Still, something was gnawing at him. Stanner had sounded flustered, which surprised him. Surely, for the TMU, a situation in which a woman being stalked had someone sitting outside her house was about as routine as life got.

Raven tapped her nails against the dashboard. 'I want to see Kevin.'

'You will.'

'You're sure he'll be safe with Ty?'

'Yes. Now, relax.'

It was getting hot inside the car. Lock pushed a button and the window slid down a few inches. The Santa Ana winds were back – they'd sprung up from nowhere. In a nearby yard the wind stirred the grass and flicked at the leaves of a bank of shrubs.

Sirens buzzed in the distance. Lock touched Raven's hand, trusting that his gesture wouldn't be misinterpreted. 'See? It's going to be fine. Whoever these guys were, they'll be long gone.'

'Can we head back? See Kevin?'

Lock waited, listening, trying to judge the distance of the approaching police units by the volume of their sirens. He counted down from fifty in his head.

At thirty-five, the grille of the grey sedan nudged its way across an incline in the road ahead, cruising slowly towards them, a shark fin in the water. With a couple of parked cars on either side of the street, Lock would squeeze past it, but only just.

He flicked his headlights on to full beam, hoping to dazzle the driver as much as possible. He got a better look at him too: a middle-aged guy with salt-and-pepper hair, carrying a few extra pounds, wearing a suit.

Lock reached down under Raven's seat and found the handle that slid it back. 'Get down out of sight.'

Raven complied. 'Usually when I'm in this position, I'm doing something other than hiding,' she said, her grim sense of humour surfacing again.

Lock bided his time, waiting for the driver of the grey sedan to try to obstruct them or to get out. He had no reason to do anything while the other was simply on the street – and both men knew it.

The grey sedan drew within twenty feet, then slid past, Lock watching it all the way, shifting his eyes from driver's window to side mirror and then to the rear-view, not allowing it out of his sight for a second.

The sirens were growing louder. But not fast enough.

The sedan was behind them now, its bumper maybe a car length from the rear of Lock's car. Lock started moving again. Slowly. Wanting to gauge the reaction of the other driver.

The grey vehicle followed, matching his speed, staying close. An LAPD radio car was heading towards them, Raven's house in sight.

Lock had decided what to do: he would swing hard into the drive, hustle Raven inside, leaving the driver of the sedan to do his explaining to the cops.

Eyes flicking between the sedan and the approaching radio car, he timed his approach, adjusting his speed accordingly. The speedometer ticked over thirty then fell back as the radio car slowed, the two uniforms in front seemingly bracing themselves to make their own move.

The grey sedan had fallen back another car length at the sight of the radio car and the cops inside. Lock grasped the moment, pumping hard on the gas pedal and spinning the wheel.

But the radio car, rather than manoeuvring round him to head off the sedan nosed in front of Lock's car, cutting off his path to the driveway.

'What the—'

His car lurched suddenly forward as he was rear-ended by the sedan behind him. Raven, still crouched down in the footwell, banged her head against the bottom ridge of the dashboard where the glove compartment ended. She shouted out in pain.

Then the passenger door of the police car exploded open and one officer was out, wielding a pump-action shotgun, which he was pointing at Lock.

'Put your hands where I can see them – right now!' he screamed, as Lock's vision was filled with flashes of blue and red light. The air echoed with shouts as cops dressed in tactical gear appeared from everywhere.

With a final look in his rear-view, Lock saw the driver of the sedan emerge at a saunter, one hand peeling back the side of his sports coat to reveal a gold detective's shield fastened to his belt.

Lock's hands stayed firmly on the wheel as the doors were yanked open and he found himself staring down the hit end of half a dozen firearms.

'Stay where you are!' the detective yelled.

He was pulled roughly from the car, and pushed face down on to the road.

Close by, he could hear Raven swearing and struggling as she got the same treatment. Then she quietened and he heard a male voice start to read her the Miranda rights. Lock groaned. Whatever welcome he'd been expecting when they got back from Vegas, it sure as hell wasn't this.

Thirty-one

Lock jabbed an accusing finger into Stanner's face. 'Why did you lie?'

Stanner gave the kind of shrug that suggested he'd been acting under orders.

Lock took a deep breath and a single step back. Uniformed officers were swarming over Raven's property, and the only silver lining so far was that no one seemed to have any knowledge of what had gone down in Vegas. But he was still angry at the way in which he'd been used. Regardless of the fact that he had believed Raven to be as much sinned against as sinner, he would have delivered his client to the LAPD without hesitation if Stanner had told him they thought they had Raven down cold for the murders of Cindy Canyon and Larry Johns.

It did clarify one thing, though. Normally any officer of the LAPD who confided details of a case to someone outside the organization was risking their career and their pension with it. So Stanner doing it had clearly been sanctioned on some level, official or unofficial. They had wanted to keep him either inside or off-balance. Lock was angry at having been manipulated, but angrier with himself for not having seen it.

He had ignored his usual mantra. *Look out for two things: the absence of the normal and the presence of the abnormal.* Stanner taking him into his confidence had been far from normal and he hadn't noted the signs.

'You couldn't have just told me you wanted to arrest her?'

'You weren't exactly co-operative and easy-going when Brogan and Wilkins wanted to talk to her originally.' Stanner motioned for Lock to move back from the house. 'Let's take a walk,' he said, striding away from the path leading to the front door where forensic techs flitted in and out.

Raven was already gone, arrested on suspicion of murder and spirited to the LAPD jail facility in Van Nuys where they would keep her until she was arraigned before a judge and a decision made about bail. Then she would be transferred to the Twin Towers, the LA County facility at the LA Century Sheriff Station in Lynwood.

'You can believe this or not,' Stanner said, 'but how we played it wasn't my call. This department doesn't like outsiders, especially not private operators. Too often they get in the way.'

'I was doing my job,' Lock said, unable to squeeze the anger from his voice.

Stanner patted at his bushy curls. 'And how do you think I feel? Robbery Homicide think the TMU was babysitting a serial killer. You think that's going to do a lot for my career?

Listen, Lock, you'll be gone, on to the next gig, guarding some rock star or holding the hand of some CEO, but I still have to work in this force. Making captain? Forget it. I'll be lucky if I'm not writing parking tickets in West Latte.' That was the LAPD officer's shorthand for the ritzy West Los Angeles Division, which contained the upscale B-neighbourhoods of Bel Air, Beverly Hills and Brentwood.

'They really think she's the perp?' Lock asked, still trying to get his head around it all.

'I can't go too deep into what they have but, yeah, they do.'

'They have forensics?'

Stanner said nothing.

Lock grabbed at his forearm. 'So they haven't. You're telling me that all they have on her is a motive and a timeline?'

'Do you listen, Lock? What they have, what they don't have, they're not giving any of that to me.'

'Bullshit. I know how it works. They might be cutting you out of the loop, but you still hear things.'

'They have some DNA linking her to Cindy Canyon. I don't know what the deal is with the Larry Johns guy back in Arizona. The fact that he tried to jump her inside the club would suggest they have DNA from there as well, but as far as what they found in his house goes – I just don't know.'

'And how are they saying she killed him? He was a grown man from what I know about him.'

'You know and I know that size doesn't always come into it. Maybe she Tasered him. Used a knife on him? He was off his ass drunk when he was attacked.'

Lock chewed it over for a moment. 'I don't buy it. I don't buy any of it.'

'Because you've been her bodyguard for all of two days? Hardly qualifies you as a character witness.'

'So why did she leave Cindy Canyon's body in her own car?'

Stanner shrugged. 'What better way to explain it than to say someone planted it there? Lot easier than dumping it somewhere, and having to deal with the clean-up. Anyway, listen, it's not your problem any more.'

Lock sighed. 'Doesn't feel that way.'

'That's your ego talking, Lock. Hey, you got taken in. So did I. Join the club. Now, do yourself a favour and walk away before you get sucked even further into the mud.'

Lock shook his head. 'I still think she's innocent, but . . .'

'Go on,' Stanner said.

'I visited the production company she worked for a few days ago. They'd offered her a new contract. There was a poster on the wall of a movie she'd done with Cindy Canyon.'

Stanner smiled. 'You still think butter wouldn't melt?'

'It's circumstantial.'

'You could have lifted the phone. Called me about it,' Stanner chided him.

'I assumed you'd already know.'

Stanner met Lock's gaze. 'You're not sure either, are you?'

Lock remained silent. Stanner was right. If the cops had Raven for the two killings that was their business, although he still didn't like the way the LAPD were playing this.

The media were already starting to arrive. Satellite vans and honey-wagons cluttered the sidewalks. A serial killer was box office. A female one doubly so. A female one who'd also worked as a porn star was a triple treat. All the press needed now was the knowledge that she'd turned some tricks on the side, maybe pull some Hollywood A-listers in on the action, and they'd have the true-crime story of the decade.

He searched for Carrie but couldn't see her. He turned back to Stanner. 'I don't have to be right about this, but you do. It's going to look real bad locking up an innocent woman, especially if it turns out she's the victim.'

Stanner met Lock's gaze with a cold stare. 'In this town, there are no victims.'

Thirty-two

Eventually he found Carrie sitting in her car, staring through the windshield as the media circus pitched its tent outside Raven's house. Angel bounded from the back seat as Lock opened the passenger door, launching herself towards him.

'She was the killer all along?' Carrie asked.

Lock ignored the question as he picked up on the flat, deadened look in her eyes. 'You okay?'

'I visited that director.'

Lock was getting a sick feeling in his stomach.

'He pulled a gun on me,' Carrie went on, still staring straight ahead.

He knelt down so his face was level with hers. 'What else happened?'

She didn't say anything.

He felt his guts twist.

'Nothing. I ran before anything could.' She turned her

head, meeting Lock's gaze. 'I thought he was going to rape me, Ryan.'

He felt nauseous, a sensation that was quickly replaced by cold rage. He reached out to touch her but she pushed him away.

'I don't know about Raven Lane, but that guy who tried to assault her in the club, if she killed him, then . . .' she paused '. . . good for her.'

'You're sure nothing happened at that house?'

'It was a close-run thing.' She shook her head. 'Maybe this isn't as simple as we'd all like to believe.'

'What do you mean?'

'Maybe the two murders aren't linked. Or, at least, not the way everyone is assuming. It doesn't make sense to me that Raven would kill another woman. But what happened to the guy who assaulted her – I could see her doing that.'

Lock took a deep breath, then exhaled loudly, giving himself a moment to reflect. 'So Raven's the common thread but we have two killers?'

'There doesn't have to be a link, right?'

'What about Cindy's body being planted in the trunk of the car? That's a pretty big coincidence for there not to be a link.'

Carrie pushed a stray strand of blonde hair away from her eyes and Lock was struck by how vulnerable she looked. 'Cindy's death might have pushed Raven to the edge, made her feel even more vulnerable. So when Larry Johns came after her, she snapped, thinking that maybe he was the guy who'd killed Cindy, and took him out.'

'But that means she would have had to follow him back to the house while still having Cindy's body in her car.' Lock stopped, worrying the scar at the back of his head with the tips of his fingers. 'You can see why, if the police think she killed Larry, she could have murdered Cindy as well.'

'So she puts the body in the trunk herself and then calls you. Why didn't she just dump it, like the head?' Carrie said, her voice stronger now. 'She was set up, Ryan.'

Lock was ahead of her. 'You think Vice did it?' he said, sounding sceptical.

'You should have seen him, Ryan. That guy's capable of anything.'

'Well, maybe I should pay him a visit. I was planning on it anyway.'

Carrie reached across to stop him getting out of the car. 'Be careful. He was armed when I was there.'

'Don't worry. I've met guys like him before. We'll see how intimidating he manages to be when he's facing me.'

Carrie smiled fleetingly, then dug into her bag and pulled out her BlackBerry. 'Yes? I need a number for an attorney's office in Century City.'

As she waited for the listing, Lock sighed. 'I thought you didn't want to be involved.'

Carrie gave him a sharp look. 'Guilty or innocent, Raven's going to need a good lawyer. And I'm going to make damn sure I get her one.'

Thirty-three

Defence Attorney Fay Liepowitz swept into the interview room in a blur of Chanel perfume and designer clothes. Her presence in the Twin Towers jail facility, where Raven was being held pending arraignment, had already drawn concerned looks between the detectives working what had been dubbed by the *LA Times* and local media as the Porn Canyon Killings.

Liepowitz was trouble. Not only could she pick apart a case better than any other defence attorney in the state of California, she was quick to mobilize traditionally liberal Californian opinion against the LAPD's supposedly institutional racism and sexism in order to cloud the issue. Los Angeles juries were capable of coming to strange conclusions and Liepowitz knew how to work them.

At forty years old her reputation as a fearsome litigator went far beyond California. A committed feminist, she had been following the case since Cindy Canyon's head had been found by that creep of an office worker downtown. He'd just noticed those copies of the paper lying there. Yeah, right. If anyone believed that, Fay had a bridge in Brooklyn she would sell them at a knockdown price.

As soon as she had heard of Raven's arrest via Carrie's phone call, she'd had her office get straight on to the phones to find out whether Raven had representation. When the answer came back that the authorities were likely to assign Raven a court-appointed attorney, she had stepped into the breach.

As far as Fay Liepowitz was concerned, this wasn't about whether Raven had killed Canyon and Johns. That was merely the corner piece of the puzzle. No, as far as she was concerned, this was about an industry that brutalized and degraded not just the women who worked in it but all women, and the male-dominated forces in society, like the LAPD, which supported that degradation.

The LAPD might think they were about to put Raven Lane on trial, but if they did, Fay Liepowitz had a shock for them. She was about to put on trial the whole damn adult industry and everyone who supported it. All of those Bible-belt hypocrites who spent more on porn than any other part of the United States, all of those two-faced cowards of legislators in Washington, who decried the women exploited in the movies while their pensions were topped up by the blue-chip companies making millions from selling porn to hotels and cell-phone users – Fay was going to put them all on the stand, metaphorically if not literally. She was going to peel back the curtain on America's dirtiest little secret, which reduced women, all women, to pieces of meat just to make a buck. This case had all the ingredients to send the media into a frenzy. And it would give Fay her biggest platform yet.

In her opinion, whether Raven Lane had committed the murders was secondary. In fact, part of her hoped Raven *had* killed Larry Johns and cut off his balls. Twenty years of practising law, and Fay had finally found the ultimate case, all wrapped up with a red Hollywood bow, that would have the whole nation watching. Now, the first part of her task was in many ways the most delicate: transforming Raven Lane, at least in the eyes of the American public, from serial-killer *femme fatale* to a woman who had rejected her role as victim and decided to fight back.

Now, in the interview room, Fay decided to drop the traditional handshake, as Raven got up from her chair, looking tiny and perfectly vulnerable. Fay went to hug her, but Raven took a step back and ducked away.

In the end, Fay had to settle for the handshake but before she had a chance to deploy the speech she had prepared on the way over (a journey she had taken from her plush suite of offices in Century City in her top-of-the-line Mercedes Benz CL65 AMG), Raven had beat her to the punch.

'I'm not a victim. I'm not a *cause célèbre*. And I'm not a serial killer. So I don't want to end up going down for life because you want to make a name for yourself, and it'll give you something to talk about at your next five-hundred-dollars-a-plate dinner where a bunch of rich anorexic bitches from Beverly Hills whine about how much they're discriminated against. You understand me, lady?'

Fay smiled. 'I've never quite had those instructions from a client before, but you can rest assured that my primary function and that of my entire law firm will be to get you out of here.'

'Good,' Raven said.

Pulling a yellow legal pad from a soft-leather Gucci folio, Fay sat across from Raven. 'Okay, so take me through this from the start.'

The flash of anger that Raven had shown a moment ago seemed to fall from her face. She took a breath. 'I got the first letter about six or so months ago—'

'No,' Fay interrupted. 'Listen, your case might go any number of ways, depending upon what the other side has, so I'm going to need some stuff I might be able to plea-bargain with. I'm not saying it'll come to that, but I want you to go right back for me.'

Raven eyed her with suspicion. 'I didn't do it. Don't you get that? I'm innocent,' she said, her voice inching up in pitch and volume with every syllable.

Fay cleared her throat. Whenever she had a client who had never found themselves jammed up in the gears of the criminal-justice system she had to explain the same thing to them. It often came as a hammer blow as it sank in, as if Fay were snatching out from under them every belief they had held, which in a way she was.

'Raven,' she said, putting down her pen. 'This is America. It's not about guilt or innocence. It's about playing the game. The best player wins. Now, thankfully for you, I'm top of the league compared to those bozos out there,' she continued, waggling a thumb at the door behind her. 'So, if you want to go home, you have to help me out here.'

Fay put both hands on the table between them, and opened her palms. 'Now what's it to be?'

Thirty-four

Darkness was falling fast in the hills above Hollywood as Lock counted down house numbers until he was sure he was close to the address Carrie had given him for Vince Vice. Despite the ebbing away of hours since she had told him about her encounter with the director, the quiet rage that Lock felt had not left him. If anything, it had taken root and blossomed.

He was going to cause Vice some pain, that wasn't in question. But he had to proceed with care. Guys like Vice were usually the first people to go squealing like a stuck pig to the cops, should someone decide to give them a taste of their own medicine.

He had talked it through with Ty earlier in the afternoon, and Ty had suggested that he call some of his homeboys from Long Beach and have them pay a visit, but Lock had declined the offer. Making the phone call to have someone else do your dirty work was, in the eyes of the law, more serious than doing it yourself. Plus, from what Lock knew of Ty's former buddies in that neighbourhood, they were apt to shoot Vince Vice in the head rather than scare him.

In the end, Ty had stayed behind with Kevin, and Lock had come alone. Much as he enjoyed Ty's company, and it was good to have someone watching your back, this felt personal enough that he didn't crave company.

Lock parked on the narrow street and got out of the car. Stepping on to the sidewalk he was immediately buffeted by a warm gust of air. The devil winds were back with a vengeance, he thought, as he walked past the open gates and started up the slope towards the house.

He pressed the buzzer at the front door. No answer. And no sign of anyone stirring inside.

Lock stepped back and walked to an open carport that held two vehicles. The first was a Dodge Viper, the second an Escalade. He touched the engines of both cars. They were stone cold. Unless Vice had walked somewhere, which seemed unlikely in this neighbourhood of twisted canyon roads, he was either asleep or hiding out.

He went to the back of the house. Walking along the concrete lip, he was almost level with the kitchen before he noticed the smashed window. He looked down at the ground. There were no shards of glass anywhere to be seen. That told him the window had been smashed from the outside in, rather than by someone breaking out of the house. Jagged glass teeth still jutted from the frame. With this type of construction it would have taken a lot to punch through a window this size.

He edged along the lip, and caught his breath. He stared

into the kitchen. There was blood everywhere. It lay in a thick, heavy sludge in the sink, patterned the walls and the counters. It was smeared across the floor. Lock had done a nine-month tour in Sierra Leone, and this was the most blood he had seen at any one time since then.

Torn about what to do next he stood there, the metallic smell burning his nostrils. The concrete lip he was standing on seemed to narrow as the drop beyond it deepened. His heart thumped a staccato beat.

If there had been a body and it wasn't moving he would have left this to the cops. But there was no body. Someone might still be inside. They might even be alive. Although how someone could survive the loss of so much blood he had no idea.

He scanned the bottom of the window frame for an entry point. Finding a fourteen-inch gap where the glass was entirely gone, he levered himself up, and quickly realized that he would have to clamber inside over the marble counter top. But the counter was slick with blood, and there was no way he'd be able to avoid it. Reluctantly, he lowered himself and called into the house. 'Hello? Is anyone there?'

The only answer was a heavy silence. Lock retraced his steps, skirting back to the front of the house. He aimed a heavy boot at the door.

On the eighth or ninth assault, the door peeled back from the frame, only by an inch or two, but it gave him the room he needed. He ran back to the Range Rover and retrieved a crowbar.

He jogged back to the front door, shimmied the crowbar into the gap and used it to pop open the door. A final kick separated the chain, and he was inside. More blood pooled directly in front of him at the foot of the stairs. Either side, the floor was clear. There was nothing for the first two steps, then a blob on the third.

The pattern trailed up the staircase, red breadcrumbs leading towards a corpse. Lock stood back. Should he follow the trail or call the cops?

A faint moan from upstairs gave him his answer. Skirting a smear of blood, he started to climb the stairs.

He took them at a steady clip, skipping the globules of blood as he went. Drops of sweat slid down his back. A click from somewhere beneath him was followed by a rush of cold air from the vents, as if the house itself was reading his mind. He checked his watch. It was dead on the hour, which suggested that the air-con coming on was a coincidence of timing rather than anything more sinister.

He reached the landing and stopped. He listened for the sound and it came again, but this time it had a rasping quality, like the wind rattling through the slats of window blinds.

It seemed to be coming from behind a door at the far end of the landing. Lock walked towards it, wishing he'd taken the chance and borrowed Ty's gun.

He toed the door with his left foot. It opened with an ill-tempered creak. His guts twisted in on themselves as he realized that the sound hadn't come from the door but from the creature lying on the bed. He couldn't bring himself to call what was on the bed a man – or a woman. It was human-shaped, but only just.

He rushed over and started to untie Vince Vice's left leg,

which, freed from its restraints, kicked out, catching him on the side of the head.

Lock rose to his feet, aware for the first time since he had entered the room that the plasma screen facing the bed was switched on. Two women writhed together on a bed.

Vince Vice's face was like a carved Venetian mask with black holes for eyes. Reaching over his body, Lock freed an arm, allowing Vice to roll over to one side into the recovery position. The movement brought a series of screams and an elbow, which had been pared down to bare bone, crashing into Lock's chest.

Lock ran to a closet, found some spare sheets and used them to mop up the blood. Within seconds the first sheet was saturated. He grabbed another, clearing the blood from Vice's face, then jamming a third bundled sheet against his groin which was a mass of gore and shredded soft tissue.

The creature strained to speak.

'Raven,' Vice whispered.

Thirty-five

Moorpark was Cop Land. A suburb of spacious ranch homes thirty-five miles north-west of Los Angeles, it had the highest concentration of law-enforcement personnel of any area in Greater Los Angeles. It was where the people who dealt with the worst that the metropolis had to offer, the endless litany of casual violence and bad choices, retired at night to raise their families. It was a long commute if you worked down-town or in one of the outlying areas, like East Los Angeles, but the compensation for those long drives was that, for the price of a parking spot on the Westside, you could get a good-sized four-bed detached house. Your daytime might be filled with ghetto nightmares but at night you could retire to the white picket fences of Moorpark to live the dream.

It was for those reasons that Marilyn Stanner's husband, Lawrence, had suggested they move out there. That and the fact that they had found a house they had both fallen in love with. They had lived there for more than eight years now and Marilyn had never regretted their decision.

She liked the house, she liked the street they lived on, she even liked the neighbours. It was also nice to be among people she felt could understand what it was like for her to be married to a man who worked in law enforcement.

Lawrence put in long hours, and while he tried to save weekends for them, that wasn't always possible. But when he was at home she had his full attention. As soon as he walked through the door, usually with flowers, he would change into shorts and a T-shirt and they would laze about the pool, drinking wine or firing up the barbecue.

He was a good man, reliable and solid. He cared about the job but not to the exclusion of her. She looked forward to see-ing him, and that was more than many wives could say after so many years of marriage.

She was in the kitchen, scrubbing the counters, when the doorbell rang. She took off the rubber gloves she was wear-ing. The doorbell rang again.

'Okay. Okay, I'm coming,' she called, flustered.

She opened the door to a neatly dressed man in his late thirties. His truck was parked behind hers in the driveway. It looked like the kind of vehicle used by building contractors. He must have got lost and, on seeing her car in the driveway, stopped for directions.

'Mrs Stanner? Mrs Marilyn Stanner?' he asked her, with a smile.

She was taken aback. She had no idea who this man was but he certainly seemed to know her. 'I'm sorry. Do I know you?'

The man cut her off. 'It's about Lawrence. Your husband.'

Marilyn felt her face flush. 'What about him?'

'May I come in?' the man asked, making a face that spoke of spared embarrassments.

Marilyn folded her arms but the gesture was undercut by a nervous peek at the surrounding homes. 'If you could tell me what this is about?'

The man smiled again, awkwardly this time. 'It's of a personal nature. It's about your husband and a young woman called Raven Lane.'

Marilyn had heard the name from Lawrence. The young woman the man had just mentioned was being stalked. She had turned to the LAPD for help and Lawrence had been assigned to her case. Then some people had been killed and Lawrence had said that the cops thought she was behind it.

She had caught sight of Raven's picture in a file Lawrence had brought home. It had struck her as unusual because he always made a point of leaving work behind at the office. The picture had got her thinking. Raven Lane was young and pretty, and when Lawrence had mentioned her, a sparkle had appeared in his eyes.

She had dismissed any thought that he might have got involved with her almost immediately. Lawrence wasn't the type. And, anyway, what would a woman like that want with Marilyn's husband?

But now this man was here and suddenly Marilyn wasn't so sure about anything any more.

'You'd better come in,' she said, opening the door and ushering him inside.

Thirty-six

Response times in this part of Hollywood Division were fast.
The first LAPD radio car had arrived within three minutes of
Lock's phone call. An Emergency Medical Service ambulance
had followed quickly on its heels. The paramedics disappeared inside and stayed out of sight as more and more
LAPD units swarmed the scene. Lock briefed the cops on
what he had found and gave the paramedics what information
he had before he was cuffed, taken out of Vice's house and
placed in the back of a radio car.

A full ten minutes later a chopper appeared, buzzing low.
At first Lock took it for a local news-station helicopter until
he saw the Helicopter Emergency Medical Service livery on
the side of the fuselage and a couple of patrol officers clearing a space for it to land in the street outside. The front door
opened and four EMS technicians appeared carrying a
stretcher, a body stretched out on top of it. An oxygen mask
covered the face rather than a blanket. Vince Vice was still

alive, but judging from the gaunt features of those carrying him it was a close-run thing.

A gurney was flicked out, the stretcher laid on top, and they wheeled Vice out towards the street. They passed the car on the way and Lock glimpsed the bandages covering Vice's eyes, medical tape holding them in place. One hand dangled free, clenching and unclenching into a fist, a hint of the agony he must be feeling beneath the cloud of morphine.

Waiting for the ambulance to arrive, Lock had tried to get a name or a description out of Vice but Vice had incanted Raven's name like a mantra before lapsing into unconsciousness. It didn't help Lock much.

The officer in the front of the radio car in which Lock was sitting shifted round, shooting a smirk in his direction. 'He fight you, huh?'

Lock gave him a grim smile in return. 'If this had been down to me, he'd be dead.'

As the gurney shifted from sight, Lock noticed a cluster of LAPD officers at the gate, suits from Robbery Homicide Division starting to appear among all the uniforms. Lock recognized one from television. Strickler. Strickling. Something like that. He was about five foot ten, with cropped grey hair. From his body language and that of the other men around him, Lock guessed he was the head honcho. He was looking at Lock now, and made his way over to the radio car.

Next thing Lock knew the officer was taking the cuffs off him and pulling him out of the vehicle.

'Mr Lock, I'm Lieutenant John Strickling, Special Homicide Division. You want to tell me what's going on here?'

Lock squared his shoulders. 'I can tell you everything I saw and heard since I got here, sure.'

Strickling gave the briefest of nods. 'I'd appreciate that.' He waved over a couple of other detectives and together they formed a small huddle around Lock as he took them through his journey to the house. He pinned down times, knowing that would put him in the clear for any involvement with what had happened to Vice.

'So you wanted to speak to Mr Aronofsky about how he had treated your fiancée?' Strickling asked, when he had finished.

'Something like that,' Lock agreed.

The front door of the house was open and Strickling glanced towards the bloody entrance foyer. 'Only someone beat you to it. Do you know when your girlfriend, Ms Delaney, was here?'

Lock told him. Strickling went quiet for a moment. 'And you're sure on both those times?'

'Give or take five minutes either side.'

'Huh,' said Strickling, frowning.

'It gives us a problem, doesn't it, Lieutenant?'

Strickling stared at Lock, deadpan, too much of a pro to say anything. 'You think?' he asked Lock finally.

'I don't think so, I know so. Between Carrie seeing him alive and me finding him, Raven Lane's been in custody. Which also means that unless we find whoever's responsible for these killings fast, more people may end up dead.'

Thirty-seven

Carrie had spent all day on the phone, filling in some of the gaps relating to the Cindy Canyon murder and chasing down what she could about the Russian businessman Raven had seen in Vegas. Cindy had last been seen alive at her apartment in Marina Del Rey, an upmarket area just south of Santa Monica, which had grown popular with singles over the years, since international cabin crew from nearby LAX had begun to spend their layover days in the area.

The LAPD believed that, as well as her work as an adult-movie star, Cindy had done some escorting on the side. She also stripped, working rarely and always as a featured dancer.

The three activities were commonly intertwined. Adult movies didn't pay well but they gave a young woman a profile that meant she could charge ten times the amount she would normally earn by escorting and stripping. And although the stripping was common knowledge, the escorting was usually hotly denied by the women involved.

Carrie also learned that, along with Las Vegas and, to a lesser extent, New York and Washington DC, Los Angeles was the epicentre of the American sex industry. Huge sums of money were involved. The adult-movie industry was worth billions, amounts that actually exceeded the revenue generated by Hollywood. Of course, ask any man on the street whether he ever consumed pornography and the answer was invariably in the negative. This meant that the men involved were even more elusive than the consumers of movies. Someone who was capable of paying an escort like Cindy Canyon several thousand dollars for an evening's companionship wasn't the type of man who would wish to have his identity known. The LAPD also told Carrie that girls like Cindy attracted not only Hollywood's A-list but also heavyweight figures from the world of business and politics. Any vice-related murder in Los Angeles was always handled with care: once you started turning over rocks, there was no knowing who might scuttle out, blinking, into the sunlight.

According to a neighbour, the last person to see Cindy had been a security guard at the complex when she had returned home in the late afternoon. After that there was no record of her leaving and her phone records, at her apartment and for her cell phone, had yielded nothing of value. Cindy, it seemed, had simply vanished into thin air – until her head had appeared in a newspaper vending machine in downtown.

The LAPD had canvassed everyone who lived in the apartment complex and run their names through local and national databases but, apart from the usual Driving While Under the Influence convictions, and some minor drug or assault charges, no one had seemed suspicious. Of course, now the LAPD had a link back to Raven, they were playing it as some kind of adult diva rivalry gone nuclear. It wrapped everything up nice and neatly. But Carrie wasn't so sure.

The evening had brought a chill to the air and a swell to the ocean running in underneath the house. Lock walked into the kitchen from the garage, throwing a set of car keys on to the marble counter. He looked like hell.

'You okay?' Carrie asked him, concerned.

'Vice was attacked. I just spent the last two hours convincing Robbery Homicide that it wasn't me. Other than that, I'm terrific.'

Carrie scrambled from her place on the couch, grabbed the remote for the TV and clicked it on. The glass and steel house came immediately into view, crime tape, ochre yellow in the fading light, marking its boundaries. 'How bad?'

'Bad. And I think whoever did it left him just about alive as some kind of warning.'

'You think Raven did it?'

Lock shook his head. 'Not unless the cops drove her there from custody. She was with me in Vegas and then she was arrested.'

Carrie whistled as she sank down on the couch. 'So she's innocent?'

'Looks that way.' Lock rolled his shoulders. 'You find anything on the Russian she met in Vegas?'

Carrie picked up a yellow legal pad from the table. 'Gregori Istanyovich. Fifty-four-year-old Russian oligarch. Richer than dirt. Various business interests. Not straight-up Mafia but connected. Likes beautiful women. That's what you already had, apart from the name.'

'And someone didn't like him seeing Raven either. Sounds like he got off lightly if all he had was threats.'

'I'm not sure that's how he sees it, Ryan. I spoke to a contact in the Justice Department. Istanyovich is pissed about getting dragged into all of this. He wants to find out who's behind these threats as much as we do.'

'Well, good luck to him,' Lock said. 'Because right now none of us has a goddamn clue who that is.'

Thirty-eight

It was late by the time Lawrence Stanner finally got on the freeway for the long drive home. He'd called his wife to see if she wanted him to pick up dinner but there had been no answer and then her cell phone had gone straight to voice-mail. After that he'd gotten the call about Vice. They were right back at square one and Raven's attorney was already doing some major grandstanding, pressing for her client to be released, even though they still had some fairly solid evidence tying her to the first two vics.

Turning into his street, Stanner noticed the white contractor's truck behind his wife's red Suburban. Perfect. Company was the last thing he needed. He didn't recognize it as belonging to anyone they knew. God, he hoped she wasn't having someone give them a quote on the kitchen she wanted.

There was no space to park behind the truck so he pulled up alongside his wife's Suburban and got out. Something jarred in him.

His twenty-five years as a cop meant that he knew when something was off kilter. Stanner's right hand immediately fell to his service weapon as he glanced back at the strange truck. The hairs at the back of his neck were on point. His heart was beating a little faster.

He ducked under the big bay window at the front of the house, then took a quick peek. The living room was empty, and everything was as it should have been. Oprah Winfrey's face filled the forty-inch TV screen that he'd had mounted on the wall. Oprah was like a living goddess to Marilyn. She never missed an edition. But Marilyn wasn't sitting on the couch watching this one.

Stanner pulled back the slide on his Glock and dropped the safety, keeping the gun at his side, out of sight of the casual observer. He glanced back across the street to Doug Preston's house. Doug was recently divorced and worked for the county sheriff but his car was absent from his drive. If he'd been home, Stanner could have asked him for help. Better to appear paranoid than dead – that was one lesson he'd taken away from his work with the TMU. Safety first.

He ducked back under the bay window and returned to his car. For a moment he thought about calling the local Moorpark deputies but he checked himself. He was a cop. He was armed.

He skirted down the side of the house, listening hard for his wife's voice. Flattening himself against the wall, he took his time, waiting until he reached the corner before he stepped out.

There was a sudden movement behind him. He went to turn but before he could face whoever had been lurking around the corner he felt a slashing pain and his neck was suddenly wet.

A man's arms wrapped around him from behind and he took another blow, this time to the side of his head. The last thing he saw was the fading sunset on the horizon, a soft orange ball settling itself above the swimming pool at the rear of the house. Then came sudden night.

Thirty-nine

Day was breaking in Malibu, and while Carrie was taking her turn in the shower, Lock sat on the end of the bed and watched live coverage of a man and a woman's bodies being removed from a quiet suburban street in Moorpark. If the window of opportunity for Raven to kill Vice had been wafer thin, and hinged on Lock knowing about it, there could be no doubt in anyone's mind that she couldn't have committed what the media had already dubbed the Copland Killings.

The TV coverage was deliberately vague, but Carrie had already been told by one of her recently acquired sources that the victims were Lawrence Stanner and his wife, Marilyn. Feeling depressed and frustrated, Lock waited until the news report started to loop round on itself, and then, having extracted as much information as there was, began to get dressed.

Although he and Stanner hadn't always been in agreement, he'd been a good man and a good cop. To murder anyone was bad enough but it was more of an outrage against society when the crime was committed against a man because his job was to safeguard society. The wife's murder took it to new levels of depravity. It was a spit in the face to decent people, but it gave Lock a new sense of purpose.

Carrie stepped from the bathroom, a towel wrapped around her. She glanced at the television. 'They definitely letting her out?'

Lock shrugged. 'They'll have to.'

'She can't go back to her place. Not after this. You're gonna have to tell her that, Ryan.'

'If she'll listen to me.'

Carrie bit down on her bottom lip. 'They could come here.'

Lock rose from the bed. 'No. No way.'

'Just for a few days.'

'It's not a good idea. Not with this maniac out there.'

'Who's even going to know? I mean, how many people do we even see out on the beach here during the day? A dozen, tops? And they're neighbours. A stranger would be noticed.'

'Carrie . . .'

'She needs somewhere she can feel safe. She needs us. I'm not even arguing with you. Ask her.'

Ten minutes later, having lost the argument with Carrie, Lock pulled out on to Pacific Coast Highway, heading for the main LA jail facility in downtown, the Twin Towers. Today Raven had been due to be arraigned on two charges of murder in the first degree, the first being that of Cindy Canyon, and the second being Larry Johns in Arizona. The killings in Moorpark had changed that, with Fay Liepowitz having led an all-out media blitz on the LAPD. Word was that the high-powered team of attorneys and investigators she had assembled was already punching big holes in the LAPD's case, and the DA's office was getting the jitters even before they'd got to the arraignment phase.

Raven Lane was about to be released from custody and her stalker had just sent a blood-drenched message to the entire city that there was no one he was scared of and no lengths to which he wouldn't go.

On the way towards downtown, Lock checked in with Ty. With the killer busy in Moorpark, Ty had endured a sleepless but uneventful night babysitting Kevin. Per Raven's wishes he was about to get him out of bed, make him breakfast and take him to the day centre. Ty could report, however, that the area was crawling with law enforcement. There were at least two LAPD patrol cars now parked opposite the house.

Lock killed the call with the jab of a finger as he rolled on to the Santa Monica freeway. Traffic was heavy, the airwaves clogged with news of the Stanner murders. The chief of police, the head of Robbery Homicide Lieutenant Strickler and the mayor were due to speak at a press conference at ten o'clock.

Lock's cell phone rang.

It was Raven. She sounded as choked as she had when she had first called him. 'Did you see the news? I can't believe it.'

Lock didn't want to offer the usual platitudes. 'How are you holding up?'

'They're releasing me.' She sounded more sombre than relieved. 'I need someone to pick me up.'

'You're asking me?' Lock said.

She sighed. 'I'm on my own otherwise. I need you, Ryan. More than I did before.'

'You're not still pissed at me over your arrest? Because if you are I want you to know that I didn't know anything about it until it happened.'

'I know you didn't. And I'm sorry if I haven't trusted you as much as I should have.'

Lock put his cell phone to his chest and took a breath. 'Where are you now?'

'Still at the Twin Towers facility.'

'They're definitely letting you out?'

'This vampire of a lawyer of mine seems to think so.'

Lock scanned the traffic ahead. 'I'll be there in forty minutes. Let them know I'm on my way – ask them to call and tell me which entrance I should use.'

'Thanks,' Raven said, still sounding upset. 'How's Kevin?'

'Ty stayed with him last night. He's fine.'

Raven's voice softened a little. 'That's good. So, see you in forty minutes?'

'I'll be there,' he said.

He used the slow pace of the traffic on the freeway to think through his strategy. He had to get Raven away from her place without anyone following them, if not because of the maniac who was still on the loose then because of the level of press intrusion they were about to face. It would make the incident with Raul, the paparazzo on the freeway four days ago, look like a warm-up. There would be helicopters buzzing overhead almost constantly. Every move they made would be monitored – not ideal for someone who was being stalked.

He put in a couple more calls, setting things up for later in the morning, then called Ty again. They'd have to present a united front or they'd have no chance of persuading Raven to do what was in her own best interests. They also had to find a way of making the whole thing seem like her idea.

Lock took a deep breath. Looking at close-protection work from the outside, most people would assume that the challenge was dealing with the threat. In truth, the challenge was dealing with the person you were supposed to be protecting.

Two minutes from the jail, as he turned right on to North Vignes Street, Lock got a call from the LAPD telling him he had to register at Reception, then come up to collect Raven. There were a couple of back entrances he could use to take her out.

As he drove past the front, he saw the media camped six deep on the sidewalk. Most of them, he knew, were there for the press conference relating to the Stanner murders, but clustered alongside them, the paparazzi were hoping for a glimpse of Raven Lane.

As he signalled to turn into a parking lot, a red Mercedes Benz CL65 AMG roared ahead of him on the outside and cut in front of his fender before disappearing down a ramp into the bowels of the jail. Lock watched it go, then made his turn. He parked, got out and walked across the street towards the phalanx of reporters and photographers.

Raul headed straight for him, but before anyone could notice them talking, Lock shot out a hand and dragged him to one side.

'What the hell?' Raul protested, his youthful features bunching into a scowl.

Lock put a finger to his lips. 'It's your lucky day.'

Raul squared up to Lock, eyes defiant. 'How that's, homie?'

'How'd you like an exclusive? Raven Lane being released from custody.'

Raul looked at him, open-mouthed.

'It's a simple yes or no, Raul,' Lock said.

'You fucking with me?'

'Okay, forget it,' Lock said, releasing his grip on the man and starting to walk away. He didn't look back.

Ten yards later Raul was in Lock's face, his camera swinging around his neck. 'What kind of deal we talking about?'

'You still driving that Accord?'

Raul nodded.

'Pull it round to the back. There's a loading bay. I'm bringing Raven out there. You drive us away, you get some pictures. You do a good enough job of no one seeing you or her, and you have an exclusive. Which makes the pics ten times more valuable, right?'

Raul glanced back to the small knots of photographers further down the street. 'Why you pick me?'

Lock met Raul's gaze. 'Because for all your posturing about what a tough guy you are, deep down in that empty shell you call a heart, you know that when I say, "If you screw me over I'll put you in hospital", I mean it.'

That seemed to make sense to Raul. 'Okay, man. You got yourself a deal.'

Lock had one final test for him. 'Any money you get for the pictures you have to split with Raven. Otherwise she'll flip out on me for letting you take 'em.'

Raul shrugged. 'You got it, man. But it has to be half of net because the agencies take a cut of the gross too.'

'Fine, but here's one more thing, and this one's a favour with no monetary reward.'

Raul took a step back. 'What is it?'

'I want you to round up all the pictures you have of Raven. All the stuff you never sold or used. You were following her before I was on the scene, correct?'

'Hey, I got nothing to do with this shit, right?'

'Answer the question, Raul.'

'She was someone I covered. But it was only pictures, okay?'

'I believe you.'

'So why do you want them?' Raul's eyes were narrow with suspicion.

'Just want to check out a little theory I have going.' Lock gave him a push. 'Now go get that car.'

Forty

Brushing off the media's questions, Lock strode up the steps that fronted the Twin Towers jail facility. A tangle of limbs and lenses filled his vision on all sides. He walked with purpose, giving no ground. He never raised his hands above his waist, just kept moving as if the ground in front of him was clear. His forward momentum caused more than one photographer to trip and sprawl on the ground. He stepped over them or, in one case, on them.

The questions came thick and fast.

'Are you here to see Raven Lane?'

'Will Raven be making a statement?'

Lock met each one with silence.

At the entrance, two uniformed cops wedged back the hordes. It didn't take much effort. It was as if there was a force field at the door. Even the paparazzi knew well enough that the LAPD were utterly humourless when it came to their turf and especially today. One of their own had been killed, as had the officer's wife. The killer had breached a taboo that lay beyond the outer reaches of even the most crazed gang member.

A sense of quiet rage seemed to permeate the walls of the building as Lock signed in. It was a rage he felt as well, although he couldn't afford to allow himself to get caught up in it. The circumstances called for calm.

In the elevator he was met by stony faces as he was led up to a conference room on the third floor. Stepping out, he noticed that the whole place was busy, reflecting that a hundred-person task force based at the Police Administration Building downtown had been announced by the chief of police that very morning.

Of course, the phrase 'serial killer' had been bandied about, but while the killer fitted the basic definition in so many ways, Lock also knew that he far exceeded it. While serial killers worked to patterns they lacked a burning motive beyond the basic need to take life. Raven's stalker seemed to be blazing a very definite trail.

Raven herself was in the room, pacing back and forth. She eyed him coolly when he walked in.

Lock put out a hand. 'Fresh start?'

She nodded. 'I'd like that. I'm ready to get out of here now.'

'This guy's not going to stop. You realize that, right? He's coming after people you know or have known so that he can get to you. None of us can be sure who's going to be next. It might even be . . .' He let Kevin's name go unspoken.

Raven's shoulders seemed to slump. 'I've never run away from anything in my life.'

Lock smiled. 'You think running makes you weak?'

'Maybe.'

'I'd say it makes you smart.'

Raven ran a hand through her thick mane of black hair. 'I have a different idea.'

'What's that?'

'This guy wants me, right?'

'Forget it,' he said. 'There's too much that could go wrong.'

'Not if you were with me. I might not have asked for any of this to happen, but lots of people are dead because of me.'

Lock grabbed a folding chair from next to the wall and slid it over to Raven, motioning for her to sit down. Reluctantly, she sat. 'Look, it's understandable that you want to put a stop to this, but this is on the LAPD now. It's down to them. They might not like someone like me being involved, but they're good people doing a tough job. You and I need to let them do it.'

Raven stayed close to Lock as he hustled her out of the rear entrance and towards the end of the alley where Raul was waiting in his Honda Accord, the engine running. There was no one else in sight. The cops who'd escorted them out had melted back into the jail. The press and paparazzi were still at the front.

Raven stepped back when she saw Raul. Lock caught her arm again. 'Hang on. He's helping us out. I couldn't have Ty come down here with Kevin for obvious reasons, and they'll all know my car by now. They're not going to look twice at another paparazzo's vehicle. It's perfect cover.'

Raul whipped off a few shots through the open driver's window.

'Sell me out once, shame on me. Do it twice...' Raven protested.

'You'll see some money from the pictures. Isn't that right, Raul?'

Raul's teeth flashed from behind the camera. 'Fifty-fifty.'

'Come on,' Lock said. 'We've got a small window to get you away from here.'

Lock put Raven in the rear passenger seat, then motioned for Raul to let him drive. Raul eyed him warily from his position at the wheel. 'Man, I've seen how you drive,' he said.

'Move,' said Lock, muscling him out of the way.

Raul shrugged, digging into his pocket and handing Lock a memory stick along with his car keys. 'This is everything I had on my laptop. Every shot going back six weeks, maybe more.'

Lock glanced at Raven but she had missed the exchange. He tucked the memory stick into his pocket and took the car keys.

After a final look around to satisfy himself that no one had seen them, Lock pulled out. As they approached the end of the alley, he turned to Raven. 'Keep your head down.' He slid the Honda slowly into the traffic on Bauchet Street. When the knots of media and clusters of photographers were dots in the rear-view mirror, he told Raven she could sit up. Raul clicked off a series of snaps as Lock doubled back towards his own car.

A few minutes later, having looped a four-block radius, and sure that no one was following them, he pulled up. 'Thanks for the ride,' he said to Raul.

Raul sat in the passenger seat flicking through the shots

he'd taken of Raven, a grin on his face. Raven peered over his shoulder. 'I look like shit.'

Lock glanced back at her from the driver's seat. 'I'd say you've got more things to be worried about than what you look like.'

Alone in his car with Raven, Lock pulled out his cell and called Ty. Raven sank down in her seat, her cap low over her eyes as they pulled up at a stop light, traffic gathering around them.

'What's it like at the house?' Lock asked his partner.

'Heavy. Lots of press.'

'Okay, listen. Raven's agreed that we need to get out of here for a while, so I want you to get together some of her stuff and meet us.'

There was silence at the other end of the line, which worried Lock. Ty wasn't exactly noted for his silences.

'Ty?'

'We got a problem with Kevin.'

'He's locked himself in the panic room again?'

'Nope.'

'So you want me to keep guessing or are you gonna tell me?'

'Two ladies just showed up. They got cops with 'em too.'

'Child Protective Services? When'd they get there?'

'Couple of minutes ago. I've been stalling 'em.'

'Did you tell them we're on our way?'

'They think I'm bullshitting them. They're saying that unless Kevin's guardian is here in the next ten minutes they're taking him into care.'

Lock checked the time to destination on his sat nav.

They were thirty-five minutes away and the traffic was heavy.

'We're going to be a half-hour at least.'

'Damn. I don't think I can stall them that long. What you want me to do?'

'I don't know, Ty. Think of something.'

'Like what?' Ty asked.

Lock shut his eyes and ground his teeth with frustration. 'Improvise.'

Forty-one

Thirty minutes later, they were home, Raven sprinting from the car before it had even come to a stop. Lock slammed on the brakes, the car mounting the kerb and scattering a couple of photographers in the process. He threw open the driver's door, the engine still turning over and tore after her.

Raven had run past a patrol car parked in the driveway and was already at the front door, slamming her hand against it, screaming for her brother.

The car journey had been fraught. She had spent much of it on the phone to Fay Liepowitz who, as well as making another appeal for a public statement, had told her that once Kevin was in the custody of the LA County Department of Children and Family Services and jammed up in the system, getting him returned to her would take some time. Lock had driven as fast as he could, which wasn't nearly fast enough.

The front door opened and Raven pushed past Ty. Lock saw a flash of blue uniform as Raven tore inside, her shoes disappearing in a blur up the stairs. Lock reached the door. 'Have they taken him?' he asked his partner.

Ty turned his face so that two patrol officers standing in the downstairs hallway couldn't see him smile. 'Not exactly.'

Lock could hear Raven screaming at someone. Moments later, a middle-aged woman in a business suit clattered down the stairs, briefcase in hand, her face white with fear, and Raven in hot pursuit.

'Get the hell out of my house!' Raven screamed at her.

The woman, presumably sent by LA County, brushed past Lock, who stepped in front of Raven. 'I think you've made your point. Maybe if we all took a deep breath it would be more helpful.'

Raven rounded on Ty. 'Where is he? Where's my brother?'

Ty pointed back up the stairs. 'He shut himself in the panic room as soon as he heard the doorbell. Nothing I could do about it.'

The woman from LA County rolled her eyes. 'We heard you telling him to do it.'

'Don't know what you're talking about, lady,' Ty said, the very picture of innocence. 'I let you in the house, didn't I?'

The two patrol officers, thumbs hitched into belts, stood there exchanging looks. Lock guessed that, especially with a cop killer still on the loose, this kind of call wasn't exactly top of their list of places to be.

'Ma'am,' Lock said, to the LA County woman. 'Kevin's legal guardian is here now so you won't be taking him with you.'

The woman grumbled a response: 'I'd still like to make sure he's okay.'

Lock met Raven's gaze with a let's-just-get-this-over-and-done-with look.

Raven shrugged. 'Fine. But make it quick.'

Together she and the woman headed back up the stairs. Lock followed them, keeping a respectful distance. In the hallway, he pulled the woman back by the sleeve while Raven went into her bedroom and knocked on the panic-room door.

A few seconds later a heavy thud announced Kevin's emergence. Raven wrapped her arms around her brother as he burrowed his face into her shoulder and neck. She stroked the back of his head as Kevin snuffled through his tears.

'Hey, it's okay,' she whispered to him.

Next to Lock, the County lady was decent enough to look awkward, staring at her shoes and developing a sudden interest in some forms she'd brought with her.

Raven continued to speak in hushed, even tones until Kevin's sobs quieted. There was the rustle of a paper tissue and the sound of him blowing his nose and then they came out of the room, brother and sister, both red-eyed.

Lock left the County woman to it and headed back downstairs, where Ty was waiting with the two patrol officers. Lock motioned for his partner to join him in the kitchen, safely out of earshot of the cops.

Pizza boxes littered the counters, dirty plates sat in the sink and the trash can in the corner was overflowing. 'Housekeeping kind of went by the wayside last night,' Ty said, by way of explanation. 'Plus I was helping him with his Hallowe'en costume. Figured it would take his mind off of everything else.'

Lock put his hand on Ty's shoulder and smiled. 'Good

work, though for now we've got bigger things to worry about than costumes. Like how to find a way of getting them out of the house without being followed. The press outside are mostly interested in Raven. How about you take her in the Pimpmobile, lose anyone tailing you, and we'll RV somewhere else?'

'Not a problem, brother. Where you thinking of heading?'

'Maybe a cabin up near Big Bear. Somewhere nice and remote where he could pick us off one by one.'

'Stop screwing with me, Ryan. I know you've got somewhere in mind.'

Lock hesitated. 'I don't but Carrie does.'

Back upstairs, Lock and Ty traded bemused glances. It was hard to decide who was taking more time over what to pack, Raven or Kevin. They were in their bedrooms, poring over their stuff as if it was the last they would ever see of it.

Lock knew from experience that he and Ty took slightly different approaches, Lock travelling light, and Ty, as befitted a former grunt marine, cramming as much shit into his bags as he could possibly carry, just in case he might need some of it at some point.

He knocked on Raven's bedroom door.

'Come in.'

She had changed into sweats. Her hair was still wet and wrapped in a towel after a long shower to wash away the smells and, no doubt, the sensations on her skin of the Twin Towers. Having spent some time in prison himself, albeit as an under-cover operative, Lock knew only too well how correctional facilities dug their way into your pores. You could smell jail on someone, and the odour lingered long after the most obvious traces had evaporated.

'How long are we going to be away for?' she asked.

'That depends on how fast the cops catch whoever's doing this.'

She picked up a fresh towel to rub away the moisture from the ends of her hair. 'What if they don't?'

Lock cleared his throat. 'That's a possibility. Your stalker's been clever so far, but killing Stanner's family is a game changer. The LAPD are going to give this the full court press. The task force they're putting together is the biggest this city's ever seen. Unless he's already on a plane somewhere he's going to be caught. Days. Weeks. Months. But the LAPD will get to him. All we have to do right now is keep our heads down and stay patient. So, no more meetings or gigs.'

'And what about Kevin?' Raven asked. 'He'll want to see Wendy. He needs to go to his centre. We can't just cut him off from his friends.'

Lock walked back to the bedroom door and closed it. 'We don't have much of a choice. Listen, we hunker down for now. When it's over, everyone can go back to their regular lives.'

Raven sighed. 'Okay, I get it.'

Lock smiled. 'Stuff like this isn't easy. It feels like you're being forced out of your own home. But sometimes retreating is the smartest way to go.'

The phone handset next to Raven's bed began to ring. They both looked at it.

'You want me to answer that?' Lock asked.

'No, I'm good,' Raven said, reaching over and snatching it from its base. 'Hello?'

Lock was on his way out of the room, eager to let Raven retain some small remnant of privacy, when he caught the look on her face, and her stiff, frozen posture.

He crossed swiftly back towards the phone's base unit and hit the speaker button as Raven stood motionless, the handset still pressed to her ear.

A man's voice filled the room. 'Hey, sweetie, did you like your new dress?'

Forty-two

Lock listened, hoping to pick up some background noise – freeway traffic, a television or radio on in the background, an airport announcement – at the other end of the line. Digging out his cell phone, he texted Ty to let the cops know they had someone on the landline. As he pressed send he gestured for Raven to keep the man talking. The discovery of the dress had not been released to the media, which left only a few options. This was either a crank who was very close to the investigation or, more likely, the stalker.

Raven held up her hands in a what-the-hell-do-you-want-me-to-say? gesture, then took a breath.

'You still there, Sarah?' the man asked.

Raven went rigid at the use of her real name. Lock felt suddenly cold. Even Kevin didn't use it, although he had told Ty what it was. The man clearly knew more about her than most.

'Yeah, I'm here,' she said.

There was a pause. Lock thought he could make out some other voices in the background but he couldn't be sure. He walked as quietly as he could to the phone base, hoping there was a record facility.

'Who's there? Who's with you?' the man said. 'I know someone's there.'

Lock waved frantically at Raven to keep talking.

'My brother. Hang on, I'll send him out of the room.'

'No, it's okay. He want to say hi to me?'

Raven's face flushed with panic. 'It's too late. He's gone.'

'Stop lying to me, Sarah.'

The bedroom door opened slowly and one of the patrol officers stepped in as the man's voice returned.

'That bodyguard's there with you, isn't he?'

Raven looked to Lock for guidance. Lock raised an open palm indicating that he would handle this.

'I'm here,' Lock said, addressing the man directly. 'And I'm not going anywhere.'

'You saw what happened to the cop and his wife. You want that to happen to you?'

'You want to have it out with me, then let's meet up,' said Lock, sensing an opportunity. 'You name the time and place. I'll come alone. We can settle this ourselves.'

There was the slightest of pauses before the reply came. 'I might enjoy that.'

Then there was a click, and a second later the room was filled with the sound of dial tone. Lock saw Raven's body almost slump with relief. The patrol officer jabbed at his radio, updating his superiors about what had just gone down.

Lock stood there for a moment, then turned to Raven. Her

face was ash white with fear, and her hands were trembling. 'You okay?' he asked her.

'Fine,' she said, opening the top drawer of a dresser and jamming clothes into a bag. 'Let's just get the hell out of here.'

A wall of lenses greeted Lock as he walked out into the front yard. Behind the photographers, two satellite vans across the street disgorged perky female reporters from the passenger seats, and a chisel-jawed male anchor elbowed his way to the front of the scrum.

Lock gave them a big smile. 'Rather than make everyone's life a misery, I want to let you all know exactly what's going to be happening this morning. In a moment, my colleague is going to be taking Ms Lane's brother to his day centre. As he's technically still a minor, and a young man with physical and mental challenges, we would ask you to respect his privacy and that of the other students and staff at the centre.'

The male anchor with the jaw interrupted: 'What do we get?'

Lock choked back his usual response to that question – 'You get to keep your legs free of fractures' – in favour of a more measured 'Ms Lane wants everyone to know that she will not be intimidated into varying her daily routine, so she will be carrying through with an already scheduled appearance at an establishment close to LAX known as the Eager Beaver Club.'

This drew a couple of disgusted looks from some of the female members of the media and plenty of smiles from the male paparazzi, two of whom high-fived each other.

'We'll be leaving in approximately ten minutes, ladies and gentlemen, so saddle up,' Lock said.

Lock walked back into the house as photographers and press

scrambled for their vehicles. Ty was in the hallway with Kevin, who was toting his Superman backpack. Hopefully, no one would notice how stuffed it was for someone going out for the day. Ty clapped Kevin on the shoulder. 'You ready, bro?'

Kevin nodded as Raven leaned in to kiss him. 'See you soon, okay?'

Her brother wiped at the lipstick she'd left on his cheek with the back of his hand. 'Yuk.'

Lock opened the door and Ty stepped out with Kevin. No one paid any real attention as the pair walked to the purple Continental, got in and drove off. A single car peeled out behind them and Lock texted the details to his partner. One car was easy to lose. Lock had a slightly tougher task ahead of him.

The one real advantage that Lock had was that, with Raven's house, there was no clear view of the back yard from the front. After dropping her off at the house when they'd arrived home, he'd moved his car into the street below, which ran parallel. Then he'd knocked at the house where the woman had the Belgian Shepherd and asked her to keep it inside.

With Raven's bags packed and most of his stuff already back in Malibu, they snuck out of the french windows at the rear. He helped Raven clamber off the deck and together they scrambled down the steep slope. At the fence he helped her over and into the neighbour's yard. The Belgian Shepherd, jaws opening and closing, barked its displeasure from behind triple-glazed windows as Lock threw Raven's bags into the trunk of his car and they got in.

He had to hope now that they didn't run into one of the paparazzi's cars leaving early to stake a pitch at the club he'd named. Pulling out on to Sunset Boulevard, he scanned the traffic behind and ahead. There was nothing out of place as he jumped on to the 405.

Lock kept scanning the traffic, adjusting his speed and changing lanes rapidly, particularly as they drew close to off-ramps, hoping to draw a sudden movement from anyone following them. Nothing. Just the relentless metal grind of Los Angeles traffic, a freeway system that ran close to total capacity, one or two accidents away from complete gridlock.

When he pulled on to the 10, which ran west towards Santa Monica, the traffic lightened a little. Then they were racing towards the McClure tunnel, Santa Monica to their right, the Pacific Ocean to their left. A couple of people were out kite surfing, and an elderly couple rollerbladed along the concrete path beside the beach, hand in hand, wrinkled brown, their speed belying their advanced years. Blue skies. Everything California perfect.

He glanced at Raven next to him in the passenger seat. She had fallen asleep, rocked into dreamland by the thrum of the car's tyres as they rolled over endless miles of blacktop. Given the setting, it was almost impossible to imagine that he was guarding a woman who was fleeing for her life from a man who had carved such a bloody trail across one of the nation's biggest cities.

He pressed down a little harder on the gas pedal, eager to put the city behind him. The sunlight flashed in the mirror as he checked it one more time. It blinded him for a second, rendering the cars behind him as black shapes on a distant horizon.

Forty-three

Ty's Continental was already squeezed into the double-space garage of the ocean house Lock was sharing with Carrie. He parked next to it, then he and Raven got out. The garage formed part of the house and backed directly on to the Pacific Coast Highway just past the stop light at Big Rock. Two doors opened from the garage directly into the house itself. Lock grabbed Raven's bags and headed for the one on the left, which took them into the kitchen.

They could hear noises overhead. There was a big deck out there, visible only to the house on the right, which was owned, as far as Lock knew, by a fashion designer who was never there. There were lots of houses like that in Malibu. Places on the beach costing millions of dollars that stayed empty, except during the summer months and at the odd weekend.

From the thumping feet and shouts, Angel had found a new buddy and Kevin had quickly adjusted to his surroundings. It sounded like Ty was up there too, trying to referee whatever game they were playing.

Lock could see Carrie on the first-floor deck. She wasn't alone either. A tall guy with a warm smile and the look of a backwoods sage was standing next to her.

Lock showed Raven to her bedroom, which was on the first floor and tucked away at the back of the house, then went to join Carrie. As he slid open the glass door leading out on to the deck, the guest rose from his chair. 'Levon Hill from the Federal Bureau of Investigation. You must be Ryan.'

Lock straightened. Beyond them the Pacific roiled lazily on to a perfect stretch of beach. A couple of seagulls swooped low overhead. 'Can I see some ID?' he asked.

'Of course. Can't be too careful under the present circumstances.' Hill dug his ID from his pocket and handed it to him.

Lock took his time checking it out, then passed it back. 'You can't have read the script, Mr Hill. Law enforcement isn't speaking to me.'

Hill smiled. 'The LAPD aren't, that's for sure. I wouldn't take it too personally though. They barely speak to me either.'

'So what's your involvement in all of this?'

'The killings flagged up on ViCAP.'

The Violent Criminal Apprehension Program was a computer database used by local law-enforcement agencies and the FBI to look for similar facts or patterns that might link crimes in different states.

'I got interested when one of the first suspects, Larry Johns, went missing in Arizona,' Hill continued. 'Anyway, long story short, I offered the LAPD my services via our field office.

They initially declined, which was perfectly understandable. Homicide is a state crime, and out of our jurisdiction.'

'But now that there's a bunch of other bodies, including a cop and his wife, things have changed,' Lock guessed.

Hill gave a sad smile. 'I'm assisting them in any way I can.'

Carrie got up from her chair, and put a reassuring hand on Lock's shoulder, letting him know that they were good. 'I'm going to make sure our guests are settling okay,' she said, and disappeared back into the house.

Levon Hill sat down, his forearm shielding his eyes from the glare of the sun bouncing off the water. Lock remained standing, a hand on the white-painted rail, eyes scanning the beach, trying to build the picture he'd been creating from day one of who belonged here, the houses they stayed in, when they walked their dogs or went for a jog. All of it would help him should he spot something or someone who didn't fit the regular pattern. He'd brought danger into his home, and into his and Carrie's lives. There was no escaping that.

'Nice spot,' Hill said, after a while.

'Why are you here to see me, Mr Hill?'

'I want to catch this individual, Mr Lock.'

'We all do.'

Hill squinted, fishing in a pocket, then pulling out a sturdy black sunglasses case. He held off putting them on – presumably, Lock thought, to emphasize his sincerity. 'Your priority is a little different. Your job is to make sure your principal stays safe. That's the right term in your industry, isn't it, Mr Lock? Principal?'

Lock nodded as Hill's eyes disappeared behind mirrored Ray-Bans. 'Correct. The client is the person who's paying.

The principal is the person you're keeping safe. Often, as in this case, they're one and the same individual.'

'So our aims diverge slightly?' Hill said.

Directly above them there was more pounding of feet and skittering of paws. Lock heard Kevin throw a ball for Angel, and Ty warn him not to throw it over the edge as Angel was about dumb enough to go after it.

'I guess they do,' Lock admitted.

'However, there might be a way in which we can bring them together. If we can catch up with the person who's making all our lives difficult, then Raven Lane is safe.'

'That would be great,' Lock said, tension creeping into his voice.

Hill gave another big, open, warm smile. 'It surely would, wouldn't it?'

Lock could feel his jaw tightening another notch. No matter how beautiful the scene laid out before them, Levon Hill's visit wasn't a social call. 'Why don't you cut to the chase? What do you want?'

Hill nodded towards the huge glass sliding door, which was still open. 'Maybe we should close that first.'

Lock took a couple of steps back and pulled it shut.

Hill angled his head better to catch the strong Malibu sun. 'This can't go any further,' he said, raising his sunglasses.

'I can't make a decision on that until I know what it is you're talking about.'

'I mean it. If it gets out that I shared this with you, my career in the Bureau is toast and you'll understand why.'

Lock very much doubted that but he kept the thought to himself. There was no way that someone who had come as far and as fast in the FBI as Levon Hill was going to start telling tales out of school without some kind of nod from someone back in Virginia. 'Spit it out.'

Hill stared into the middle distance. 'We think we have the killer.'

'How?'

'The phone call. We're a bit further ahead on the technology than people think.'

'One phone call doesn't prove anything, apart from the fact that he knows Raven's real name and about the dress.'

'That's correct,' Hill said. 'Which is why I want to draw him out further into the open. The acceleration of the time between the killings shows that he's clearly in a state of some psychological turmoil. I think he wants this to be over as much as we do.'

'Why do you think that?'

'I don't believe in accidents, Mr Lock. If an individual gets sloppy, it's usually because on some level they want to be caught. Not a theory you can easily sell to law enforcement, I might add, but it's the truth.'

'And how do you intend to draw him out?'

'We have a name, we have a location, but we need more evidence before we can bring him in.'

'One last time, Mr Hill. What is it you *want*?'

Hill pulled out a pack of nicotine gum and popped a piece into his mouth. 'I want to put Raven right in front of him.'

Forty-four

Directly above them, Lock could hear Raven talking to Ty as Kevin continued to chase Angel around the house's upper deck. He took a moment, allowing Hill's request to sink in.

'We have a lot of circumstantial evidence, but nothing firm enough to get through the arraignment. Last thing the LAPD want to do is arrest someone then have to let them go – especially after what happened with your client,' Hill continued.

Aware of their voices travelling up, Lock moved to the sliding door. 'Let's talk more inside.'

Hill followed him into the main living area, then through to a small study with a sofa bed, desk and computer. Both men stood in the cramped quarters, as a screensaver of a lightning storm bounced around the computer.

'So this guy, what's his name?' Lock asked.

'I can't tell you that. Not right now anyway.'

'But you have him under surveillance?'

'Like white on rice,' Hill said. 'But we have to be careful. We don't want this going the way of the Phantom Lover case.'

The reference was to a man known as Vercanto Diaro, also known as the Phantom Lover. A serial killer in Colorado who targeted college girls around the Denver campus of the University of Colorado, Diaro had racked up more than a dozen victims before he'd become a suspect. Without enough direct evidence to arrest him, the FBI had mounted a huge surveillance operation, but Diaro had worked out he was being watched and fled the country.

'You think our guy's aware that you're on to him?' Lock asked.

Hill frowned. 'I think he's matching us every step of the way. This isn't some mouth-breathing sociopath we have here. Our guy might be crazy, but he's also very accomplished at this.'

Lock sat on the arm of the couch. 'You can't share a name with me?'

Hill shook his head. 'No.'

'Worried I might go after him myself?'

'I don't know whether you would or you wouldn't. But I do know that there are still questions over the ATF agent who died in that stairwell up in San Francisco.'

Lock felt himself bristle. In San Francisco, he'd shot an ATF agent who'd been conspiring with white supremacists and whose treachery had cost the lives of one of Lock's friends and the man's family. Despite the provocation, Lock had killed the man in cold blood and there wasn't a week that went by when he didn't question what he had done. 'That was self-defence. You know that. Look, let's cut to the chase: you want to use Raven as bait to draw your suspect out.'

'And if we do, this can all be over in less than twenty-four hours.'

'And what if something goes wrong? You said yourself that our guy's smart. You don't think he'll get a little suspicious if we offer Raven up to him on a plate?'

'He's smart, but he's also obsessive to the point where his intelligence is overridden by his baser needs. Right now his basest need is Raven. I'm willing to bet that this will trump his not wanting to get caught.'

'Wait here for a second, will you?' Lock asked.

'Sure.'

Lock walked out of the room, opened a side door and took a set of external steps up to the top deck. Everyone stopped to stare at him, even Angel who cocked her head to one side. 'Ty? You got a minute?'

Ty looked at Kevin and Raven. 'Holler if you need us. Okay?'

Raven took the ball from the deck and tossed it to Kevin. Angel almost did a back flip trying to intercept it. 'Sure.'

As they walked back down the stairs, Lock quietly brought Ty up to speed. Then they strolled to where Hill was sitting at the computer playing a game of Patience.

'So? What's it to be, gentlemen?' he asked.

Ty and Lock shared a look.

'I want Ty here to make sure there's no spin put on this at a later date – any suggestion that somehow we've not co-operated.'

'So you'll do it,' Hill said.

'No,' Lock responded. 'We won't. My responsibility is to make sure that Raven and her brother stay in one piece.

Staking her out like a goat for a mountain lion would be an abrogation of that responsibility. Keep running your surveillance. Hope he slips up.'

Hill closed down the game and got up. 'What if we lose him? What then, Mr Lock?'

Ty stepped in close to Hill. 'Then we'll deal with it.'

A door led out on to the Pacific Coast Highway where the traffic choked the northbound lanes as people made their way back towards the San Fernando Valley. Lock noticed a huge outline of a ghost tacked to the house next door, a reminder that tomorrow evening was Hallowe'en.

Hill opened his car door, putting a hand out to Lock. 'I'd have said the same thing if I was you. No bad feelings?'

Lock shook. 'We're good. I hope we get him soon.'

'Oh, and you're gonna keep this on the down-low, right?'

'Wouldn't do me any good to broadcast it.'

'And your fiancée?'

'We have an agreement about stuff like this. She knows I have to be able to do my job. Plus, I'm guessing that the LAPD would bring a world of hurt down on a reporter who let slip that you have this guy in their sights.'

As Hill got into his car there was the steady trill of a cell phone. He dug it out of the light grey windbreaker he was sporting and studied the display. 'Wait up. Let me just take this first.'

He hit the call button, the phone pressed to his ear. A full ten seconds later he said, 'When?' Then he listened some more. He finished the call and turned back to Lock and Ty, who were still standing outside the house. 'You familiar with someone called Raul Dominguez?'

'What about him?'

'His car was just found burned out by Central Division,' Hill said.

'And what about Raul?'

'He was in the trunk.' Hill looked away. 'Looks like he'd been stabbed.'

Lock felt the muscles in his neck and shoulders tighten. Despite the friction between them, Raul had been a good kid. It made no sense that he was dead. But it showed that the killer was growing increasingly desperate. As the initial jolt of shock ebbed away, something occurred to him. They had the suspect under surveillance. Yet Lock had seen Raul not that long ago. 'But you just said that you have—'

Hill interrupted: 'That's the kicker. The surveillance team lost eyes on him about six hours ago.'

'Right when Raul would have had to go missing,' said Ty, as he glanced towards Lock.

'You know,' Hill said, 'if he slips away again, and finds Raven . . .'

'Then we'll be ready,' Lock said firmly.

'What do you think all this stress is doing to her?' Hill asked. 'Listen, we'll have cops wall to wall. Raven will be totally safe. If this drags on, can you say the same? Can you be certain of that, Mr Lock? Let's get some closure to all of this.'

Lock sighed. 'Fine, ask her yourself. But if she says no, then you drop it.'

Hill smiled. 'You have my word.'

Forty-five

Lock looked at Raven, who faced him in the kitchen, her arms folded. Her eyes were yellowing slightly, and her skin had moved beyond pale to transparent. The strain was finally showing.

Tiring of the deck, and at Lock's suggestion, Carrie had taken Kevin on to the beach with Angel. The one thing you could rely on in Malibu was the neighbours' discretion. Even if someone did spot Kevin and work out who he was, no one would be calling the media. People came to Malibu because they had money and because they wanted to be left alone.

'I'll do it,' Raven said, her face set in a frown.

'It's your call,' Lock said.

Hill looked surprised and Ty shocked. Raven unfolded her arms. 'What?'

'I said it's up to you,' Lock replied.

'You're not going to give me some big lecture about how I'm being irresponsible? About how I might get hurt?'

Lock answered with a shrug of his shoulders. 'Would it make a difference?'

'Nope. My mind's made up,' she said.

'Well, then, I'll save my breath.' Lock turned to Hill. 'But I'm going to be there. That's part of the deal.'

Hill sighed. 'The LAPD won't like you being involved.'

'Tough shit. I also want to be able to recce the location first.'

Hill reached for his cell phone, which was lying on the black granite counter. 'I'm going to have to make some calls.' He looked over at Raven. 'You're good to wear a wire?'

'Whatever it takes. I just want this done.'

Lock raised his hand. 'I have a question.'

'Go ahead.'

'How are we going to know where this guy is?'

'He popped back up on the radar right after we found Raul.'

'You spotted him?' Ty asked.

'No,' Hill said with a sad smile. 'He strolled back into his apartment in West Hollywood like he'd been out for a pack of smokes.'

'He's got to know you're watching him,' Lock said.

'Maybe he doesn't care.' Hill walked out on to the deck and started making calls, pulling the heavy glass door shut behind him. Lock watched him pace up and down, one hand in his pocket: Mr Cool, Calm and Collected.

Ty clapped a hand on Lock's shoulder. 'Are you for real? We're sending her into the lion's den.'

Lock smiled. 'No, we're not.'

'What do you mean?' Ty asked.

Raven flicked a stray strand of jet-black hair away from her face. 'Yeah. What do you mean?'

Lock stared at her, the smile gone. 'You're not going into any lion's den. Trust me.'

Ten minutes later, Hill stepped back inside. 'All set.'

'What's his name?' Raven said suddenly.

Lock, Ty and Hill all turned to look at her.

'I already said,' Hill said. 'I can't tell you that yet.'

'This guy has been making my life hell. I want to know what his name is or the deal's off. I'll sit here until you work out what you want to do.'

Hill looked at Raven, then at Lock, and then back at Raven. 'Clayton Mills.'

'And you think he's the guy who's been sending the notes?' she asked.

'We know he made the phone call and he knew about the dress. The dress wasn't information that ever went public, so—'

'Jesus, why did he pick me?' Raven broke in, her voice cracking with strain. 'There are lots of girls who do this. Why me?'

Hill gazed at the dark hardwood floor of the kitchen. 'We'll be able to answer those questions once we have him in custody.'

'You think he won't know he's been set up?' Lock asked. 'If he's been obsessing about Raven all this time, what's it going to be like for him to be talking to her?'

Hill grunted noncommittally. 'The honest answer is, we don't know.'

'And what if he tries to hurt me?'

'We'll have armed officers everywhere. He makes a move to harm you, he's dead meat.'

'He is?' Raven asked, her brow furrowed.

'He's a cop killer who's going to be surrounded by cops,' Hill said. 'No one's going to hesitate to take him down if there's an excuse to do so.'

Raven sighed, then made for the door, shoulders hunched. 'Okay,' she said. 'Let's do it.'

Forty-six

The sun was starting to set as they arrived at a café in West Hollywood. It was a few blocks away from where the police knew Clayton Mills was living and where the surveillance team had observed him eating. Hip West Hollywood with its large gay population was not an area that Lock would have associated with this type of predator but, then, nothing about this job had been normal so far.

Lock and Raven sat down, ordered coffee and scanned the menu. Lock was nervous. This was not his plan, and even though there were maybe two dozen cops all around, including a couple of undercover officers at nearby tables, he knew that if Clayton Mills was here or walked in, and if he sensed some kind of betrayal, his and Raven's lives could be snuffed out in a matter of seconds.

He scanned the other patrons. There was a man sitting inside on his own. He was wearing a cut-off wife-beater-style T-shirt designed to showcase his massive biceps.

Clayton Mills, Lock said to himself. It was the arms. They were prison-muscle. No tone or definition to them, just bulk. The kind of arms you got from a bad diet and lots of big weights.

Lock saw a slight tremble in Raven's hands as she rested them on the table. He had no gun but he did have his Gerber knife tucked into a pocket, ready to jam into Mills's neck at the first sign of any aggressive move on his part. While the LAPD had shown little respect for him, Lock had equal distrust for their abilities in a situation like this. Their focus was on making sure they had their suspect. Lock's focus had to be on making sure that Raven walked away in one piece. Difficult when she was being dangled like a piece of bait in front of a man who had already slaughtered several people in cold blood.

'You okay?' he asked Raven.

Fear, and proximity to the man who had made her life hell, would be a powerful gravitational pull, and her desire to look at Mills must be strong. Yet they both knew she had to pretend he didn't exist.

'Fine,' she answered, shoulders rigid with tension.

'So, what you gonna have?'

'I'm not hungry.'

Lock glanced at the two men at the table directly to their left. They were tucking into their meals with a relish not often seen in a part of town so obsessed with appearance. 'The eggs look good.'

Raven scrunched up her face. 'I hate eggs.'

An avenue for small-talk. 'How come?' he asked.

Raven made another face, carefully plucked eyebrows

darting upwards for a split second. 'You really do not want to know.'

'Try me.'

'It's gross.'

Lock had once had to scoop a friend's lower intestine back into his abdomen. It was like gathering slippery rope. He didn't get grossed out easily any more. 'Go ahead. I love gross stories.' Behind them, through the murmur of café chatter, he picked out the man he had down as Clayton Mills talking to one of the waiters. Now, from the tone of the man's voice and how he was speaking, he was sure. Ex-cons were nothing if not direct.

'You started work here today?' Mills barked, interrogating the waiter.

Jesus, thought Lock. The cops had put one of their guys in as a waiter. It was about as newbie a piece of police work as Lock could imagine. It came down to the same rule that Lock applied in his job: what do you look for in a situation that tells you things are off? The absence of the normal. The presence of the abnormal. The bad guys looked for the same thing as the good guys.

Putting Raven in here was pushing the second part. Throw in a new waiter, and you might as well have replaced the *faux*-fifties neon sign hanging outside with 'Police Stakeout In Progress'.

As Clayton Mills's voice rose in volume, an embarrassed hush descended around them. Lock reached for the handle of his knife, the fingers of his right hand closing around it as he watched him continue to remonstrate with the undercover cop doing a bad job of playing a waiter.

Lock kept his eyes on Raven. If she reacted, he would move.

The intensity of his focus meant that the big guy coming down the sidewalk towards them was less than ten feet away before Lock recognized him. It was the bodyguard from Las Vegas, the guy doing the security for Raven's Russian client.

He winked at Lock as he passed, then took a seat at a table in the middle of the café, as a few more pieces of Lock's puzzle fell into place. Lock's knuckles whitened as he tightened his grip on his knife. Violence crackled in the air. Someone was about to get hurt – badly. The only question now was who.

Forty-seven

Ty stood back as Wendy pushed open the front door. She and Kevin hugged, Kevin planting a kiss on Wendy's cheek as her mother watched. Whatever went down in West Hollywood, whether the stakeout worked or not, Ty knew that they finally had an opportunity for Wendy and Kevin to meet up without looking over their shoulder too much. Wendy's mother had taken a lot of persuading, but Ty, with a little help from Carrie, had broken her down. The plan was for Ty to drop the kids off at the mall, then leave them for a while so that they could catch a movie together and get something to eat. Alone. Without someone monitoring their every move. Like regular seventeen-year-olds did.

Kevin, freshly showered, his hair still a little damp, kept his arm round Wendy. One of the things that Ty had noticed about him was how tactile he was, with none of the inhibitions that seemed to affect kids as they grew into their teenage years when parental contact was about as welcome as herpes.

Wendy's mother hovered inside the hallway, arms folded, eyes filled with uncertainty. Ty smiled at her. 'They'll be fine. You have my guarantee.'

'They'd better be,' she said firmly.

Ty knew better than to argue. He'd rather go ten rounds with a field full of Taliban than an overly protective Valley mom.

'You crazy kids ready?' he asked Kevin and Wendy, who were already hand in hand, consumed not so much by a teenage surge of lust as by a simpler delight in each other's company after an extended separation.

On the way out, Wendy's mother pulled her daughter to one side, drawing an eye-roll and 'Mom!' as they ran through a checklist of 'Do you have your cell phone?', 'Okay, keep it on silent in the movie theatre', along with what seemed to Ty like a thousand other rules and strictures. After the fourth or fifth do or don't, he tuned out, keeping his eyes on the quiet suburban street behind them, with its neatly trimmed lawns and American flags snapping tight in the warm Santa Ana winds.

Finally, she was done, and there was a hug for both Wendy and Kevin. 'Remember what I said,' she said sternly, to all three of them.

'It's burned on to my mind, ma'am,' Ty said.

In the car, Wendy and Kevin rode together in back, Ty doing his best to keep any rear-view glances disguised behind his sunglasses. He kept his eyes on the traffic around them, alternating his speed. A car full of *cholos* dug past, with a dramatic blare of its horn, as they drove down Van Nuys

Boulevard, its occupants' arms dangling out of windows, a gang sign thrown by one, the kid's fingers contorting into an unlikely tangle as he showed his allegiance.

Ty thought about Lock and Raven, and how worried they were about the stalker, but the dangers in Los Angeles were more random, more casual, more mundane than any shower-scene finale in the last reel of a low-budget slasher flick. A quick glance revealed Kevin with his arm around Wendy, oblivious to anything else.

Ty smiled to himself. Young love, man.

Despite all his bravado, he regretted not having found the connection that Ryan and Carrie shared. Ty didn't have a problem attracting women. Didn't have a problem getting them to go to bed with him either. It was the stuff that came after that he struggled with. In his twenties it hadn't bothered him. That was what your twenties were for. Love 'em and leave 'em, although in Ty's case it had been more hump 'em and dump 'em. But that shit got stale. Maybe Kevin had something to teach him, not the other way around.

Kevin was at the front of the line for the concession stand, his arm still around Wendy's waist. Cradling a big tub of pop-corn, he carefully took out a twenty-dollar bill from his jeans pocket and handed it to the kid behind the counter, watching carefully as he was given his change. Ty had noticed that for Kevin everyday transactions seemed to require unflinching concentration.

People filtered past, mostly families with kids. The movie Wendy had chosen was the sequel to a huge kids' franchise by

Pixar, a selection that made Ty's job easier. A lone adult walking in to watch the movie would stand out. The thought made Ty's next decision easier as well. He went across to Kevin and Wendy.

'You have your phone on, Kev?'

Kevin struggled to wrangle the monster tub of popcorn and vast container of soda to one side long enough to pat the lump in his left pocket where his cell phone was tucked away. 'I'll switch it off. I know the rules,' he said, with an eye-roll for Ty, much to Wendy's amusement.

'No, keep it on.'

'What?'

'Put it on silent. I'm going to hang out here. Let you two guys have some space. You don't want me sitting behind you like some old maiden aunt, do you?'

Kevin and Wendy exchanged a look, delight creeping in at the edges of their mouths. Then Wendy frowned. 'But Mom said . . .'

Ty put up his hand. 'I won't tell her if you don't. Now, listen, I'm going to be just outside the door. If anything happens you yell out. Okay?'

Kevin gave a solemn nod.

'Okay, go have a good time.'

Kevin scrambled to take Wendy's hand. Ty watched as they headed across, handed over their tickets and disappeared inside the movie theatre. He waited a few moments, followed them, handed over his ticket but stopped shy of the door leading into the theatre. He took a seat next to a big cardboard promotional display, featuring a family of cartoon racoons and settled in. Besides the fire exits, there was one door in and one door out. He kept an eye out for any lone adults but it was only families, or single parents with kids.

He sat back and watched a young middle-class African-American couple and their kids as they raced ahead through the door, squealing with delight, and felt suddenly empty. Man, Lock didn't know how lucky he was.

Forty-eight

Raven's hand shot to her mouth. 'He's staring at me.'

Lock realized she was referring to Clayton Mills. But he was more interested in the presence of the bodyguard. 'Ignore him.' He put his hand out and touched hers. 'Pretend like we're two people having breakfast. You were going to tell me why you can't eat eggs.'

Raven put down her menu and folded her napkin over her knees. 'Okay, so Vince Vice, his movies went way beyond hardcore, right?'

Lock shrugged, still tense, still waiting for it all to kick off. 'I wouldn't know. I'm more of a Tom Hanks guy.'

'Well, they did. He got off on pushing the actresses as far as he could. The sex got violent too. He'd choke you. Force you to gag.'

Lock put down his menu on the table. 'And that has what to do with eggs?'

'He'd ask you to eat fried eggs before a shoot so that when you threw up it was more visual.'

A waitress circled the table. She was pretty and blonde and perky, in the way that only people who don't really understand what the world is truly like can be. This part of LA was full of people playing at being waiters, or parking attendants, or fitness trainers or, Lock thought cynically, in this case, cops. 'Are you folks ready to order?' she asked.

'I'll take some coffee but make sure it's really hot,' Lock said. 'I mean scalding.'

'Anything else?'

'Just some toast, thank you.'

'No eggs?' Raven prompted.

Lock smiled. 'I'm not really in the mood.'

'And you?' the waitress asked Raven.

'I'll take the French toast and some coffee.'

The waitress jotted down their orders.

'Hey,' Raven said, 'I did tell you it was a gross story.'

But Lock had tuned back into the conversation between the world's most unconvincing waiter and Mills.

'This isn't what I ordered,' Mills was saying, his voice low and barely contained, the words spat out, clipped and deliberate.

'I'll take it back and get it sorted with the chef.'

'No, forget it. Just gimme the check, will ya? In fact, here.'

At a nearby table two men, way too well dressed and manicured to be straight, craned their necks to get a better look. One whispered something to his companion, which drew a laugh that was a little too loud.

Lock took it as a signal to turn round and take a quick

look. As he did, he caught Mills tossing a ten spot on to the table in disgust before rounding on the two men.

'What the hell are you looking at?'

Eyes down, they sank back in their chairs as Mills rose from his table and stalked past them. Lock tensed, his right hand wrapping around the handle of his Gerber knife once more.

By now Mills was level with him and had caught his eye. Lock looked right back.

'You have a problem?' Mills snarled.

Lock got up from his seat, his focus on Mills's hands. In the movies, bodyguards seemed to search people's eyes but it was hands and feet that always posed the most danger.

Very slowly, he inched the handle of the knife to the very top of his pocket, ready for fast deployment.

Mills raised his hands, muscles tense as he shifted into a fighting stance.

But the bodyguard was making his move. He had a gun in his hand and it was aimed towards them.

Lock dove towards Raven, taking her to the ground and covering her body with his.

All hell broke loose as diners scrambled for cover. The shot went high and wide. Cops appeared from all directions.

Lock twisted his head in time to see the bodyguard take a bullet to the chest, going down slowly as screams filled the café. A nearby table went over, spilling food and coffee across the floor.

More cops appeared, as patrons pushed each other out of the way, making for the door. Two, in plain clothes, rushed past Lock. He watched as a baton crashed into the back of

Mills's knees. His legs folded, and someone grabbed the scruff of his neck and forced him to the ground.

Lock took Raven's arm and pulled her to her feet. As she staggered up, he saw Mills turn and look at her. There was something in the way he did it that told Lock they had met before. Clayton Mills knew Raven and she knew him. He was sure of it.

Behind them, the bodyguard convulsed, as blood poured from his mouth. Then he made a rattling sound and went limp. Paramedics rushed to help him, but Lock knew it was too late.

Forty-nine

Legs spread, hands cinched tight behind his back by cuffs, Clayton Mills was draped across the front of an LAPD cruiser. Lock stayed within earshot as Hill went through Mills's wallet for ID.

'Go on, man,' Mills was saying. 'Check me out. Then let me go.'

'And why do you think I would do that?' Hill asked.

Mills's head twisted again, neck muscles rippling like taut steel cabling. 'Because I haven't done anything you can arrest me for.'

'You admit making a threatening phone call?' Hill pressed.

'Making a phone call? That's a crime now?'

'Nope, but killing someone is.'

Mills broke into a grin, then began to laugh. 'Dude, I just got out of the pen a few days ago. I've been in there for the past four years. My probation officer's number is in my wallet. Call him if you don't believe me.'

Hill's face betrayed nothing but the slight sag of his shoulders told Lock that this was news. The FBI agent walked away to make the call as Mills was hauled to his feet and put into the back of the radio car. He sat there with a look of amused satisfaction on his face.

Less than two minutes later, Hill was back. He nodded for one of the uniforms to let Mills out of the car. 'Release him.'

Mills stared at Lock, and grinned. 'Nice meeting you, tough guy.' He rounded on the cops. 'You'll be hearing from my attorney about this. Police brutality is what that was.'

Outside the café, the bodyguard was being wheeled out on a gurney, ashen-faced cops watching its progress towards an ambulance. Down the street, next to the radio cars, the crowd that had gathered to watch the show parted as Clayton Mills walked through. Lock followed as far as the Range Rover, which was parked less than half a block away.

No one else was following Mills as he turned to stare at Lock for a few seconds, laughed and walked on, whistling to himself.

Fifty

From inside the sanctuary of the Range Rover, Lock watched Levon Hill approach an agitated Raven. The cops stood around outside, and studied the sidewalk, sipped coffee or, in one case, kicked the kerb in impotent frustration.

Outside the café witness statements were being taken from those who hadn't already fled. Forensics personnel were moving around carefully inside. A police shooting of a civilian, even under these circumstances, had to be investigated thoroughly.

For his part, Lock was less focused on the screw-up than on the look that Mills had given Raven and the way she had reacted to it. She was scared of him – Lock didn't doubt that for a second. As someone who was intimate with fear in its many incarnations, he knew when someone was faking it. Raven hadn't been. She was terrified. But that, and the shooting of the bodyguard, still left a residue of questions. Questions that he knew he wouldn't get a straight answer to.

Clayton Mills couldn't have killed Stanner because he'd been in prison.

Popping open the central console, Lock clicked on the wi-fi system and extracted a small Windows-based laptop computer. He dug out the USB memory stick that Raul had given him, jammed it into a port at the back of the laptop and waited. A few seconds later a folder popped. There they were: the photos Raul had taken of Raven.

Lock double-clicked – and groaned. There were at least a thousand images. Although most would be near duplicates, it still left a lot of ground to cover, especially as he wasn't a hundred per cent sure of what he was looking for.

He clicked on the first picture. It was dark and grainy and it took him a moment to work out what it was. He only managed by studying the lighter edges of the frame, which revealed the open door of a limousine and a strand of red cord drawn tight to a brass pole. It was what was known to photographers as an up-skirt shot. Presumably it had been taken when Raven had got out of the limo and Raul had held the camera low enough to get a shot angling up between her legs.

Lock clicked on to the next image. This one was the same shot but slightly clearer, the flash bleaching the top of Raven's thighs linen white.

He skipped ahead a few pictures. Finally he was on safer ground, although these images seemed in some ways as intrusive as what had gone before. They were mostly of Raven going about her day-to-day routine: leaving her house, dropping Kevin off, picking up dry cleaning, shopping at the mall.

For the next fifteen minutes Lock glanced between the pictures and what was happening outside as Levon Hill talked Raven down.

He was reaching the midway point in the folder when he stopped and went back a couple of images, shifting in the seat as he did so, making another check that Raven wasn't heading back to the car.

The picture itself was innocuous. Raven's BMW was in the foreground, parked close to the kerb, and she must have got out of it a few moments before, judging by her direction of travel and distance from the car. She was pushing open the door of a mailbox store. In the top left corner of the frame there was an intersection, but the street signs weren't visible from the angle that the picture had been taken, which was going to make his task a hell of a lot harder.

He'd been so engrossed in the picture that he'd forgotten to keep an eye on Raven. Now when he looked up, it was to see her coming towards him. Hill had given her a hug, a strange gesture for an FBI agent, but then Raven seemed to elicit strange gestures, especially from men. Once again, Lock thought of Stanner and his relationship with her.

He knew he had to move quickly as he clicked on the picture and moved it over to the desktop. Then he opened a web browser and, using his gmail account, sent the image to his own email address for safekeeping before deleting it entirely. Then he closed the image viewer and the folder. Next he powered down the laptop. While he waited for that to happen, he pulled out his cell phone and called Ty, reaching over at the same time to Raven's purse, which was lodged in the footwell below the front passenger seat.

'Just checking in,' he said, opening the bag and momentarily struggling to find what he was looking for in the mess of cosmetics, cigarettes and half-empty packs of gum. There it was: a small, harmless-looking mailbox key. Quickly, he put it in his pocket.

'He take the bait?' Ty asked.

'No, but I'll fill you in on the details later. Did you take them to the movie at the Beverly Center in the end?' He, Ty and Wendy's mother had been unable to agree earlier on venues and show times.

'Yeah, they're just coming out now.'

This worked for Lock. The Beverly Center was only a few blocks from where he was parked.

'Good,' he said. 'Take your time. Raven might be calling you in a few minutes to pick her up.'

In the background, Lock could hear Wendy and Kevin talking, their voices light and giggly, all psyched up from their date together. He did his best to tune them out. Raven was steps from the car now.

'But you're with Raven, right?' Ty was saying, confused.

'Just hang back and this part of our conversation never happened, okay?'

'Roger that,' Ty said.

Lock killed the call as the door opened and Raven climbed in. He waved his cell phone at her. 'Just checking in on the kids. Everything's cool.'

'At least one thing's going right then, I guess.' Raven sighed, sitting next to Lock. 'You okay?'

'Sure. Why?'

'I don't know,' she said, digging into her designer purse

and retrieving her makeup. 'You look kind of spooked.'

Lock did his best to force a smile. 'You're not?'

Raven's head ducked into her purse and Lock tensed. Then she came up with her cigarettes and he relaxed again. 'Levon really helped to put my mind at rest,' she said.

'That's good,' said Lock, noticing a slight shake in her hand as she lit her cigarette. 'Listen, I have a couple of quick calls to make before we leave. Is that okay?'

Raven nodded, blowing out a puff of smoke, which clouded the air between them. 'Take your time.'

Fifty-one

Outside the Range Rover the sun hung low over the rooftops of West Hollywood. At the nearby Beverly Center, cars laden with trick-or-treat goodies streamed out of the parking exits and families headed home to celebrate Hallowe'en.

A couple of little girls, chaperoned by their mothers, walked past, one dressed as Cinderella, the other as Snow White. Raul's memory stick was digging into Lock's thigh. He had to find the time to go through the images, if for no other reason than to put his mind at rest. In the passenger seat, Raven sat quietly and watched Cinderella and Snow White. Then she opened the door and got out, reached into her purse and handed them each five dollars. 'I don't have any candy. I'm sorry,' she said.

Their mothers prodded the two little girls to thank her before one of them must have recognized her. The woman's smile curdled and she hustled a bemused Cinderella on down the sidewalk. Raven got back into the Range Rover. She rubbed at her temples, her head slumping forward and her black hair falling over her eyes.

'What do you think the bodyguard was doing there?' she asked.

Lock shrugged. 'Did you tell the cops you knew him?'

'Didn't have much choice,' Raven said. 'But it's that Mills guy I'm worried about. If they won't arrest him, isn't there something you can do?'

Lock started the engine. They had been parked a few blocks from the café for the past half-hour. After speaking to Ty, he'd called Carrie but her cell phone had been switched off. He'd tried the landline at the house and left a message. He felt a twinge of concern, then told himself she had probably taken Angel down to the beach and forgotten her phone.

He drummed his fingers on the steering-wheel, then twisted in his seat so that he was looking straight at her. 'You've known him all along, haven't you? He's your stalker and now you want me to kill him. That's it, isn't it? That's what this has been about.'

Raven reached over to turn on the air-conditioning, her arm brushing against his chest, her hand settling there. He made no attempt to move it.

She looked at him, her violet eyes glistening with tears. 'You know, by rights he should still be in prison. I mean, what kind of a life is he going to have? Is he going to be a benefit to society? No, he's not. And now that he's good and pissed, he's going to kill me. Maybe not today. Or tomorrow. But at some point.' Her voice cracked. 'And then he'll come after Kevin.'

'The police are watching him,' Lock said, still aware

of the weight and warmth of Raven's hand on his chest.

'There are those who watch and there are those who take action. If I asked you now, would you do it for me, Ryan?' She moved closer until her lips were less than three inches from his. 'Like you did to that ATF guy in San Francisco?'

'What would be in it for me?' Lock whispered.

'Whatever you want, cowboy.'

He had planned on pushing it further, but Raven using the word 'cowboy', a term of endearment that Carrie used for him, made it tougher than he'd thought it would.

'Forget it,' he said, pushing her away. 'Get out. I'm done.' He reached over and opened the door. 'I said, get out.'

'But I've hired you to protect me.'

'Get out before I drag you out.'

She grabbed for her bag, which fell from her grasp, the contents spilling out on to the sidewalk. She got out after it, then turned back, tears running down her face.

'You're just like all the others,' she sobbed. 'You can't leave me like this, not after everything that's happened.'

'Watch me,' said Lock, slamming the door. 'Ty'll give you a ride home. Call him.'

Fifty-two

Lock drove less than six blocks, and pulled into the rear parking lot of a small antiques store. Far enough away that neither Raven nor Hill and the cops would see him – at least, he hoped they wouldn't because he needed to be alone for the next part, and unless he got lucky it would take some time.

He opened the centre console again and retrieved the laptop, then powered up the wireless Internet router, which pulled signal from whatever was closest. As he waited for a connection, he opened the photo he'd saved on the desktop and studied it a little longer.

Raven was receiving mail at a second mailbox location that she had told neither him nor the LAPD about. But before he could figure out why, he first had to find it. The photograph was the only clue he had.

Like someone solving a jigsaw puzzle, he worked from the edges of the frame in, searching for clues to its location. Although it was daylight there was no sky in the picture, which wouldn't have been a problem if Raul's framing hadn't also omitted the store front's signage. Lock groaned. Knowing what the place was called would have made his task a lot more straightforward. There was a large Federal Express notice in the window but that didn't help as those signs were promotional giveaways used by a lot of mail-collection businesses.

At the top of the glass door there was a street number, but no street name. A parking meter bisected the glass store front almost exactly down the middle. That was it. Not a lot to go on.

He opened the browser, pulled up Google Maps, then Raven's home address. He began to search for mailbox services, methodically pulling up the street-view picture on each one and comparing it to the image he had.

The process took him back to his Military Police days when he had worked on criminal investigations. Seconds spent crashing through doors to give a bad guy the good news, but days occupied with the seat of your pants to the seat of a chair, grinding through thankless tasks.

Nothing turned up in Raven's immediate neighbourhood so he kept moving outwards. North a few miles. Then south a few miles. Then east. Then finally west. Each time he inched a mile further outwards.

West finally worked. The mailbox was in Encino, the other side of the 405 freeway from Raven's home. From the street-view image on Google it looked like a little mom-and-pop operation. It was on a busy street, with a Korean restaurant on one side and a chiropractor's office on the other. Lock got the directions, packed everything away and switched off the wi-fi. He'd have to move fast. It was getting close to rush-hour and it was an hour's drive.

He decided to take surface streets. You hit the lights but it was better than the relentless grind of sitting stationary for minutes at a time on the freeway as you approached an off-ramp only to get up to a less than exhilarating thirty miles an hour before a shoal of red brake lights brought you back to a standstill. At least with the streets there was a feeling closer to perpetual motion.

About halfway there, as he pulled out of a side-street and back on to Ventura Boulevard, Ty's name flashed up on his cell phone.

'What the hell did you say to her, man?' Ty asked, skipping the pleasantries.

'She came on to me, asked me to take out the guy the cops had in the frame.'

There was a moment of silence before Ty spoke again. 'You know, it would kind of make sense.'

Lock spun the wheel, pulling over into a parking space, and took the phone off speaker. 'Ty?'

'I'm here.'

'I'm going to forget you said that. Okay?'

'Only saying,' Ty said, a hint of injury creeping into his voice. 'Anyway, it might not be our problem for very much longer.'

'What do you mean?' Lock asked.

'Well, she's talking about replacing us. I mean, I tried to smooth things over but I think she's serious. She's already made a couple of calls.'

'Then let her,' said Lock. 'Tomorrow you can get back to

your vacation and Carrie and I can head for New York. The deeper I go into this, the less I like it.'

'What do you know that you're not telling me, Ryan?'

'Right now? Nothing very much. But I'm working on that.'

Fifty-three

This one had taken some tracking down. With Stanner it had been easy. Cops don't usually look out for someone following them home. Not if you were careful about it, anyway. Apart from gangbangers and morons, people generally don't kill cops, not unless one walked into a liquor store when it was in the middle of being held up or something. Even then a lot of the cops he had met would most likely have walked outside and called it in, waited for someone who was being paid to turn up and deal. So, yeah, finding Stanner's home had been easy. Same went for Vice's. But this one – this one had been a lot more difficult.

He had got there in the end, though. And now here he was. Parked up outside. Waiting. Watching. Choosing his moment.

He liked to get a feel for a place before he made his move. He liked to see who was around and who wasn't. You could learn a lot just by sitting quietly. He'd realized that as a teenager rolling drunks in Arkansas. You could always tell the ones who would put up a fight and the ones who wouldn't. He'd seen some supposedly reformed criminal on one of these talk shows telling all the squares in the audience about how he'd always selected his victims.

But his selections had changed once he'd come out of the joint this last time. He no longer went after the weakest. Some of those he'd gone after, like Stanner, definitely hadn't been weak. But then again, his old movements had been blurred and fuzzy, first money and then, later on, sex. But now he was working for a higher purpose. The highest purpose of all, some might say. His motive was love, with a capital L.

Right then the door leading into the next-door house opened and a woman appeared dressed in shorts and a T-shirt. Man, all this dough and people dressed like absolute slobs in this neighbourhood. Although maybe, he guessed, that was the point. Make enough money and who gives a shit what other people think of how you look?

The woman was moving a trash can out to the side of the road. Guess it had to be refuse day, he thought. She couldn't have brought her keys because she'd wedged the door open with some kind of fancy doorstop in the shape of a Chinese dragon or something.

Beyond the door there was a long narrow wooden walkway, which dead-ended with a large glass-fronted guard rail and beyond that, if he listened hard enough, he could hear the roar of the Pacific surf, sea air mixing with the exhaust fumes from all the traffic speeding past him on the Pacific Coast Highway.

Exhaling, he stretched his legs. It was almost time to make his move.

Fifty-four

Lock was relying on one simple facet of human behaviour. To a greater or lesser degree, we are creatures of habit.

He was outside the mailbox store in Encino, and he was gambling on the fact that, although Raven had decided to use a different box for some correspondence, she had used the same number. With no indication on the key as to what it was, if she had switched to a different one, she risked forgetting it. It was the same for people who used the same password on the Internet, or the same PIN for bank accounts. There's only so much stuff that we can store in our heads at any one time. That had to be the case for Raven.

The key turned first time in the mailbox lock. With a sigh of relief, Lock dug his hand inside. He had been expecting one or two pieces of mail but the box was so stuffed with letters that his palm got wedged for a second and he had to wiggle it free before he plucked out the letters one and two at a time.

When he had everything, he closed the mailbox and locked it. Unless Raven had another key secreted somewhere, it was unlikely she would be able to come here in the next few hours, open the mailbox and find it empty. Lock wanted to make sure, though.

He crossed to the counter, which was staffed by a smartly turned out Asian woman in her late forties. 'Excuse me? Ma'am?'

She looked up from the puzzle book she was working through. 'Can I help you?'

'I was wondering, do you keep a spare key for the boxes? Only I lost my back-up copy.'

'I'll have to ask my husband.' She went out the back to where a man Lock took to be her husband was sorting through various courier packages, which they signed for on behalf of people.

Lock waited at the counter, watching the security camera focused from behind the desk on the main body of the store. She was back in less than thirty seconds.

'If you need another key it'll be twenty dollars.'

Lock smiled. 'I'm good for now, but thanks,' he said, then headed back to the box, picked up the contents and went out of the door.

He clambered into the driver's seat of the Range Rover, dropping the letters in a pile on the passenger seat. Most had been opened, with maybe only two that hadn't. Opening mail and leaving it in a secure mailbox was suspicious in itself. Raven clearly did not want anyone reading the contents.

Lock drove round the corner, out of sight of anyone who

might be watching him from the mailbox store. The light was gone outside now, taken by the darkness.

He flicked on the overhead console light and picked up the first letter at the back of the pile, checking the postmark. Then he did the same for a few others, building a quick timeline.

The oldest letter dated back almost four years. The most recent, one of the unopened ones, was from a week ago. The postmarks were interesting too, as were the return addresses or, in the case of the last letter, the absence of a return address. He wondered if Raven had even seen it. He thought for a second about going back to the store and asking if they kept their CCTV recording but thought better of it. Even if they did, the storekeeper wouldn't share with him. More than likely she would just call the cops and he didn't want the cops involved yet. Not until he had a handle on this. No, he wanted this whole deal clear in his mind before he did anything else.

He picked the first letter out of its envelope, with the California Department of Corrections and Rehabilitation postmark embossed on the front, and started to read. Skipping through the first few paragraphs, he quickly worked out that this was not the first time this particular inmate had written to Raven or she to him. Judging from the stack of envelopes and the franks on the front, prisons had been a rich source of fans for Raven Lane.

The letter went on:

Raven, you writing me back has been about the best thing that's ever happened to me in my hole shitty life so far.

Knowing that you're gonna be there for me when I get out, my little angel, my beautiful angel, well it makes life about bearable in this place.

Sometimes at night when everything's about as quiet as it gets in this place, I lie awake and imagine our life together. All three of us, together. It might seem like kind of a weird deal to anyone who don't get it but what do we care about what anyone else thinks about us? As long as we all have each other, and we can all get along then that's all that matters, right?

I count the days my darling. You should too. Because when we're together then nobody and no one is ever going to hurt you like they did in the past.

I also think about us together.

Lock skimmed the remaining few paragraphs as they descended into a series of luridly graphic accounts that would have made the Marquis de Sade blush. For a guy who wanted to protect her from all the other perverts, he sure as hell had some strange ideas about the fullest expression of romantic love between two adults.

Lock checked the postmark again, jotting it down on a piece of paper, alongside the name of the inmate and his prison number.

De Shawn Wilder. Corcoran Prison, California. Prisoner Number 9786324.

Lock put the letter to one side and started on the next. This one was from Pelican Bay, an institution Lock was familiar with. The tone and content weren't that different from the other. It talked about the person writing it getting out and what he would do with – or, more accurately, to – Raven. It was dated four months back.

He scanned the rest of the letter, seeing if anything would jump out. He was going so fast he almost missed it.

One word, a name, tucked away in the penultimate paragraph.

Fairfax.

The name chimed. He'd heard it somewhere in connection with Raven. He looked outside at the gathering dusk, then back at the letter, reading the sentence.

Let me know if there are any more creeps like Fairfax hassling you.

And then it came to him. Fairfax had been the first porn director whom Raven had threatened, the one before Vice, the one who'd ended up dead.

His heart pounding, Lock took another look at the sender.

Reardon Galt. Pelican Bay Prison. Prisoner Number 675310.

Fifty-five

Carrie was sitting out on the lower deck, and didn't hear the whir of the garage door. It was covered by the sound of the ocean rolling in under the house.

It was only when Angel stirred from beside her feet, head cocked to one side, then started to bark in the direction of the kitchen door that she swivelled round. Ryan must have got home early, she assumed. Or maybe Maria, the woman who came to clean the place twice a week and had left only an hour ago, had forgotten something and come back to retrieve it.

As the door into the kitchen swung open, this was who she thought it was. At least, for the first second or so. Her mouth dried and she felt a raw squall of fear creeping over her skin and burrowing its way into her stomach.

She squinted, her eyes struggling to adjust to the relative gloom of the kitchen after facing the dazzling sunlight sparking off the water. The shadowed outline of a man stood there.

He was short, shorter than Lock anyway, but wide and muscular. She picked out his features for a second before he took a step forward and the changing angle of the light from behind her revealed that he was wearing a clown mask. The nose was red, but around the eyes was purple, and the normally exaggerated smile was blue in colour and had been inverted into a frown.

He seemed to hold himself in an almost semi-permanent squat, like a bull ready to charge. He was wearing a pair of dark slacks and a dirty-white sweatshirt, which was streaked with slicks of a green, oily substance. In his hand, which dangled casually by his side, there was a large knife, taken from the block next to the fridge.

Through the mask she could see dull hazel-brown eyes staring at her. 'Trick or treat?' he said. A pink tongue poked slowly through the blue mouth slit of the mask as he licked his lips.

Before she could stop her, Angel, who had retreated back to Carrie's feet, made her own charge, racing through the gap in the glass door towards the man. Carrie's breath caught in her throat as she rushed the man, tail flat, teeth bared.

The man stood perfectly still. When Angel was within three feet, his chin shot forward and he shouted at the dog: 'Go on. Git now.'

Angel stopped dead, then slunk away, her tail between her legs. A feeling of relief swept over Carrie that he hadn't harmed her. She'd also noted his accent. Southern. But not Deep South. More south-west. Arkansas, maybe. Or northern Arizona.

The man seemed to chuckle, before his eyes rose from

Angel and his black pinprick pupils settled on Carrie. His head lowered again so that she could see where the greasy sheen of his forehead slid into his dirty brown hair. He seemed at ease, and as if whatever fear he could read on her face was giving him an intense amount of pleasure.

The smile snapped Carrie out of her fear response long enough to take a breath. She took stock of the situation quickly.

Shit. Her cell phone was on the dining table, which lay beyond the sliding glass door separating the deck from the inside of the house. She might reach it before the man did but she'd never have time to make a call too.

Right now all that stood between her and him was the sliding glass door, which locked from the inside. She could try to hold it shut but she doubted that would work for any length of time.

She glanced back. The tide was coming in but not fast enough to make a jump from the deck anywhere near safe. The sand robbed from the beach by the Santa Ana tides had left a crop of black rocks jutting directly underneath. Jump into wet sand from thirty feet and you might break a leg. Hit the rocks and you'd likely break your neck.

The man had been moving towards her, and was now level with the coffee-table. He picked up Carrie's cell phone and switched it off with the meaty pad of his left thumb. He was looking at her now, running a wet tongue across his lips as he stared at her breasts.

Something about the gesture snapped a thought into her mind. She had been running through escape routes, but Lock had taught her some basic defence moves. She doubted an elbow strike was going to cut it against this guy wielding a knife, which meant that there was only one smart thing to do. It went against everything she believed in, but it was her only chance of getting out alive.

She took a deep breath and started to scream the one word guaranteed to focus the mind of any multimillionaire Malibu property owner likely to hear her.

'Fire! Fire!'

The man's eyes flared wide at her cries. Before she got to shout it a third time, he had wrenched the sliding door back so hard that Carrie, who was trying to hold it shut, tumbled backwards. Next she felt a sharp tug as he grabbed her long hair and began dragging her into the house.

She kicked and punched, at least one fist melting into the man's chest with no apparent effect. Then the knife was in her face.

'Be quiet,' he grunted, as she slid, her sneakers squeaking, over the polished wooden floors.

She screamed again, a guttural sound, raw and without either form or shape. It was the scream of someone being brought to a place beyond rational thought, a scream perhaps only heard from a soldier who'd just caught an IED – or from a woman at the height of childbirth who has only one sentence running on a loop through her mind.

Oh, God, please let this stop.

The man's face was level with hers now, his big red nose almost touching her cheek as he whispered into her ear, 'One way or another, you're coming with me.'

Fifty-six

Reardon Galt. It wasn't a name that Lock had heard before. Not even in passing. But the porn director Gary Fairfax was significant. He thought about calling Levon Hill but decided to wait until he had sorted through the rest of the mail.

It took him the best part of an hour. It looked as though Raven had been using two mailboxes for fans: one for civilians, which she checked regularly and which he'd visited with her that first evening; and this second one for prison inmates. What he really needed now was to see Raven's side of the dialogue, but those letters would be tucked away in cells deep within the bowels of prisons like Corcoran, Pelican Bay and San Quentin.

Lock knew that Raven's letters would have been read by the correctional officers. However, he doubted that copies would have been made. Neither was it likely that they would have drawn much attention. The prison guards who went through mail were usually on the lookout for something other than romantic correspondence. Prison mail held a whole host of horrors, from liquid amphetamine soaked and dried into birthday cards all the way through to very sophisticated code messages that were employed to order assassinations on both sides of the prison walls.

There were two envelopes left. Both unopened. Both having arrived in the past week. Neither bore a name on the outside of the envelope or any return address. Lock put them aside while he made a phone call to an old acquaintance, someone he'd hoped he would never have to talk to again.

The phone rang twice and Lock asked to be put through to Louis Marquez, the warden at Pelican Bay Supermax Prison. A few moments later there was a click at the other end of the line.

'What can I do for you, Lock?' Marquez asked, sounding harassed but not as unfriendly as Lock had guessed he might.

'I need to know if you still have an inmate by the name of Reardon Galt, either with you or somewhere else in the system.'

'I have three and a half thousand men in here, Lock. You know that. They filter in and out.'

Marquez had overstated the filtering part, he thought. Seventy-five per cent of the inmates inside Pelican Bay were serving life without possibility of parole. The only place those men filtered between was general population and the Secure Housing Unit, with an occasional transfer out to San Quentin or Corcoran for the lucky ones who kept their noses clean.

'I have a prison number for him too.'

Marquez coughed. 'What's this about anyway?'

Lock told him that his current client had stupidly entered

into a correspondence with an inmate. He was now concerned that said inmate was out and looking to make good on some of the promises he'd made in his letters.

'Do you keep copies of incoming letters?' he asked the warden, double-checking his understanding of the procedure.

'Not unless the Gang Unit has an ongoing investigation and is keeping stuff back as evidence. Otherwise, once mail goes to the inmate that's it. We'd need another hundred acres and about as many staff to archive everything these guys get,' Marquez said. 'Mail's one of the few things they got going for them.'

'So would you be able to tell me if you still have Reardon Galt?'

'Chances are we do, but off the top of my head I'd have to get back to you. Listen, Lock, I can tell you if he's here or not – I can maybe even stretch to what's on his jacket. Beyond that, information's with the probation service. If he's on the outside and causing this lady problems, I'd put my house on him not being at the address he gave his probation officer.'

'I understand,' Lock said. 'How long do you think it will take you?'

There was a very deep sigh at the other end of the line. 'Because, Lord knows, I don't have anything else to do.'

'I'd appreciate it,' said Lock, terminating the call.

He went back to the pile of mail on the passenger seat beside him, picking up the first mystery envelope – the one with no return address and an illegible frank mark. He dug a nail under the corner, then stopped. He reached into his pocket, pulled out his Gerber knife and used that to slash open the top of the envelope. Then he pinched out the letter that was inside using the nail of his thumb and forefinger.

At that second Lock's cell rang. He smiled, thinking it was the warden at Pelican Bay returning his call. It wasn't.

A minute later, he was drenched with sweat and the Range Rover was barrelling down Ventura Boulevard, scattering other drivers in its wake, the engine running flat out, as Lock summoned every iota of concentration to get to Malibu as quickly as he could.

Fifty-seven

The Pacific Coast Highway was at a standstill. From Santa Monica all the way up to Trancas the traffic was inching forward in increments of a few feet every minute. The main tourist route from southern to northern California, this particular stretch also served as a major artery for people commuting back and forth from the Valley to the Westside or down towards LAX airport. And at rush-hour on All Hallows Eve it was gridlocked.

Lock spun the wheel and pulled into the breakdown lane, drawing furious horns and more than a couple of one-fingered salutes from other drivers. The road surface wasn't great so he had to keep his speed below fifty as he tore up the highway.

His stomach was knotted and his guts twisted as he thought of the phone call. A report of a fire had come in from Malibu. The address was 19967 Pacific Coast Highway, the house he had been sharing with Carrie.

The breakdown lane ended, the surface giving way to slopes that buttressed the other side of the highway, and he was forced back into traffic. In typical LA fashion the car ahead wasn't about to let him merge until he swung violently across, giving the driver of the Mercedes behind him no choice but to let him in ahead. The guy was middle-aged, with long white hair that ran just below his collar. He was gesticulating. Then his door opened and he started to get out.

Lock got out too, and the man saw the look on his face and got back into his vehicle without a word passing.

Lock got back into the Range Rover and squinted through the tinted windshield at the traffic snaked along the coast. His knuckles were white from clutching the steering-wheel too hard. This was impossible. It would take him over thirty minutes to get to the house at this rate. With a clear road, even going at the speed limit, it should have taken five.

The car in front of him moved a few feet giving him hope before its red brake lights extinguished it again a second later. Ten car lengths ahead, the stop light at the turn that took you up into Topanga Canyon was at red – not that it mattered because, apart from a clear gap in the junction, a solid line of immobile cars was all you would meet on the other side.

At the stop light, a weekend warrior type was gunning the engine of a Harley Sportster. Judging how clean and fresh his leathers were, Lock guessed he was probably a personal-injury lawyer or a gynaecologist undergoing some kind of mid-life crisis. Lock had a crisis of his own right now, one that really did call for a fast motorbike.

In less than a second, Lock was out of the car and running

towards the weekend warrior on the Harley. 'Get off. I need your bike.'

The man popped his visor up and stared at Lock. 'Are you out of your goddamn—'

Lock grabbed him by his jacket, but the man managed to shrug him off long enough to gun the engine and take off at speed, ignoring the red light and narrowly avoiding a car stalled in the turn lane in his desire to get away.

'Fuck,' Lock said, kicking out at thin air.

He worked his way back towards the Range Rover and got into the driver's seat but didn't close the door fully. Every second seemed to drag. A minute seemed like eternity.

He waited, keeping his eye on the side mirror and cursing his stupidity. He'd given the guy on the Harley the split second he'd needed to get away – and he'd taken it.

Less than a minute later, he saw another bike darting north-wards between the stationary cars and trucks.

He tensed, choosing his moment. This bike was more of a tourer, the person on it clad in jacket and helmet but with only denim shorts covering his legs. He was taking his time, picking his way past side mirrors, having to squeeze through when he encountered parallel SUVs.

Lock focused hard. Then, at the very last second, as the bike inched past him, he threw open the heavy door of the Range Rover. The handlebars of the bike shifted but not far enough, as its front tyre slammed hard into the door, wrenching at the hinges.

The person on it went over the top of the handlebars and landed awkwardly on the tarmac, but Lock was already out of the Range Rover. The bike was toppled over on to its side, with the engine still running, and he wrestled it backwards, then closed the door. The biker was getting to his feet, dazed but okay.

Lock pulled the bike upright, climbed on to it and took off, almost pulling a wheelie and sending himself to the ground. He eased off on the throttle, the tyres found traction and he was on his way.

Fifty-eight

The work truck had been perfect cover. In this part of the city, the men who drove them were invisible to the wealthy white population. As he white-knuckled around hairpin bends, gunning the engine on the straights, not one person gave him a first glance, never mind a second.

He finally dumped the truck on a fire road up in Malibu Canyon and switched to his regular car, a 1995 Saab 900. Then he drove home to the guest house he rented on Colina Drive in Topanga. Under the seat he had a semi-automatic, which he'd bought when he'd first moved out to Los Angeles. Growing up where he had, guns had been a part of everyday life. His father had hunted. So had his brothers.

The move to Los Angeles, like everything else that had happened in the last six months, had been for Raven. Everything he did was for Raven. The way he worked hard to keep in shape. The notes he spent hours crafting, even though he hadn't sent most of them. The people who were out to hurt

Raven, and whom he had taught a lesson: Cindy, who wanted
to usurp Raven's star status; that asshole in the bar, Larry
Johns; and that scumbag director who had hurt her and was
an affront to all men.

The first one, Cindy, had been the most difficult. He didn't
want to admit it to himself, but with it being a woman, he had
felt a sexual charge. But the swelling he had felt between his
legs when he had abducted Cindy and had her under his
control seemed a betrayal of how he felt about Raven, so he
had packed those thoughts away.

People might have imagined that it was an easy thing to do
but it wasn't. Approaching Cindy in the underground parking
lot, he had been close to backing out. His stomach had filled
with tension, and his mouth was so dry that he had barely
been able to utter her name loud enough to get her to turn
round. He'd hit her with the stun gun, and once that had been
done, once he had crossed that initial line, it had been much
easier. There was the rush of adrenalin for a start, the fear of
knowing that if someone saw you now it would be bad, that
you would be arrested and people would know what you had
done.

The thought of people knowing had been the scariest of all
in some ways. He had floated through life with no one
noticing him. That was what life was like when you looked
like him. The only thing worse than being ignored was the
barely concealed looks of disgust you got, especially from
beautiful girls when they saw you. From an early age he had
done everything in his power to fade into the background.
Then he'd made a mistake, a terrible mistake, and he had been
drawn into the light, albeit momentarily.

He got out of the Saab, walked to the rear and opened the door. The blonde stared back at him wide-eyed, gagged, and with her hands bound behind her back. He climbed in and pulled her up into a sitting position. Then he helped her out of the car and on to her feet. Pushing her ahead of him, he walked inside the one-bedroom wooden guesthouse that he rented from the old lady who lived in the main house and whom he never saw except when he paid his rent every month.

'You can relax. You're not my type,' he said to the blonde. 'I'm saving myself for someone else.'

He needed to speak with Raven alone. Just five minutes would do it. Five minutes when he could explain why he had done what he had. That was all he needed. If that bodyguard hadn't got involved he would have had those minutes by now and one less person would have had to be hurt. But he wouldn't listen.

Well, he was listening now.

Fifty-nine

Riding with no helmet, the acrid sting of burning wood along with the dust thrown up from the highway stinging his eyes, Lock smelt the fire long before he saw it. He tried not to think of Carrie trapped inside the house as flames licked the walls but couldn't help himself. With the image came a deep rage that welled up inside him.

His mind drifted back to the letters but he couldn't put any order to them now. He had to stay focused, direct his energy first at getting to the house, and then to finding Carrie. Nothing else mattered.

He took the curve wide before the house, then cut in front of the line of cars that had been stopped by a California Highway Patrol radio car on the ocean side of the road. He climbed from the bike, not stopping to bother with the kick stand. It fell with a crash on to its side, the front tyre spinning round and round.

He could see flames licking out from the garage and two

separate City of Malibu fire tenders parked close by, fire fighters in breathing apparatus dousing the roof and those of the houses either side with two monumental jets of water, trying to dampen the blaze before it took a proper hold of the main structure.

He ran towards the house, pushing past a couple of neighbours who had gathered to watch. As he shouted Carrie's name, a Malibu sheriff's deputy crossed towards him. Lock could feel the intensity of the fire now, a wall of heat that buffeted towards him as the wind changed direction.

The deputy put out an arm in front of him, barring his progress.

'My fiancée was in there,' Lock said, pushing away his arm.

'Sir, the crews have already checked inside. There's no one inside.'

Lock stepped back away from the deputy and began to look around. There was an EMS ambulance parked across the street on the other side of the highway, and he sprinted over to it. Two crew members were in the front cab, and he tapped on the window. He asked if they'd seen Carrie but they replied in the negative. No one had needed medical assistance so far.

As he was talking to them a call came in about an injured biker south of their position on the Pacific Coast Highway. Overhearing the radio message snapped Lock back to some semblance of reality. Regardless of the circumstances, he would be arrested for taking the guy's bike. The present chaos might delay matters but the Range Rover was still there, and it would be traced back to him eventually.

He needed to get away – and fast. But he also wanted to

make sure that what the deputy had said was correct, that there was definitely no one inside the house.

With this thought in mind, he jogged northwards towards a beach-access gate, which lay about fourteen houses further down.

He took the steps two at a time and started back along the beach in the direction he'd just come. Two houses short of the beach house, he stopped, blowing hard from the running and the wisps of smoke that had caught in his lungs. Bent forward, palms pressed to his knees, he tried to catch his breath.

The front of the house was almost perfectly intact, which lent a surreal air to what he'd just witnessed from the highway. Looking up he could pick out a couple of details. He couldn't get far enough back without going into the ocean to see the top deck, but the glass door leading to the lower deck seemed open. He knew Carrie wouldn't have left without locking it, which told him she'd gone in a hurry.

The beach would have been the obvious escape route, not just because of the water but because the belly of the fire lay near the road side of the house. He clung to the thought. He'd start walking back north first, trying Carrie's cell phone as he did so, even though it was still switched off.

He walked close to the shoreline so that he could get a view into some of the houses in case Carrie had sought refuge with one of the neighbours. As he walked, the tide rushed in behind him, erasing his footprints.

Two hundred yards down the beach, the smell of the cloying smoke began to abate and the sirens drifted away to a whisper, snatched away by a hot south-easterly Santa Ana. Looking north, the chaos that lay behind him seemed almost impossible. Up ahead he could see a dog, head down, wandering back and forth in the surf.

Angel.

The realization hit him like a slap. He'd forgotten about her. He broke into a run, wet sand making it hard, his thighs and calves stinging as he reached her. She trotted up to him, tail wagging but with her head down. He knelt down to stroke her head and she defaulted to her usual position, lying on her back, legs akimbo, waiting for him to rub her belly.

It was the first ray of light he'd had so far. There was no way Carrie would have left Angel in a burning building or vice versa. For one of them to be safe meant both had to be.

Lock's cell phone chirped and relief swept over him as he saw Carrie's name flash on the display. 'Christ,' he said. 'You had me worried sick. Are you okay? Where are you?'

There was a moment of silence, then a man's voice: 'She's fine. Now, here's my offer. I'll trade you. Your bitch for mine.'

Sixty

Fear descended slowly over Carrie, settling on her like a shroud. She'd struggled on the journey out until she'd felt a horrific jolt of pain in her lower back, which had almost lifted her off the floor. At first she thought he had stabbed her with the knife. It was only a few moments later that she realized he had Tasered her. The knife had been there to scare her, the fifty thousand volts of the Taser to gain her compliance.

He had set the fire using a can of petrol he'd found in the garage. Then they had left. He had given her a clown mask to wear as they crossed the street, thus shielding her face from any passing commuters. It would be like they were a couple goofing around on Hallowe'en.

It had worked. They had attracted a few strange looks, but this was LA, after all, a city where strange behaviour was the default setting.

Now she was bound and gagged, trussed up on a couch in a living room that smelt of dried semen and stale, ten-day-old laundry. Her hands had been tied in front of her and her legs bound quite tightly together. A third rope linked the two and meant that if she attempted to stand up she would fall forward on to her face. She knew this because she had already tried it – twice. The second time the man had walked in on her. He was still wearing the clown mask, which she took to be a good sign.

Lock must have mentioned in passing that kidnappers who hid their identity usually didn't want a surviving victim identifying them. If you were kidnapped by someone who had no such reservations then the chances were far higher that you were going to die.

Hauling her back on to the couch, the man had run his hands over her body. He'd unbuttoned her blouse and slid a hand inside her bra.

In the end, a phone had rung in the small kitchen off the living room and he'd withdrawn his hand to go and answer it, leaving Carrie on the couch, her heart thumping with fear.

She could hear him talking a few feet away but had to strain to pick out any words. She thought she heard her own name, then Raven's, but the rest was muffled.

Then he was back, sitting next to her on the couch, a lecherous hand sliding to her knee. The horrible clown mask tilted towards her at an angle that made the face, which hadn't changed, of course, seem inquisitive, as if Carrie was a specimen pinned to a high-school science-lab table, ready to be dissected.

'Now, where were we?' he said.

Sixty-one

Ty had stashed his purple Continental at Burbank airport and hired them a fresh ride, a new model Ford F-150 truck. It had been selected via phone by Lock because there was a near identical one (same model, same colour) parked three doors away from where he and Ty were now.

Outside Raven's house two Cadillac SRX SUVs were parked up, the only visible outward evidence of her new security team, who were already inside. Four men, all of them ex-law enforcement, though thankfully not LAPD.

Lock looked across to Ty. 'You do realize that if we mess this up we're going to prison, right?'

Ty clenched his right fist and held it out for Lock to bump. 'Then let's make sure we don't mess it up.'

It had taken Lock less than five minutes after the phone call to decide what had to be done. He could have called the cops and laid the whole thing out for them, but he would have lost any control over what happened to Carrie. And after the stunt they'd pulled with Clayton Mills earlier that day, and the betrayal with the bodyguard, he couldn't trust them to do this right.

From his private security work, Lock knew that kidnappings were far more common than you would realize from watching the news. There was a simple reason for that. People were kidnapped. Demands were made. Demands were met. People were freed. It was a black market of criminality that operated under the cops' and the federal authority's radar. Kidnap and ransom insurance, usually abbreviated to K&R, and the attendant specialized security companies to which they subcontracted extractions, were big business.

This meant there was a straight line here. There might be kinks in it, and Lock would have to deal with those, but essentially it was straightforward. Lock kidnapped Raven and handed her over in return for Carrie. There was a part beyond that too, but for now that was the equation.

He could only hope for one thing: that Raven hadn't yet heard that Carrie had been taken.

He looked from the front of Raven's house back to Ty. 'Let's do this.'

He got out of the car while Ty stayed in the driver's seat. He could feel the weight of Ty's Sig Sauer 226 pressing against the small of his back as he tucked it inside his waistband. A properly held concealed-carry permit seemed suddenly redundant and almost comical in light of what he and Ty were about to do. Regardless of the extenuating circumstances, kidnapping was hard time for a long period. Let Carrie die and he'd be good with the law. Try to save her and he'd be on the wrong side. There was only one way to go.

Lock walked down the path to the front door of Raven's house and rang the bell.

There was no surprise when the door opened. A shaven-headed guy, big but with a paunch, glared at him. 'Can I help you?'

He was typical of most private security contractors. To an outsider he might have looked the part but Lock knew that, when it came down to it, he'd be about as much use as a glass trampoline. Lock smiled at him, burying any residual anxiety he was experiencing. 'I'd like to speak to Ms Lane. I'm—'

'I know who you are,' the guy said.

'Can you tell her I'm here? If she says she's busy or doesn't want to see me, give her this.' He handed the guy a blank white envelope, which held the key to the mailbox that he'd taken from Raven's purse.

The guy took it and the door closed.

A minute later it opened again and Raven stood on the threshold. The envelope had been opened and she was pale but doing her usually good job of holding things together. She stared at Lock.

'The key must have fallen when I pushed you out of the car,' he told her.

'Thanks,' she said. 'Look, I'm sorry. You were right – back there in the car, I mean. Things were a little confused. I was a little confused as well.'

If Carrie wasn't being held God knew where, Lock would have laughed. 'You were wasted in adult movies, Raven,' he said, pulling a single sheet of paper from his pocket, the top sheet of one of her many prison letters.

She took it. 'So? Lots of people write me. You know that.'

'I found the other mailbox, Raven. I know everything,' he said.

Her expression didn't shift but her pupils flared wide. Lock sensed one of her new escorts in the hallway behind them. He jerked his head in that direction. 'You might not want to be overheard.'

Raven stepped outside and began to close the door, but Lock put up a hand to stop her. 'Let's go for a drive. We have a lot to talk about.'

'And what if I don't want to talk? Those letters don't prove anything.'

'They can go away. I can get rid of them, if you like.'

She glanced back inside the hallway. 'I'll just be a second,' she called, then pulled the door all the way closed. Lock noticed that her feet were bare, and her usually perfectly painted toenails were chipped at the edges.

'What do you mean you can make them go away? Are you trying to blackmail me?' she asked, her hand still on the door handle.

Lock grabbed her arm while, at the same time, reaching round for the gun, making sure that she saw a flash of it before he jammed it back under his jacket. 'If only it were that simple. He has Carrie, and that means you're coming with me even if I have to kill everyone in that house. Your brother too.'

That Lock had mentioned Kevin, never mind threatened his life, seemed to register with Raven. He felt it as her violet eyes turned black. The truth was he would never have touched Kevin. But he had shifted something in Raven's mind and that was all he needed. Raven might have craved a protector but she understood much more keenly, on the most base level, the behaviour of a predator.

'You understand me?' he asked her, his tone low and level, his eyes never leaving hers.

She nodded.

'Good.' He smiled, aware that they might be being watched. 'Now tell them you'll be back in an hour. If I even suspect you've tipped anyone off, I'll make good on my promise.'

She started back inside and he made a point of stepping in with her. Once the front door was closed his chance would be gone for ever.

The guy who had answered the door said nothing as Raven threw on a pair of sneakers, and gathered her jacket and bag.

'I'll only be an hour,' she said.

'One of us should come with you,' the guy said.

'He's a bodyguard. I'll be safe. Isn't that right, Ryan?'

'Of course.'

'Do I have time to say goodbye to Kevin?' she asked.

Lock squared his shoulders. 'He won't even know you're gone.'

They left together, the door closing behind them. Lock had no idea if she would see her brother again. But he had no idea if he would see Carrie again either. At least in one regard they were even.

Halfway down the path, Raven stopped and turned to him. 'I'm sorry about Carrie,' she said, her eyes watery.

Twenty-four hours ago, he might have bought the line. Now he knew better.

Sixty-two

The doors sealed with a muffled *thunk* as Lock made sure that Raven sat in the front of the truck, wedged between him and Ty. He glanced at his watch. It was just as well that Raven had put up little resistance. In five minutes the man who had said he had Carrie was going to call back, and if he didn't hear Raven's voice, he'd promised that Carrie would be dead by the time the call ended. He'd also said that Lock could listen to this if he wanted, maybe even say a last goodbye. After all, he knew what it was to love someone too.

Ty was driving with no particular destination in mind. That would come with the phone call. Lock told him to head for the intersection of the Santa Monica-10 and the San Diego-405 freeways, which ran east to west and north to south respectively. At least moving forward gave them something to do and made them more difficult to track.

Raven had been silent since they'd got into the truck but now she spoke. 'You have to understand, I never meant for anything like this to happen. For it to go so far.'

'You know,' Lock said, staring out through a windshield that was dotted with raindrops, the first he'd seen since he'd arrived in California, 'it was Carrie's idea that I look after you, and that you and Kevin came to us. She made the call to get Fay Liepowitz to represent you too.'

Raven's hand went to her mouth and stayed there. 'What do they want?'

Ty glanced over and Lock stared at her. 'They?'

'It's an expression.'

'Not the way you said it,' Lock said. 'Are you saying there's more than one person involved in this?'

'I don't know.'

Lock motioned for Ty to pull over by the side of the road. 'Pick somewhere quiet.'

Ty pulled tight to the kerb at a spot equidistant between two streetlights. 'Ryan, take it easy,' he said.

Lock's jaw tightened until his teeth were grinding against each other, then he pulled out the Sig and pressed the barrel to Raven's face. 'How many are there? How many lunatics do you have out there doing your dirty work for you?'

Raven swallowed hard. 'I think there are two. Clayton and this other guy.'

Lock's cell phone rang. Breathing hard, he lowered the gun, and passed it to Ty. He poked a finger into Raven's chest. 'Stay quiet if you know what's good for you. You understand me?' He clicked the answer button on his cell phone. 'Lock.'

'I have some information on that prisoner for you, Mr Lock,' the voice on the other end of the line said. It was Marquez, the warden from Pelican Bay.

'Go ahead.'

'Reardon Galt was here all right. He was released on probation about six months ago. You want me to tell you what this gentleman was serving time for?'

'Sure.'

There was a shuffling of papers at the other end of the line. 'Let's see what we got here now.'

Lock closed his eyes, the phone cradled between chin and shoulder.

'Huh, this is slightly unusual. Usually he would have gone to at least a lower-level facility first but we had him in the Transitional Management Unit right up until release day.'

Lock knew that was where they usually kept prisoners who would be under threat from those in the general population, most notably prisoners who were leaving one of the prison gangs, an act that carried with it an automatic death sentence on the yard. 'Do you know where he was from originally?'

'An inmate's hometown isn't the kind of information we have,' the warden said. Then there was more rustling of papers. 'Wait. I do have something in here about him having committed a felony or two in Arizona.'

Arizona was where Larry Johns was killed although this might have been coincidence. So Galt had been out for six months – just in time for the rampage to start.

'So what was Galt inside for? The jacket tell you that?' He was watching Raven, checking for any reaction to the name. He was not disappointed. She visibly stiffened, her back as rigid as an ironing board.

The warden sighed. 'You'll want to keep a real close eye on this lady you're watching out for.'

It was Lock's turn to tense as he thought of Carrie. 'Why's that?'

'Lord only knows why he wasn't serving life without parole. Must have had himself a good lawyer or a liberal judge.'

'Warden?' Lock prompted.

'He was in for abduction and rape. Kidnapped some woman from right inside her own home while her kids were asleep upstairs. Drove her across the border into California from Tempe and – well, you can guess the rest.'

Lock's blood ran cold. 'One more thing.'

'Go for it.'

'You wouldn't happen to have a name for Galt's cell mate before he was released, would you?'

There was the sound of more papers being shuffled. 'In fact I do. The guy got out a few days ago too. Crazier rap sheet than Galt had. Lots of violence too.'

'What was his name?' Lock asked, as a cold bead of sweat worked its way down his spine and into the small of his back.

'Oh, yeah, here it is. The inmate's name was Clayton Mills.'

Sixty-three

They were parked on South Sepulveda, across the street from a drug store, waiting for the phone call from the kidnapper, which should come at any minute. Raven was sandwiched between Lock and Ty, shifting in her seat.

Heavy drops of rain spattered the windshield, exploding on contact with the glass and trailing down like tears towards the lashing wiper blades. Overhead, the sky had darkened, heavy banks of grey cloud folded under each other in every direction. A nearby storm drain was already backed up, water flooding on to the street causing a couple of drivers coming towards the truck to aquaplane.

Marquez, the warden from Pelican Bay, had given Lock a description of Reardon Galt, wished him luck and then hung up. Again Lock thought about calling Levon Hill.

The FBI and the LAPD had far greater resources than he and Ty had: of that there could be no doubt. Despite his run-ins with them, they were one of the most professional and well-run law-enforcement agencies in the country. However, their size and their command structure meant that, in a situation like this, they would be behind Lock and Ty in their speed of response. Also, they were hampered by protocol, and by constitutionally guaranteed things, like Miranda rights and search warrants.

Bottom line: the LAPD, like any police force, was in the business of catching the bad guys and placing them in front of a jury. Lock had only one objective: to save the woman he loved.

His decision was made.

He turned towards Raven. 'No more lies. It goes no further than this vehicle, but I have to know the truth.'

She started to speak but he cut her off. 'The truth. You know Clayton Mills. I could see it in your eyes this afternoon. I bet Hill could as well. That was why they wanted to put you two together in that café.'

She took a deep breath. 'I never asked for any of this.'

Rage surged inside Lock. 'Any of what? Cindy's head cut off? A cop and his wife killed? Carrie kidnapped? He's doing it for you. Or his buddy Reardon Galt is.'

'He did Fairfax for me. That's all.'

Lock was shocked. 'That's all? Fairfax was murdered, and you're saying he did it for you?'

'It wasn't like that. I met Clayton in a club. He was working security for the girls. Fairfax was hassling me, wouldn't leave me alone. I didn't ask Clayton to kill him. Clayton was just supposed to frighten him off. But things got out of hand.'

'So he did kill him?'

Raven nodded, tears streaking her face. 'But no one knew

about it apart from me. Then he got caught on a parole violation for something dumb, and I thought that was the end of it.'

'Then the letters started?' Lock prompted.

Raven nodded. 'First from Clayton, saying how he hoped I was waiting for him. Then his cellmate must have found my letters because he started writing to me too. I thought about telling Clayton but I knew he would have killed him.'

'So why did you write back? Why didn't you just go to the cops?' Ty asked.

'I was there when Fairfax died. Clayton said that if I went to the cops, he would tell them about it. Tell them that I had practically begged him to kill Fairfax.' She turned to face Ty. 'I couldn't take the chance of going to prison. Not with Kevin to look after.'

'You think they're competing for you?' Lock asked.

Raven scratched a nail across her nose. 'I don't know. All I know is that people are being killed and everyone is acting like it's all my fault.'

Lock stared out at the rain, thinking of Carrie and what she was going through. He'd had a bad feeling about this job from the start, and he'd been right. He hadn't trusted his instincts and now there was a terrible, terrible price to pay.

'I need to pee and I can't wait,' Raven said suddenly.

'You'll have to,' Lock said. 'You can go when we get somewhere quieter.'

'I can't. If I don't get out, I'm going to pee in the car.'

Ty glanced over. 'I'll take her.'

'Okay,' said Lock, grabbing Raven's arm as Ty opened the driver's door. 'Leave your bag here and remember – if you do anything stupid, it's not just Carrie who gets hurt.'

Ty gave Raven his windbreaker to hold over her head as they made a dash across the waterlogged street towards an International House of Pancakes. By the time they reached the door of the restaurant they were both soaked and Ty pulled her in under the canopy.

'Listen, you made your choices a while back and now you have to live with them. I'm all out of sympathy for you, so whatever Lock threatened you with, you can double it from me,' he said.

She stared at him, drops of rain running down her face. 'You wouldn't hurt Kevin.'

Something like shock must have flickered across Ty's face because Raven put a hand on his arm. 'He's gonna hand me over to this sicko in return for Carrie, and walk away, isn't he?'

Ty shook his head. 'We'll get you out as well.'

'I don't believe you,' Raven hissed. Taking a small step back, she brought her knee up into Ty's groin with as much force as she could muster before taking off down the street, water detonating up from the puddles as she sprinted through them.

Across the street, Lock watched Ty go down in agony. He moved into the driver's seat, but Ty had taken the keys with him. *Fuck*.

He reached over to open the door and get out as Raven fled. He'd skirt round the block in the other direction and try to head her off. But as he got out of the truck his phone rang. He jabbed down on the answer button.

'You have her ready for me?' the man on the other end of the line asked, as casual as someone ordering a takeout meal. 'The clock's ticking.'

Sixty-four

Lock started towards the alley, then stopped. Alleyways were for someone wanting to hide. Raven knew she had two men looking for her and that if she tried that she'd be found. It might take a few minutes, but it would happen.

She could have easily burst through the doors of the Pancake House and screamed the place down. A black guy chasing her who looked like Tyrone did? Hell, there would have been a line of people to call the cops.

But she hadn't. Because she was up to her neck in this. Because what she wanted was escape, and people don't escape in alleyways.

Lock raised his cell to his ear. 'Forget the alleyway, Tyrone. What's the next street?'

'Bentley,' said an out-of-breath Ty.

'Okay, make for that.'

'Roger.'

Lock alternated between a fast-paced walk and a jog, hands

dug into the pockets of his jacket as the rain tumbled all around him. He took another right at the corner of Sardis and Bentley, scanning for cabs that would provide Raven's most likely passage out. She could have stepped into the traffic and flagged down a passing motorist, but again this would almost certainly have alerted the cops. By her actions Raven was revealing herself: every decision she made peeled away another layer until, Lock figured, only her guilt would be left visible.

He saw her halfway down the block, pressed into a doorway, eyes scanning the street. He kept close to the storefronts.

Loosening into a walk, he reached behind his back and pulled out Ty's Sig, keeping it low and down by his side. He called to her as the traffic slid past them on the rain-drenched street, angling the gun in his hand so she was sure to see it. 'He didn't say whether he wanted you alive or dead, and right now I'm not fussed either way.'

He had forty minutes to get Raven into the car and to the drop-off point up in Topanga Canyon. Over that by even a minute and Carrie was definitely dead.

'I got her,' he told Ty. 'Go get the Ford and bring it round.'

Raven's shoulders slumped and she stayed put while he closed in on her, Lock wondering what he had become, and whether the moral chasm between him and the man who held Carrie was still as wide as it had once been.

Sixty-five

Clayton Mills had the music cranked up loud, the bass line from Kool and the Gang's original version of 'Ladies Night' moving the floorboards underneath his feet. Hell, yeah, the feeling was right, he thought, as he slung a T-shirt on and headed for the window at the back of his apartment, levered it open and crawled out.

He landed with a hip-shuddering thump, his left boot almost slipping out from under him on the damp grass. He looked around. The rain had driven everyone, even the small knot of local kids that had come to his door earlier trick-or-treating, from the streets.

The van was still parked across the road, but no one would be able to see him here where the building catty-cornered to the next apartment block. There was a wall to negotiate so he put on his gloves and hauled himself over. Then it was a straight walk to the car he was using, a piece-of-shit 1989 Camry, which was one of the easiest cars there was to steal.

When he'd first seen it parked here it had seemed like a sign from God. Mills had learned so many things from the penal system over the years – jacking cars wasn't the half of it.

More than anything he'd learned about people. How to read them. What drove them. And how to use those two pieces of knowledge to get them to do what he wanted them to. That was what the other cons had never understood about him. His command of a situation wasn't physical. There were plenty of guys in the pen who were physically stronger or more violent than he was. No, his strength was psychological.

Back in Pelican Bay, he had taken a lot of shit for sharing with Reardon Galt because of what Galt was inside for. By rights, he should have sliced and diced him that first night in the cell. But he had never quite understood how a guy who'd taken some asshole bank manager's family hostage, and maybe beaten the snot out of the guy in front of his family, could feel morally superior to another guy just because he hadn't slipped his hands into the bank manager's wife's panties while he was doing it.

Kids . . . well, kids would have been different. He wouldn't have stood for sharing with a cellie who'd hurt little kids. But a little misunderstanding between a man and a woman? Well, shit happened. It happened between guys in the pen, and no one was lining up to dish out a beating to the guys inside the joint who forced their affections on another man.

So, Mills had let Galt live, even kept an eye out for him, and they'd started to get along. And Galt, it turned out, had had his uses. He was out before him for a start. He could use him to clear the decks.

What had taken Mills aback, though, was how seriously

Galt had taken to his task. Once he was outside the gates, Mills had had no direct control over him. He'd gotten inside Galt's mind, and maybe he'd done it too well because all he'd asked the man to do was take care of business – to make sure that Raven was nice and single for him getting out. But Galt had taken his instructions way too literally and Cindy had been the surprise.

Back in the pen he'd known all about Galt writing to Raven. He'd thought it was funny and something he could use. He'd promised Galt that he would get to spend some time with Raven too. He had lied.

What was that saying? Two's company and three's a crowd? Well, Mills had no desire to share Raven with anyone, least of all Reardon Galt. But before he got to that, there was some business to take care of. Tricky business with that mother-fucker and his bodyguard buddy. He'd need Galt for that. Later, maybe not so much.

First things first, though, Mills thought, the engine of the Camry turning over. He had to get to Topanga Canyon.

Sixty-six

To dry their clothes Lock had the truck's heater running full tilt as, next to him, in the driver's seat, Ty edged steadily along the winding canyon road. A flimsy sheet metal barrier was all that separated them from a near vertical drop to the canyon's floor. Rain continued to pour and a muzzle flash of lightning broke somewhere out over the Pacific. The water carved gullies from bone-dry soil and rock as it tumbled down from the mountains and splashed on to the narrow road.

Lock hauled up a canvas bag and started to dig inside. A few seconds later he came up with what looked like a matt black nail gun or one of those devices you bought at the hardware store to locate wires or studs in your walls.

Raven studied it for a moment. 'What the hell's that?'

'It's what might just keep you alive tonight. It's an RFD tracking device. Or, rather, it's the device I'm going to use to implant an electronic chip under your skin so we can find you. Don't worry, you'll barely register it going in.'

'And what about it coming out? I started out not wanting to be stalked and I finish up with something inside me that's registering my every move.'

Lock started to load it with the chip. 'It's a straightforward procedure to have it taken out.'

Raven closed her eyes. 'Go ahead. Believe me, I've had weirder things than that inside me.'

The chip itself was around 0.5 millimetres wide and the same height with a depth of around half of that. In other words it was smaller than a grain of rice, and the device popped it under the skin. It might leave a slight red mark or abrasion, so Lock had decided to put it near the nape of Raven's neck where her long black hair would conceal it.

The only drawback with the technology was that he was going to have to stay within a certain range of the chip or he'd lose signal. He knew Carrie's kidnapper would be looking out for someone following him. If Lock got too close to him, he might freak out and kill Carrie. If he stayed too far back, he'd lose the kidnapper entirely. Getting Carrie and Raven out alive came down to a grain of rice balanced on the edge of a knife.

'Pull your hair up at the back,' he instructed Raven.

She gathered it in one hand and shifted her hips in the seat so that he had a clear view of the back of her neck. He held the device up, pressing it to the skin.

'Count of three, okay?' he said to her.

'Okay,' she said.

'One,' he said, squeezing the handle on the device to launch the chip into her.

She jumped. 'You said count of three.'

'I lied. The more you tighten up the more painful it is,' he explained, as her hand went up to the tiny reddening rise in her skin.

'Don't rub at it,' he said, looking at Ty who was hunched over the wheel, picking out the road through the silvery tumble of rain past the headlights.

'Is it okay if I ask a question?' Raven said.

Lock shrugged.

'What if you don't find me in time?' she asked, as, ahead of them, the silver rain cascaded through the light and disappeared into the jet-black void.

Sixty-seven

Carrie lay on the couch and listened to the rain battering at the windows. Gusts of wind came every few moments, whistling down the chimney into the tiny fireplace. Inside, everything was perfectly still, Carrie included.

The front door had slammed ten minutes ago, followed by the noise of a car engine turning over. The crackle of gravel, muted by the rain, had ebbed away to silence. Her kidnapper was gone.

He'd left Carrie on the couch, eyes dead, but heart still beating. She hadn't even heard him lock the door on his way out. He seemed to have deemed her an item on his list that he didn't have to worry about.

But Carrie had one thing going for her. After what had happened she wasn't entirely convinced that she wanted to go on living. Before, such a thought would have seemed melodramatic. But not any more. It wasn't that she felt suicidal. It was simply that she was floating in a place where not to live seemed equal to going on. If life was somehow premised on faith, which it always had been for Carrie, then in the past few hours she had shifted towards a position of agnosticism. Her indifference, she realized after a few minutes' reflection, might give her the strength to get out of here.

If she wanted to live to see the sun rise, this was her chance. Before her kidnapper had left, she had heard him talking on his cell phone about an exchange, but she didn't believe for a second that he would hold up his end of the bargain. Once he had Raven, he would kill her. Unless, of course, he chose not to come back to the house at all. But that didn't seem likely, not the way he'd been talking. He'd told her that he wanted to be with her one last time before he left. With her and Raven. All three of them together. Carrie would rather die before she let that happen.

Pushing aside the tides of shock and nausea that were still washing over her, she began to work herself into a sitting position on the couch. With the way he had tied the ropes, even this much movement left her arms and legs burning with lactic acid. Finally, she ended up squatting on the edge. The mid-section of rope linking her arms and legs was the problem as it restricted her ability to stand, which presumably was the idea.

Unable to stay in the same position, there was only one thing for it. She allowed herself to fall face first on to the hard wood floor. She angled herself as she did so, protecting her nose and mouth but taking a hefty whack to the side of her head in the process. There was a loud booming crack, which could have been thunder but was as likely her temple meeting wood.

A shooting pain slammed all the way from the side of her head down her neck and then along her arm. She took a couple of deep breaths, then started on the next section of what she needed to do, visualizing it in her mind's eye.

Using her elbow and knee she pushed herself across the floor, her view of the room skewed and distorted by the low angle. Then her foot found purchase and she discovered that, by pushing off on it, she could move maybe ten inches or even a whole foot forward. In between pushes she took two good breaths. Then on the third inhalation she would push off again.

Time was difficult to track. The thought of Galt walking back in seemed to accelerate it; the throbbing pain in her head slowed it down. No matter: all she had to do was count to three and remember to breathe.

The door leading into the kitchen lay open. She had already checked that before setting out on this epic voyage across the living room. Stone tile against her face marked her entrance. She stopped for a moment and rolled over a little more on to her back, seeking out a view of what was above her, and searching for a drawer that might hold cutlery – a knife.

The kitchen counter was in a single length against one wall. There were three drawers, each of equal depth and about six inches wide. She tried to move into a position where she might be able to raise herself back into a squat, which proved to be a hell of a lot harder than she'd thought it would be. On the couch she'd been able to use the drop to lower her legs. With all her limbs on the floor now and at an equal height, this wasn't an option.

She stopped struggling, and took another moment to think it through as a wall clock ticked away nearby.

The wall. That was it. She needed something to lever herself up against. She started to back up a little, as her head banged against plasterboard. She kept shuffling back, and inched up against the wall, her thighs and calves doing the work. Then her shoulders were vertical. The sensation of having something at her back spurred her on and soon she was sitting up and pulling in her heels. With one final effort she wiggled her arms and pushed up with her calves at the same time. Then she was back in that half standing, half squatting position.

She didn't stop now. The pain in her quads, in every part of her legs, was next to unbearable and she knew that if she stopped for any length of time it would overpower her and she would fall.

She shuffled as fast as she could towards the first drawer. Her hands were at the right level to open it, a realization that came to her with a surge of excitement as she stretched her fingers out and hooked them over the handle, easing the drawer open.

Apart for a sheet of faded yellow wallpaper, which had been placed inside as a liner, it was empty. Excitement chilled to self-pity and she almost lost her balance as she swayed back.

Three more shuffles. The second drawer. It was harder to open than the first, which didn't seem like a good sign. But when it did open, she had her reward in the shape of a small paring knife with a blade no longer than three inches.

Digging the tips of her fingers into the drawer, she grabbed the handle of the knife and, after a full minute of contortions, she had the blade facing towards her as she sawed away at the rope that linked those that bound her hands and feet.

Sweat poured off her forehead as she worked the blade, stinging her eyes and making it difficult to see. But she kept going. She had a task, a purpose, something tangible to focus on. It might even be what would make life worth living again. If she could survive the night.

As the rope separated into threads her heart pounded faster. She waited for the sound of the car squelching its way back up the drive. But then the rope broke, and she could straighten her spine and stand. The knife tumbled to the floor. All she had to do now was reach down and pick it up again.

Now there was a dilemma. To free her hands or her legs? Thinking of Galt's strength and what Lock had often said about bodyguarding work being 'organized running away' she chose to cut the rope around her ankles first.

Five minutes later, with the knife tucked away, and her hands still bound she was out of the house and engulfed by the storm. The rain felt sweet against her face, and a sense of elation in having escaped, in having tricked Galt, came at her without warning.

She looked around, moving into the shadows and the cover of the trees as she did so. There was a bigger house a little way up the slope. Its presence startled her. Someone had been less than a hundred feet away the whole time. Did they know what had been going on? Were they complicit in it? Could they see her?

The thought spooked her so much that she turned back

down the drive and headed for the road. She was soaked to the skin, her hair plastered in strands at the front of her face, her limbs still aching and tingling with the fear of recapture, but pushing all of that to the side she felt more alive than she could remember.

She was on the road now. Cindy Canyon. Larry Johns. Vince Vice. Lawrence Stanner and his wife. Carrie Delaney wasn't about to become the final footnote in another demonic chapter of the history of the City of Angels. She had survived.

The driver barely had time to register the ghostly apparition in the middle of the road before he stood on his brakes and skidded, hitting her side-on, her body tossed like a rag doll up and over the hood of the car.

She travelled twenty-five feet, reaching a height of ten, before landing in the trees at the side of the road. She lay on her side, broken and unable to move. Her eyes flickered open and her mind flashed to Ryan and the thought of never seeing him again. It was a sharper pain than anything physical. Unbearable. Excruciating. Tears began to roll down her cheeks. No sobs. Only the tears.

Where was he? Where was the man who protected everyone that mattered and left no one behind? Where was he now that she needed him? When she needed to say goodbye.

Sixty-eight

The only sound inside the cab of the Ford F-150 for the first three seconds was that of breathing. No one moved. One moment they had been driving along, all of them tense: Raven because she was being handed to her stalker; Lock and Ty because Carrie's life was in danger and a long few hours lay ahead of them. Then the woman had appeared on the road. At least, Lock thought it was a woman. He had only seen her for a split second before she had gone up and over the hood of the Ford.

He blinked, trying to wish away what had happened. Then he glanced at Ty, who was staring dead ahead, his hands white and gripping the steering-wheel.

They had to stop. Lock clambered out, reaching for a torch before he slammed the door behind him.

The rain was coming at him almost horizontally, driving into his eyes, making it difficult to see. He clicked on the torch and swept it over the terrain. On one side the road fell away down a tree-filled slope. On the other the ground rose up sharply. There was an open gate a hundred yards back. Further up, beyond the gate, he could just about make out a couple of lights shining through the windows of two houses.

The torch beam swept across the road behind them. Nothing. Lock began to walk back down the road. Ty was behind him, Raven forgotten for now.

'I didn't even see her, man,' he could hear Ty saying.

Lock reached back his free hand, signalling for Ty to quieten. If she was alive, they might hear her.

Lock listened, but all he got was the static of ten thousand raindrops meeting the earth and the howl of the wind up through the canyon. He motioned for Ty to start checking the upward slope side while he used the beam from the torch to ferret into the wooded undergrowth beneath his feet.

Thirty yards back he got a flash of pale skin about ten feet down the bank. He turned back to Ty. 'I've found her,' he shouted.

He caught sight of Raven standing beside the truck, sucking on a cigarette, the red tip bobbing backwards and forwards from her mouth.

'Go keep an eye on her,' he said to Ty, who had arrived at his side. If she'd wanted to make a run for it, now was her chance.

Ty stared down into the culvert. 'Fuck, man.'

'Ty?' Lock prompted.

'Okay. Okay,' Ty said, and jogged back towards the truck.

Lock stared down the slope, his shoes struggling to find traction on the sodden ground. It was even steeper than it looked from the road. He almost went over a couple of times and had to reach out to grab tree branches to steady himself.

He could see the woman's body now. It wasn't moving but he wasn't close enough and it was too dark, even with the torch, to tell if she was breathing.

He straightened up for a second, one hand against the trunk of an oak tree and the beam on the shape in front of him. What the hell could anyone be doing out on the road in this weather? he thought. Then the answer came to him in a single, sickening blow.

Please, God, no.

He summoned everything he had to shift the torch a few inches to his left. Lifting the truck would have taken less out of him than this slight shift of his wrist.

Her eyes were open but without focus. A trickle of blood ran down the side of her face, matched by two streams from each nostril.

Lock had seen enough dead bodies in his time to know that she was gone. He sank to his knees, the slope pitching him forward so that he was on all fours, his hands ploughing into the soft earth, his knees and ankles soaked with water.

A penitent with no possible hope of salvation, he crawled down towards her. Somewhere above him he could hear Ty shouting but he didn't have the breath to answer.

Without being conscious of having covered the ground, he was suddenly next to Carrie, her head cradled in his lap. He took his sleeve and dabbed away the blood before craning forward to kiss her forehead, the coldness of her skin against his lips sending a fresh torrent of grief sweeping through him.

Seconds passed. Then a minute. Ty's voice grew louder,

then fell away to a whisper as Lock felt his friend's hand close around his shoulder.

'Oh, no, Ryan,' Ty said. 'Oh, no. Oh, Christ—'

Ty was next to him now, also on his knees, his arm around Lock's shoulders. They stayed like that for a while before Lock reached behind Carrie gently to untie her hands.

Her wrists were red and raw from the rope, which brought him swimming back to the surface of the present. He rose unsteadily to his feet. Ty did the same. They looked at each other, then down at Carrie.

'I can't leave her,' Lock said. 'Not like this.' He handed the Sig back to Ty, who took it. 'He'll still be waiting for Raven,' he said. Ty nodded. Both men knew what had to be done.

Lock watched Ty climb back up the slope, the gun swallowed in his hand. A few moments later he could hear Raven's questions as Ty ordered her back into the truck at gunpoint. Then there was the roar of an engine and Lock was left alone with Carrie as the storm blistered his skin and the wind sang among the trees.

Sixty-nine

The Ford F-150 eased through the break in the chain-link fence, its tyres struggling for traction in the muddy ground, and came to a halt. Inside the cab, Ty and Raven sat together in silence. Ty looked between his watch and his side mirrors. There were minutes to go until the planned handover.

Raven had sobbed pretty much the whole way here. It had got so bad that he had put his arm around her. 'It's all my fault. All of it,' she kept saying, until finally he'd had enough. Pulling her round to face him, he'd set her straight.

'There's going to be plenty of guilt to go round, so why don't you leave some for the rest of us, okay?' he'd said.

High beams flashed behind them and he felt her stiffen. He racked back the slide on his Sig and cocked the trigger before sliding his right index finger along the side into a ready position.

The car that had driven into the lookout point swung

around so that its lights were blazing towards them, blinding them.

Ty opened the door and nodded for Raven to come with him. He'd already explained that he needed her to stay close the whole time. If he had got out on his own then there was nothing to prevent Galt killing him where he stood and taking her. As a precaution he'd thrown on a ballistic vest, which he wore under his jacket.

With Raven in front, they stepped out into the mud. The driving rain had let up a little, and the lights of the San Fernando Valley spread out in front of them as Ty waved for the driver of the car to get out.

The door opened and Reardon Galt got out. He was carrying a handgun. With the blinding lights behind him, Ty couldn't make out what kind it was; nor did it matter.

'I've brought our part of the bargain,' Ty shouted over. 'Now where's yours?'

'I'll give you the address soon as I have her. You look real pretty by the way, darling. I've been a long time waiting for this.'

'What's the address?' Ty asked. 'My partner has to check it out first.'

Galt glared at Ty. 'Stop fucking around. I said I'd give you it once you hand Raven over.'

'Tell him,' Raven said.

Galt reached up with his left hand to wipe away the rivulets of moisture that were running down his face. 'Tell me what?'

Ty raised his gun, pointing it at the centre of Galt's chest. 'Put down your gun, Reardon.'

Galt seemed to rear up, his shoulders rotating back, his chest puffed out as he tried to re-establish that he was in charge here. 'You do this and she's dead.'

Ty looked at him steadily. 'She's dead already, Reardon.'

Galt spat on the ground. 'Bullshit, man.'

'She escaped,' Ty went on. 'Got hit by a truck. It's all over for you. Put down your gun right now.'

Ty's index finger moved to the trigger as the red dot from the laser sight mounted on top of the 226 carved a pattern around Reardon Galt's heart.

Galt smiled. 'Okay, you got me. I'm going to put it down. Real easy.'

There was something in Galt's face that Ty didn't like. Galt wasn't looking at him or Raven, but behind them. Was it nerves – or something else?

Galt hunkered down, and started to place the gun on the muddy ground as Ty heard the squelch of a boot planting firm behind him. He swivelled round – only to catch a fist in his face. Slipping the punch, he pushed Raven away from him, giving himself room to manoeuvre as Clayton Mills moved in on him, launching a kick that caught him in the stomach.

His abdomen already tensed, Ty shrugged it off and, raising his hand, brought it down in a hammer grip so that the butt of the gun caught Mills flush in the face. It was a messy blow, one that crunched cheekbone but slid down and off Mills's face, as the 226 slipped from Ty's hand and on to the ground.

Mills's mistake was to make a dart for it. As he bent down, Ty kicked him in the face as hard as he could. There was a cracking sound, Mills's neck whiplashed back and he ended on the ground, gasping for air.

Ty turned to find Galt less than ten feet from him, with his gun raised towards Ty's head. A difficult shot to miss. After what had happened to Carrie, Ty wasn't sure that he cared.

The next sound was a gunshot but it was Galt who sprawled backwards, as a red rose of blood blossomed across his chest. Raven stood holding Ty's gun, her face etched with shock.

From behind them came a voice.

'I can't feel my legs, man. You have to help me.'

It was Mills. Still holding the gun, Raven took a step towards him, the taste of Galt's death still evidently fresh in her mouth.

Ty reached over and clasped her wrist, easily enveloping it in his hand. 'No,' he said softly. 'There's been too much killing. It's time to call a halt – don't you think?'

Seventy

Two weeks later

Century City, Los Angeles

On the fifteenth floor, the receptionist looked up from behind the mahogany desk where she and another young woman were fielding an endless succession of phone calls. Lock and Ty were perched opposite on a couple of gaudy green-velvet club chairs that would have seemed more at home in a Vegas casino than the waiting area of a white-shoe law firm. Ty fiddled with his cell phone while Lock checked his watch. Both of them wanted to get this done as quickly as possible.

'Mr Lock, Mr Johnson, you can go in now.'

Lock picked up the thick brown manila envelope from the low-rise coffee-table in front of him and rose with Ty.

Ty's hand fell on to Lock's shoulder.

'You sure you're ready to do this?' he asked Lock.

Lock nodded.

They walked down a short stretch of grey-carpeted

corridor and into a conference room that looked out over the Avenue of the Stars. It was a crisp late-autumn day, the temperature outside a California-perfect 72 degrees.

The storm of two weeks ago had brought with it an end to the devil winds, and the spasms that had racked the city had quickly ebbed away to a memory. Lock wished he could have said the same. In the two weeks that had passed he had woken after fractured sleep, showered, forced himself to eat and moved through life like a ghost. Trapped by the investigation, he was in limbo, and every second of every day he ached for the woman he had been due to marry. It was a wound that refused to stop bleeding.

Ty had been affected too, and Lock had taken his only comfort in the fact that he could reassure his friend that there had been nothing he could have done differently. It was an event that happened to remind you that life could be cruel, unfair and random. Lock played it over in his mind, a series of what-ifs that led him deep into a maze of anger and self-reproach, and left him nowhere.

Behind them, Fay Liepowitz, Raven's attorney, walked in, trailing with her the cloud of expensive French perfume that, right now, smelt to Lock a lot like sulphur. She reached out a perfectly manicured hand to each of them in turn.

'Mr Johnson. Mr Lock, I am very sorry for your loss, as is my client. Carrie was a remarkable young woman.'

Lock said nothing.

'Please, gentlemen, take a seat,' she said at last.

Lock and Ty both pulled out a chair and sat opposite her. This table, like the one outside, was mahogany, the surface smooth and perfectly polished. Everything within sight was the same, including Liepowitz, whose furrowed brow suggested that it was now time to get down to business.

'Let's keep this short, shall we?'

Lock nodded.

'Fine by us,' Ty growled.

'As you are probably aware, my client has said nothing to the LAPD about your less than ethical, and undoubtedly illegal, actions on the evening two people died,' Liepowitz said.

That much was true, thought Lock. There was a reason for that, a lot of reasons, and they were all in the envelope that Lock was holding.

'Kidnapping, I think we can agree, is a very serious charge,' Liepowitz went on. 'However, in return for her personal property,' she said, looking at the envelope, 'she is prepared to sign a legally binding confidentiality agreement, which says that she will not discuss any further aspects of the relation-ship she had with you and Mr Johnson here beyond what she has already told the authorities. That includes what happened two weeks ago.'

Lock and Ty had already known this was coming down the pike so there was no need for any further discussion between them.

'You have a deal,' Lock said.

She looked towards Ty. 'Mr Johnson?'

Ty shot her a bitter smile. 'Sure.'

Lock slid the envelope fast across the table towards her. It went a little wide and she had to dart out a hand to stop it falling off the edge. She opened it and spent a cursory few minutes going over the contents.

Finally, she looked up. 'There are no copies?' she asked.

Lock shook his head. 'That's everything. We want this over as much as you do.'

'Very well,' she said. 'You understand, of course, that anything that's signed is merely a way of formalizing what both parties here agree?'

Lock sighed. 'You mean that if anyone opens their mouth then we're all in trouble.'

'Quite,' said Liepowitz, with a smile that was all teeth and lipstick, reaching over to press an intercom button. 'Lisa, could you come in here for a moment? I have some material that needs to be dealt with straight away.'

By 'dealt with', Lock guessed that she meant that the letters in the envelope between Clayton Mills and Raven would be shredded and then burned to ashes. He got to his feet. The smell of the place, a mix of money and hypocrisy, was getting to him. He needed some fresh air.

'You don't want a copy of the agreement from my client?' she called after him.

He stopped in the doorway, Ty behind him. 'Mail it to me.'

'And where should I mail it?' the attorney asked.

The question was one that Lock hadn't given much thought to. He'd been living in a hotel just off the Sunset Strip for the past few weeks with only Angel for company. The apartment in New York belonged to Carrie, and the thought of living there without her was more than he could take.

He had no home, he realized. Not in any real sense anyway. Carrie had been his home and now she was gone.

'Mr Lock?' Fay Liepowitz prompted him, with a shrug of her shoulders.

'Send it to Ty,' Lock said finally. 'He'll be able to find me.'

As Lock passed the South Pasadena exit of the 10 freeway heading out of Los Angeles, the dense, choking wall of vehicles surrounding him began to clear. Ahead of him lay open road. He clicked on the radio, then clicked it off again after the first few bars of music. It didn't matter what song it was: upbeat songs held a mark of disrespect, and love songs, even the cheesier ones, reduced him to a maudlin mess. He had never before been so aware of the power of music. He settled instead for an imperfect silence.

He glanced at the front passenger seat, expecting to see Carrie. It was empty; another cruel lapse of memory.

For the past few weeks he had been surrounded by people who told him that he shouldn't dwell on what had happened. But not to dwell seemed like a betrayal. And yet he knew that at some point he would have to let go. The weight of doing that felt more painful right now.

He had lost friends before. He had lost family. He had killed and seen those he loved killed in return. His was an existence populated by the ghosts of those who had passed. He knew he was not alone in that regard.

He slowed the car a little, the muscles in his shoulders and back tightening. For a rare second, and for the first time since he had landed in Los Angeles, the highway ahead was completely clear. Ahead of him lay the nation he now loved and hated in almost equal measure; loved for all the good reasons – life, liberty, the pursuit of happiness – but hated because it had allowed men like Reardon Galt and Clayton Mills back on to the streets to destroy those same rights for others.

Finally, blinking away the weight settling on his eyelids, he decided to take the only option open to him. Pressing down on the accelerator, Ryan Lock kept moving forward. He had no destination in mind. He trusted that he would know it when he got there.

Acknowledgements

A huge thank-you to my family, friends, agents and publishers for their continued encouragement and support. A special mention also to my brother-in-law. Lieutenant Ron Spicer of the Los Angeles Police Department, for his guidance. I should stress, however, that any procedural or other errors are entirely my own. Above all, though, I would like to thank Ryan and Ty's fans, my readers, who make it all worthwhile.

About the Author

Sean Black grew up in Scotland, studied film in New York, and has written the screenplays for many of Britain's best-known TV dramas.

To research the first two Ryan Lock thrillers, he underwent weeks of intensive bodyguard training and spent time inside America's most dangerous maximum security prison, Pelican Bay Supermax in California. In *Gridlock*, he takes his readers deep inside the murky world of America's multi-billion-dollar adult-entertainment industry.

For more information on Sean Black and his books, see his website at www.seanblackbooks.com, or follow him on Facebook: www.facebook.com/seanblackthrillers.